# JACOB ROSS

# THE BONE READERS

sphere

SPHERE

First published in Great Britain in 2016 by Peepal Tree Press Ltd
This edition published by Sphere in 2018

1 3 5 7 9 10 8 6 4 2

Copyright © Jacob Ross 2016

The moral right of the author has been asserted.

A CIP catalogue record for this book
is available from the British Library.

ISBN 978-0-7515-7446-3

Printed and bound in Great Britain by
Clays Ltd, Elcograf S.p.A.

Papers used by Sphere are from well-managed forests
and other responsible sources.

MIX
Paper from
responsible sources
FSC® C104740

Sphere
An imprint of
Little, Brown Book Group
Carmelite House
50 Victoria Embankment
London EC4Y 0DZ

An Hachette UK Company
www.hachette.co.uk

www.littlebrown.co.uk

For Maurice
For the disappeared . . .

## ACKNOWLEDGEMENTS

I owe the realisation of *The Bone Readers* to Jeremy Poynting, who promptly pointed out the potential of a short story I sent him, and whose positive interest in the development of the novel triggered me to deliver.

Many of the final-draft refinements were due to Jeremy's, Dave Martin's and Lindsay Waller-Wilkinson's incredibly useful feedback, which made for a more satisfying novel.

An anecdote from Chris De Riggs sowed the seed of the story which became *The Bone Readers*.

Yvonne Malcolm facilitated a short conversation with Officer Findlay which informed several elements in the novel.

From a list of proposed titles, Rod Duncan had no doubt that *The Bone Readers* had to be it.

Loss is loss, and nothing is gained by calling it by a nicer name.
Tony Judt, 'Night', *New York Review of Books* (Jan 2010)

I'd left school with no job to go to and exam results that my teachers said could get me to any university anywhere in the world. If I had the money.

I mentioned the sum to my father and he laughed. The bank managers I went to didn't laugh – at least not in my face. They asked for equity, then my family name. I gave them my mother's. They pointed out how generous they were by giving me their time, then nodded at the door.

I went south to the Drylands where the hotels were. For two tourist seasons, I peeled back my lips and exposed my teeth, served drinks barefoot in a rainbow-coloured synthetic shirt, wide-brimmed straw hat and pantaloons which no Camaho man would be seen dead in outside of Beach Bum Bar. Then a half-drunk old bull from Germany, red like a barbecued lobster, closed his hand around my crotch and I punched him in the face.

The Englishman who owned the place leaned in close and demanded I apologise, else he fire me without pay. I told him to haul his arse and walked.

I took to the sidewalk of San Andrews watching the tourists, the pretty cars, the office girls stepping in heels that raised their arses almost as high as their ears, and young men shuffling bow-legged in waistless trousers with rappers' caps and speaking in made-up American accents. I watched, especially, the bright open faces of the little boys in school uniform heading home every afternoon to parents who might someday laugh at them. I didn't doubt that they would end up like me with their shoulders propping up a storefront in San Andrews.

Then one Wednesday afternoon it happened right in front of

me: a huddle of youth-men arguing over something. I paid them little mind. They were wharf-rats who made a living begging money off the tourists. When the ocean liners weren't in, they drifted around the town pulling at the skirts of school-girls and pushing their pelvises against them. Many parents waited at the school gates and escorted their daughters home.

A single protesting voice rose up from their midst, pitched high and desperate. Heads turned, followed by a patter of fast-approaching feet. Market people loved a fight.

There came a flare of voices from the knot of hooligans. I heard the word 'respect', then 'fuck', then 'fuck-up', then 'fucker', then a thud like a fist sinking into a pillow. A gasp, followed by the rapid scattering of feet as the young men fanned out, adjusted their hoods over their heads and sprinted off.

A boy lay on the sidewalk in the same uniform I wore to school for seven years. He was laid out on his side, right arm curled in front of his stomach; the other, bent at the elbow, was under his head as if he were asleep.

I followed the red trickle that seeped from under his hand, its abrupt change of course as it met the invisible incline of the concrete gutter and flowed into it. I thought I knew the boy. I felt I ought to.

An office girl with a tight, high bun of expensive Indian hair, nails glinting gold in the sun, brought her phone to her ear, her arm making a delicate stylish curve just before she spoke into it. I watched her crimson lips moving.

I walked across the road, knelt and touched the boy's forehead. I stood up, ignoring the shock on all those faces fixed on me. They were reading me, I knew, studying my expression, waiting per-haps for the howl that would confirm for them that this dead boy was family.

I did none of that. I simply stood over him.

When the police came they rushed me. The largest one slammed my back against the wall, jammed a knee into my stomach and pressed an elbow against my throat. I choked on my breath and held his eyes. He did not like that. He threw me on the pavement, dropped his weight on my spine, then dragged my hands behind my back and handcuffed me.

2

A little car arrived. It stopped in the middle of the road. An apparition got out: a white head of hair; eyes like two knobs of flaming coals; lips that would look perfect on a battered leather purse.

White Hair shouted something. The words came out of him like gravel on a grater.

The weight came off my back. I was lifted to my feet, the handcuffs removed. Rough hands bundled me into the little car.

All the while, people were out there protesting at my arrest. All women. The men remained silent. They were, no doubt, less interested in my fate than in the way injustice takes its course. It made for better rumshop conversation.

They took me to an old brick building backing the bus terminal, which stood over the sea. Above the entrance in big white type: San Andrews Police Central. Inside, I caught the faint smell of tar from the island schooners berthed against the jetty. Partitioned rooms retreated all the way to the back of the building. From them came the shuffling of paper and, occasionally, the boom of men's voices. Outside, the blasts of horns, the rise and fall of market women's voices, the penetrating bray of the coconut seller we called Cocoman.

Amid the thunder of vehicles arriving in the concrete courtyard, White Hair sat me down in a chair by an untidy desk. He pressed a sandwich into my hand and a glass of orange juice. He lowered himself in front of me and jabbed a finger at his chest. 'Detective Superintendent Chilman. You?'

'Digger.'

'That's the name on your birth certificate?'

'Michael Digson.'

'How long you been out there?'

'Out where?'

'On the street.'

'I have a home.'

'How long?'

'Eighteen months three days.'

'You been counting?'

'Uh-huh.'

'Why?'

3

'Keep my sanity.'

He looked me in the eye. 'You still got it?'

'You got no basis for arresting me.'

'Calm down, youngfella, you not under arrest. Now talk to me. What happm?'

I pushed aside the sandwich and sipped the juice. 'Monkeys demanding respect from humans,' I said. 'They killed the human.'

Detective Superintendent Chilman leaned forward and squinted as if he were examining a speck in my eye. 'You upset. That's good. You could point them out?'

'They hide their faces from the start, before the argument. Is obvious they plan it.'

Chilman rubbed his chin and looked up at the ceiling. 'Right,' he said, rising to his feet. 'Come with me.' He stopped at the door and raised his voice. 'Okay fellas, bring them out.'

Twenty-three young men – all in rapper's hoods rolled back from their heads – filed out of three vans into the yard. Some looked nervous, some angry, most of them relaxed. A few were so terrified they could barely walk. A couple of them didn't drop the monkey swagger.

The officers lined them up against the wall of the building.

Chilman prodded me. 'Recognise any?'

I shook my head.

'Let's try something else then.'

On his word, Chilman's officers pulled the hoods over the young men's heads and ordered them to run across the yard.

Chilman looked at me. 'Anything?'

A few of the youths threw threatening glares in my direction. I squared my shoulders and glared back.

'Make them talk,' I said. 'Let each one ov 'em say something.'

An officer grumbled under his breath and sucked his teeth – the same one who'd flattened me on the sidewalk.

Chilman leaned into my face. I caught a whiff of rum. 'Listen, youngfella, I'll make them lil sonuvabitch across there skin kuffum and walk upside-down on one finger if I have to, because I want a result, unnerstan? I want a result right now. So don't play the arse with me. If that is what you doing.'

4

Beneath that tired old face he was seething. He was so full of fury I felt myself leaning away from him. I had never seen such rage in another human.

Still, when he turned to address the young men his tone was conversational. 'This is the way I see it, genlemen. I could let everyone of y'all walk out of here scott-free. I could do that right now and turn my back. But y'all won't get far. People out there know who been arrested. That's why I order these officers to stand y'all together in the market square and give the whole damn town a good look at y'all face. I know for sure that word already reach the brothers and the uncles and the cousins. They don't know which of you just murder their boychile. They won't want to know. All they'll want is blood. Your blood! As much of it as they can get until they satisfy. They'll come after every one of you. My job is to prevent that. So… one-by-one, you say your names and where you live exactly. Youngfella, you ready?'

I nodded and pressed my back against the old white vehicle. I closed my eyes while the boys shouted their names and co-ordinates. I relived the heat of the afternoon, the sound of oncoming vehicles, and the heavy fruit-and-earth smell of the marketplace; the hot pitch of words, the exact timbre and inflections of the voices. I have that kind of memory.

I picked out every one of them. Eight. One was missing.

It was easy afterwards. They betrayed themselves by pointing at each other.

When it was over, Chilman's hot eyes were on my face. The old fella was smiling. He pointed at the sandwich. 'I know you hungry. Eat.'

He lowered his voice, his eyes still probing. 'Ever been arrested before today or charged for anything?'

He must have seen the irritation on my face. 'Sorry, youngfella, I have to ask them questions.'

I got up to leave.

He pushed out a stiff hand. 'You not leaving right now.'

DS Chilman led me back to his office and sat me on a chair in the corner nearest the door. Officers in plain clothes criss-crossed the uneven wooden floor. From time to time, one of them stopped and placed his mouth against Chilman's ear. The old fella's lips barely moved when he replied. All I could hear was the throaty rattle of his voice.

Occasionally, I caught his eyes on me – a steady, coal-fire gaze. I pretended not to notice. He said something to an elderly woman who sat in the middle of the room under a big white ceiling fan. Two girls in swivel chairs, on either side of her desk, were stapling papers and slipping them into light-green folders. When the old man straightened up, the woman's eyes took me in briefly, then slipped away. Because of that look, I felt my heartbeat quicken. She had a detached, almost dreamy face, thick, charcoal-black hair swept back in a bun with a single streak of white following the curve of her head all the way from the hairline of her forehead.

Chilman came over to me. 'You want to know?'

'Know what?' I said.

'The lil fella name is Ryan Weekes. His mother working she arse off in the nutmeg pool in St Johns to give him an education. Only child – you unnerstan what that mean?'

I stood up. 'You finish with me?'

'You telling me it don't concern you?'

'I don't have nothing to do with this.' I'd raised my voice. The office fell silent. A slow turning of heads in my direction. Expressionless faces.

Chilman showed me a row of yellow teeth. 'That's not the way I see it, youngman: y'was there, like all them other *citizens* who stannup like jackass in the middle of the govment road and watch eight harden-back ram goat gang-up on a lil child and murder him. That make you a witness. At least! Prime! I could make it worse. I could say you were handling the body when we got there. That's tampering with evidence. And if that don't stick, I could get you for loitering.' He patted my arm and winked. 'I will let you go home, but not before you tell me where you live.'

'Nuh.'

His forehead bunched in a sudden frown. The old man raised his hand and curled a finger. A young officer in a crisp white shirt and impossibly pressed trousers rose from his desk in the far corner of the room and strolled over. He had the darkest eyes I'd ever seen and a tight unsmiling face. We locked eyes, his nostrils flared and something in him stiffened.

'DC Malan, this is Michael Digson. The youngfella refusing to cooperate. I want you to handcuff the gentleman and escort him through San Andrews market in the hot sun. I want you to take your time so everybody could see you frogmarching the sonuvabitch round town.'

DC Malan gave me a long, dark-eyed look. I squared my shoulders and held his gaze.

'No probs,' he said, slammed open his drawer and straightened up with a pair of handcuffs in his hands.

I dropped back in the chair and told Chilman where I lived.

'Thank you, Sirr! Now you free to go.'

I marched through the door, my ears burning with the chuckles of the people in Chilman's office. His voice – coarse as rock-salt – followed me outside. 'Don't try to run away. I not done with you. Y'hear me?'

When Chilman released me, I went to Grand Anse Valley to visit a girl who'd made promises to me. She wasn't there, or maybe she was, but decided not to answer my calls from the road. I hung around in the yard of a little roadside shop named Grace's Place, watching four men and a woman with bottles of Carib lager at their elbows, slamming dominoes on a rickety table.

## 2

Daylight was already draining out of Old Hope when I got home. The air was heavy with the threat of rain. In the distance, the peaks of the Mardi Gras mountains caught the last of the dying sun.

My grandmother left me a two-roomed storm house on the side of Old Hope valley, a gift from the colonial government of her time after a hurricane named Janet flattened everything and left the island destitute. In the days when she worked in cane, she'd added another bedroom.

On lucky days, a bowl of something boiled or stewed or steamed would be on my step, anchored there with a hefty stone to keep away the chickens and the dogs. Weekends, I repaid the women's kindness by sitting with their children and helping with their homework.

Nothing today.

I had not eaten anything apart from the sandwich the DS gave me earlier. I wasn't feeling hungry but I decided to force myself to eat.

I lit the two-burner kerosene stove and warmed the pot of vegetables I'd cooked the night before, sat on my steps with the bowl in my lap and stared out at the evening.

A lump had settled in my chest and my head was throbbing. The murdered boy was on my mind. I couldn't get rid of the image of his crumpled body on the edge of the drain. Killing looked too easy, the taking of that child's life so sudden and so casual, the whole thing felt unreal.

I chewed on the tasteless food while staring down at Old Hope Valley where concrete roads cut white winding ribbons toward unfinished houses on the foothills. My grandmother used to tell me that this valley was filled with sugarcane. Now bamboo, dandakayo trees and flaming love vines had taken over. I didn't mind this place. Most days, it was full of wind and light and bird cries, and always cool in the shadows of the Mont Airy hills.

*Fuckim*, I thought. *Fuckalladem*.

I went inside and lit the kerosene lamp, then returned to the steps. The sound of a vehicle pulled me out of my thoughts. I watched a little car skew abruptly to a halt on the verge of the road directly below. The engine shuddered, then cut off.

I hurried inside, dropped my bowl on the table and covered it with a plate.

DS Chilman took his time coming up the hill. Now and then he paused to survey the bananas that bordered the stone path up to my grandmother's house. When he got to the yard he hitched up his trousers, tightened his belt and stood there breathing hard.

'Okay. So, you happy to see me again. And so soon. Right?'

He dropped a bruised leather bag on the step – his stringy neck jerking like a turkey's as he inspected the house. He pushed past me and walked inside.

He took in the little stove, the kerosene lamp, the stacked bookshelf I'd built against the partition, the photographs I'd pasted on the walls. He reached for the picture of my grandmother, then changed his mind. I saw the outline of the pistol under his shirt, stuck into the waist of his trousers.

I remembered the books I'd taken from the library with no intention of returning them, and sure enough he slipped a couple from the shelf.

'You read a lot?'

I nodded.

'All of these?' He made a gesture that took in the whole shelf. I nodded again.

He'd taken out several more and laid them on the table, muttering the name of each one as he did so. 'Poems of Resistance... Social Anthropology – A Beginner's Guide... Bending the Mind – Principles of Persuasion...' He turned around to face me, holding up the last. 'How Yourope Underdevelop Africa...' Government banned that one in '74. You planning a coup?'

He dropped the book; lifted the two smallest of my trophies from the top of the bookshelf. He read the inscriptions, then slid his eyes at me. 'You don't look like no sprinter to me.'

Chilman replaced them one by one. Had I not been there it would have been impossible to know that my belongings had been tampered with.

When he took up the shoe-box with my documents, I sprang forward. He stopped me with a glare.

He sifted through my papers, picked up my black notebook. He hefted it. 'You glue all them front pages together, why?'

'Is personal,' I said.

'The rest not personal too?' He turned a couple of pages, brought the notebook closer to his face. 'And the church bell tolls, fading, ever-fading beneath its shell of stones. Hard as the heart of blue-eyed men... long gone...' he raised his head at me, laid the notebook on the table and turned to go. 'Pretty words. No rhyme, though. So! How come you didn' win the island scholarship. Who they give it to? Because from what I see...' He tapped his pocket and I heard the jangle of keys 'Who they give it to?'

'Not me,' I shrugged. I did not care to talk about it.

He stood above me, arms making handles on his hips. 'So! you got nothing preventing you from taking the job then?'

'What job,' I said.

'The one I offering you right now.'

It took a while before his words sank in.

I went outside and sat on the step. He lowered himself beside me. I stood up and stepped away. He leaned forward, reached back and adjusted the gun. He fixed me with those eyes of his. 'It wasn the way you identify that bunch of fellas who kill the boy today. Some people will call that obeah. Was a stupid thing you say that make sense to me.' He showed me his teeth again. *They hide their face before they start the argument so was obvious they plan it.*

'Now, youngfella, a good lawyer could make a fool of you in court for saying that. But I not a good lawyer. You want the job? You tell me, yes, I fix the rest, and to hell with procedure.'

'I want nothing to do with police.'

'You prefer to keep rolling in this shit? That what you prefer? Lemme tell you what I just work out, Pretty Boy. You bright as hell. You got enough brains to give away most ov it and still have nuff to bamboozle everybody, but vexation make you stupid. You remind me of my first daughter. Look at you, you starvin. Is poor people round here you depending on to feed yuh? I offering you a chance to get off yuh arse and do something and all you could do is twist your mouth and say, "I want nothing to do with police" – eh?'

'I got my reasons.'

He threw me an awful grin. 'You think I dunno your reasons? What job you think I do?' He got up, walked into the house again and inspected the photographs on the wall. Chilman raised an index at the picture of my mother.

'Lorna Digson, not so? May 1999. Rape Riot.' He was silent for a long time. He'd creased his forehead and his fingers were making useless movements at his side. 'That one really upset me. Real bad. I was on leave at the time. Off the island, yunno. But that don't make no difference to you, right? I think I unnerstand that.'

For the first time DS Chilman would not look at me.

'I not saying we perfect. Ain got a police force in the world with a clean cupboard. We not no church. Sometimes the thing they do to stop a crime is worse than the crime itself. Used to be a time when they never recruit the smart ones – fellas with the soft hands and fingers long-and-slim like yours. They too quick to talk back and ask hard question, so they didn't qualify because they too qualified if-yunno-what-I-mean. Nuh – in them times what you want is the kinda policeman who got just enough language to follow orders. You could instruct him to shoot his mother and he'll do it without question. That's not what I offering you. What I…'

'Nuh.'

The old man snapped to his feet, a movement so sudden it startled me. He pointed at the house. 'You sinking and it stinking – and that's a rhyme, Missa Poetry. Maureen, my secretary, say, "Chilly, leave the boy alone; you wasting your time. He look like he finish. He gone through." So I say to mihself, for once I going to prove she wrong. Is the waste I can't stand. That's all I see around me now. Waste! Like that boy-child them ramgoat kill today. A blasted waste!'

11

He dug into his shirt pocket and pulled out a tiny notepad, ripped out a leaf and scribbled on it.

The red eyes turned on me. The old lips barely moved. 'Loitering is a punishable offence, yunno that? Stay away from San Andrews unless you got a valid reason to be there.'

He laid the square of paper on the step, cleared his throat and sidled a look at me. 'After I look you up and find out about all what happen, it cross my mind that mebbe, if you accept my, erm, proposition, you kin work out a way to… yunno… make your own enquiries, so to speak. Call me if you change your mind.'

He hitched up his trousers, turned his back on me and began picking his way down the hill.

Down below, the car shuddered to life, the headlights came on – a glow so faint, I wondered how he saw the road. I followed the farts and belches of the vehicle until the racket melted in the quiet evening.

Night filled the valley. Fireflies flecked the air. The fruit bats in the eves of the house launched themselves into the darkness, their geiger-counter chittering painful on my eardrums. I knew of no one else who heard them. Me – I could single out each creature by the difference in their cheeps.

I went back in and sat down. The shoe-box was on the edge of my vision where Chilman had left it on the table. The photograph of my mother lay on it. It was clear he had been digging up my past. But in all his talk about policing and my mother, he made no mention of my father and the part he played in killing her.

## 3

I used to wake with my grandmother's face above mine, her hand on my forehead, her voice soft and shushing. She would stroke my forehead and my throat until my shivering subsided. My head would remain clotted with the remnants of the dream: the vague shape of a woman in a white cotton dress sitting on our step, her right hand around my stomach, rocking me on her knee. There would also be the dim remembrance of a laugh. It is the dream-image of my mother.

Awake, I see her differently: I am eight years old. She is in the yard in a yellow t-shirt and dark-blue jeans, a white bandanna holding her dougla hair in check.

The air is thick with rumours of some disturbance in San Andrews. The women of the village crowd her with their questions. Whatever the trouble is, its awfulness is in their voices. They are talking about men – *fuckin wicked men*.

My mother's upset is sleepier. I could smell it on her skin like the leaves of the borden tree that I'd strip in later years and bring to my nose to remember her.

I remember following her to the main road where a car was waiting.

She noticed me on the grass verge; saw perhaps the fear that held me there. She lifted a finger at the driver, came out of the vehicle and stooped in front of me. Her breath on my face was dry and sweet. I remember that. I remember her kissing my ear, the sockets of my eyes, feathering her lips on mine, pulling me close, her mouth against my ear: 'Don't worry, Sweetman, I home a lil later.'

She never came back.

My grandmother gave no explanation for my mother's absence. She did the things my mother used to do, and the village kept its silence, as if, whatever the reason for her disappearance, there were no words for it.

Over the years, my brain tried to make some sense of it by feeding on the few words from other people's mouths, and the newspaper cuttings I dug up in the old library, since washed away by a storm surge.

What I learned was that it was a demonstration. A school girl had been raped somewhere in Canteen on her way from a revision class in her school. It was perhaps what they'd done to her that stirred the women of the island. They had not only killed the girl, they'd desecrated her in other ways – bits of wood and dirt in every orifice. They left her splayed out in the open field in Canteen. When the news broke, the ring leader, the son of a politician, had already been smuggled off the island to some place in America.

The women took to the streets of San Andrews; the police arrived with guns. And whichever way I looked at it, it had to be my father, the Police Commissioner, who ordered his men to shoot. But then it would have hardly mattered to him since she was just his servant girl that he'd impregnated, and I was no more than an 'outside' child.

From the time my mother disappeared, my Fire Baptist grandmother became a cane-stalk of a woman. She began shedding her flesh as if she were lightening her body for her final flight to Zion. She had meandering conversations with a growing assembly of childhood friends and family. Dead brothers with Old Testament names popped out of her mouth like a new language: Hezekiah, Nathaniel, Zebediah...

She had fretful arguments with a man named Suresh. I deduced he was my great grandfather who wanted her to return his belt. 'It is for the boy!' she said.

Sometimes she disappeared. When I got back from school, I dropped my books and walked the village. Someone always intercepted her and kept her in their yard until I came to pick her up.

The old woman went wherever her mind told her that her daughter, Lorna, might be buried. Once I caught her staring into a woman's face and calling my mother's name, as if she had become a soucouyant and dressed herself in the skin of another person.

I cooked, I cleaned; I tended the kitchen garden and sent myself to school.

One Friday afternoon I entered the house, called out to her and got no answer. I dropped my books, was about to go out again when something stopped me. It was the brightness of her bedroom. The single window in there was open wide. The old woman was on her bed in the white raiment of her religion, her string of prayer beads laid out around her headwrap like a broken halo. I knew she wasn't sleeping.

She'd left me messages. The room was full of them. She trusted me to understand them by the colours of the bits of cloth she laid on every item: yellow for the things that would matter in the future – a will for the house and a rectangle of land somewhere in the barren south of Camaho. I did not know the bit of land existed. She'd folded her eight silver bracelets with white ribbons. They were for the girl-children I might have.

She'd topped a large clay jar with a wad of notes and left it on the floor. Around its base were five gold bracelets and a couple of fine-linked chains. She'd surrounded the jar with a blue fragment of cloth and by this I understood that these were the things that I could sell in desperation.

Four donkey-eye seeds were on the white tablecloth, each representing a corner of the earth.

Beneath the open window, among a toss of shells, she'd laid a picture of me in my school uniform.

When her mind belonged to her, my grandmother preferred seashells to the bones of birds for her floor X-rays. She would throw them like a handful of dice, bring her face down to the patterns, spend hours on her knees muttering to herself – part of her ritual of discernment of the shadows and silhouettes that preyed on troubled minds. Things the doctors in San Andrews neither detected nor understood. I wondered if this last reading had been for me – my granny seeking some assurance from Oya, her personal orisha, that I would manage on my own.

I left the room, felt the welling in my chest, heard my own voice pitched high and tight and desperate as I laid on the stones in my grandmother's yard, hugged myself and broke.

Chilman's threat prevented me from going back to hang out in San Andrews. He'd decided to make me prime witness in the case of the murdered boy. That meant the courts, a trial, my name and face in the papers, and I would not put it past the sonuvabitch to implicate me. I thought of his digging eyes and the way he talked to me as if he had a right. I decided I hated him.

I counted the money I'd put aside during the time I worked in Beach Bum Bar. I combed my hair, pulled on a tee-shirt and a pair of jeans and walked to the Drylands.

They turned me down at every bar and hotel where I asked for work. The owner of Beach Bum Bar had passed my name to his employer friends. They reminded me of the incident; spoke as if they'd been there to witness it. The owner of Nutmeg Bar and Grill ordered his security man to escort me off his premises.

Sometimes I returned home soaked and dripping. A whole week of bad weather and, according to the radio, it was just the beginning. A low-pressure front which they had not given a name to, because it was not yet a hurricane, was marching down the East Caribbean islands, trampling the trees and houses that could not stand up to it. The weatherman said that it would hit the south-east hardest and there was no place more south-east on the island than Old Hope.

I drove nails through the wooden posts that the little house stood on. I crawled up on the roof and hammered a handful through the galvanised roof. The old woman had surrounded the place with wind-breaking trees – mainly cutlet and mango. As a last line of defence, she'd grown a semicircle of wild pine whose roots reminded me of mangroves.

The sky above the Mardi Gras had become the purple of an

infected wound. Everything had gone still. I could hear the growling of the sea beyond the hills, the knock of cutlery against utensils in the houses down below.

The animals were always first to know. Chickens began huddling under houses hours before roosting time. Sheep – restless and plaintive – pulled loose from their tethers and hurried home to their pens.

The valley vibrated with the sound of hammering.

I was in bed when it struck, woke up to the house straining against the assault of wind and water. Some time close to morning, a sheet of galvanise peeled back from the rafters and began thrashing. The weather stormed in and kept me hostage in my little bedroom until daylight broke. When it passed, I unlatched the window and looked down on a dripping, roughed-up world – trees laid low, the little river down there raging, the gurgle and tap of water everywhere; and directly above my head, an angry strip of sky where the sheet of galvanise had been.

I spent the next two days bailing out the house, fixing what I could, and cleaning.

*

I got up and walked the three miles out of Old Hope to the main road. I stood at the junction for a while, then counted the change in my pocket. The rain of the night before had stopped, but the grass on the verge was still glittering with droplets. A hard wind was pushing against me. I leaned into it and lengthened my stride.

An hour later, I tapped the side of the door of San Andrews Central Police Station. Chilman raised his head from the paper he was writing on, the pen held level with his ear. He curled a finger at me and I walked in. The sonuvabitch was smiling.

A young woman stood at a photocopier at the far left of the room, neatly dressed in white bodice and purple skirt, her hair pulled back in a slick bun. Big round eyes travelled down the length of me, stopped at my shoe, then repeated the journey upwards to my face. I felt myself shifting under her gaze. She smiled and I relaxed.

DS Chilman dropped the pen on his desk. His voice rasped at me. 'I glad you come, youngfella. Come in.'

A couple of men in plain clothes approached his desk with papers in their hands – potbellied men his age who spoke under their breaths. At a nod from him, the officers retreated with barely a glance in my direction.

'Best thing that happened to me today.' He rose from the desk, placed a hand against my lower back and propelled me toward the middle of the room.

'People,' he said. 'Meet Michael 'Digger' Digson. Y'all might remember h'was here before under different circumstances.'

One of the men chuckled and promptly lowered his head.

'That young lady there name Lisa; the one that showing you her prettiest smile name Pet. You met Malan already. Miss Maureen is my right hand and foot. I run this office; she run me. She will do the paperwork. Most of it done already.' He patted me on the back. 'Follow me, I'll introduce you to the others later.'

His office was a tiny room, empty except for his desk, stacked at the rear with box folders. A small table hugged the corner of the space, two plastic chairs pushed right up under it. He pulled out a chair, gestured for me to sit.

'Now that you make up your mind, how you feel?'

'Conscripted.'

Chilman rasped a laugh. 'I prefer recruited. I didn't tie a rope around your neck and drag you here.'

He planted his elbows on the table and lowered his voice.

'What make you change your mind – desperation or the temptation to find out what happen to your mother?'

I held his gaze and said nothing.

'You got what I lookin for,' he said. 'And if you thinking Commissioner Joseph Lohar got anything to do with this, you wrong. But…' He looked me in the eyes. 'I will have to tell him.'

'Fuckim,' I said.

'Sorry, youngfella, I can't oblige you.'

I was surprised that he'd heard me. He stiffened, a sudden finger in my face. 'Make this the last time you speak in front of me like that.'

'I take the job on one condition, Sir.'

He raised his brows.

'One month pay in advance.'

'It don't work like that.'

'I got to fix my roof.'

'What happm to your roof?'

'Part of it blow off.'

'How?'

'Bad weather.'

'Okay, so you take the job to fix your roof. I must be thankful for bad weather, then.' I thought he was going to laugh. He did no such thing.

He pushed himself to his feet and went through the door. He was out there a while, his lips close to Ms. Maureen's ear. The DS returned with a brown envelope and dropped it on my lap.

'I know you don't have an account. Open one. When your employment's confirmed, borrow from the bank and fix your house.' He dropped a book and a pile of typewritten sheets in front of me. 'Recent cases and this…' – he tapped the book – 'Operational Handbook: offences, basic legislation, police powers and procedure, sentencing and punishment. Learn everything. What's not in there you'll pick up on the job, or learn from me.

'Now for the other matter.' He placed both hands on his desk and leaned into my face. He'd dropped his voice to what sounded like a deep-throated rattle. 'You mother is *your* jumbie. Nothing to do with San Andrews CID, y'unnerstand? I dunno nothing about what you looking for. You get that?'

I nodded.

'Only thing I goin say to you is, walk careful, because if you walk too hard, you going to stir up snake.' He jabbed a finger at the envelope. 'Remember, you have to pay this back. Now get out of my face and go fix yourself. You starting work tomorrow.'

## 5

DS Chilman reminded me of geezers I saw sitting on wooden stools by roadside rumshops with their backs against the sagging walls. But, here, everyone turned to him.

Eleven weeks and two days later, he stood over my desk. 'Digson, I want you to pick up a man. In other words, today you make your first arrest. Forget all that stuff you read about the Miranda rights. Just arrest the fella and bring him in.' He tossed a pair of handcuffs on my desk.

I found myself travelling by bus along the western coast. I watched roadside villages slip past and it crossed my mind that two hundred square miles of island territory, pitted with valleys and mountains and rain forests, was a lot of country. Enough for the Europeans to kill each other for a couple hundred years ago, and to frighten the hell out of Ronald Reagan in my mother's time; enough to have him put an aircraft carrier on our horizon and launch Blackhawk helicopter gunships and F16 bombers to pound us into the sea. Small island my arse!

I sat sandwiched between two women, one with a child on her shoulder who seemed fascinated with the collar of my shirt, gripping and tugging it with surprising strength its little fists.

By now I knew that I, along with Malan, Lisa, Pet and Chilman's 'recruits', whom I had not yet met, were part of the DS's plan for a separate office from San Andrews Police Central, with its own staff and resources. Chilman wanted a squad of men who could navigate the forests and the valleys of Camaho blind-folded, with guns at their disposal. 'Because is not nice what I see coming in a coupla years time.'

According to him, San Andrews CID had to be at the crime scene first. The four Police Divisions on the island – The North, The South, the East and the blaastid West – must be at the service of San Andrews CID when the department needed them. And the Justice Minister must show him some respect.

He was getting there, he said, but slowly. The Commissioner understood him, the Permanent Secretaries did what they were told. The politicians ignored him.

There were times when I thought I saw his point, like the Friday evening, having been away from the office all day, Chilman turned up in such a rage he almost broke down the door. We let him talk until he stopped to draw breath, then we dragged our chairs to the centre of the office space and sat down.

'How many of y'all heard about the Dorian case in Cherry Hill?'

We exchanged looks, then shook our heads.

'That's my point,' he said. 'Here's how it go. Four days ago, young woman name Dorian didn turn up at her mother place to pick up her lil two-year-old daughter. Mother keep phoning the husband on his cell phone, but he not answering.

Next day, the mother phone West Division to say she can't find her daughter. By way of information, it turn out that the daughter married to an English fella name Edwin Jack. He 32, she 27. He run a business supplying fish to them hotels in the Drylands. Is six years that he and the Dorian woman married. Now hear this, she disappear on the anniversary of their marriage.'

The DS dragged a chair and planted himself between Lisa and Pet. 'West Division out there four days looking for the woman and San Andrews CID don't know nothing about it. It not even on the news. They say they called me and they couldn't get through.'

*Drunk*, I thought. *That's why*, but I said nothing.

'I only hear about it this morning. First thing I do is ask the neighbours and the relatives a coupla questions. Here is what they say.

'English fella used to beat up the woman all the time. They didn think it odd because that's what fellas here do. Make it worse, the wife couldn't leave the house when she want because

22

this fella train his dog to tear her up if she put a foot outside, unless he want she to leave the house. He used to be a dog trainer for some prison or other in England.

'The neighbour also mention *in passing*, people, *in passing*, that the husband have a girlfriend living in one of the houses next door and it been going on for some time. The girlfriend seventeen years old; she still in school.'

Chilman scanned our faces, then narrowed his eyes at me. 'How you would've proceeded from there, Digson?'

'Pick up the schoolgirl, Sir. Question her.'

'Why?'

'She's intimate with the fella, chances are she knows something. Besides, she has a vested interest. I'd instruct her to call the husband from her cell phone – ain't got nobody who don't have one these days. Most likely he will answer. I'd make her ask him, under duress if necessary, where he is.'

Chilman turned to Malan. 'You?'

'Find the dog, shoot it. Find the fella, shoot him.'

Pet chuckled. Malan frowned at her.

'Digson not wrong. I had the fellas from West Division arrest the girl and make her call the fella. The rest was easy. He lead us to the wife in a shallow grave that he and the schoolgirl dig. Grave 3 feet 6 inches wide, 3 feet 8 inches long in a patch of land that belong to the family of the girl. Mister Jack zip up his wife in a suitcase and plant her there.'

Chilman shook the sheaf of paper in his hand. 'Preliminary autopsy: death by blunt-force trauma and asphyxiation by strangulation. Four days and them still looking! It take me a coupla hours to find the wife.

'So, y'all unnerstand me now when I say is rapid response I want. Young people without rum guts, who could think fast and move fast. Not no ole fellas who, before their duty over, run home to their wife and their kingsize plate of food. And if I got to lift young people off the street and plant them in this office, I will make it happen. Watch me!'

The DS directed his chin at Malan. 'Why you want to shoot the fella?'

Malan muttered something about blasted foreigners.

'So you think is only Camaho man got the right to maltreat Camaho woman, right? My eldest daughter will tell you is we fault. Whitefella come here; he see how some of y'all behave with woman, so he think is normal. Y'all give him licence.'

'I asking for permission to question him, Sir,' Malan said.

'About?'

Malan pushed his back against the chair, folded his arms and crossed his legs. 'What's the charge?'

'You want to guess?'

'Non-capital?'

'Non-capital murder, yes. You got a problem with that?'

'Yes, we have…'

'Death penalty, right? And since that not happening, you want to go to the jail and bus' the whitefella arse, not so? You think you different? You married, but tell me how much woman you got around this island?'

'Is different,' Malan said.

'How?' Chilman said.

They locked eyes until Malan twisted his mouth and shifted his gaze.

I prised my collar from the child's grip, knuckled the roof of the minibus and dropped off amid the smell of the ocean and fermenting cocoa.

I was on the northernmost tip of the island. On my right was the rising spine of Saint Catherine mountain. Leapers' Town huddled at its base, almost tipping over into the sea.

A whitening sun beat down on the road. Unpainted galvanized roofs simmered with heatwaves, and it was just mid-morning.

Chilman had given me no instructions, and when I asked about backup, the fellas in the office chuckled. I would need transportation, I insisted, to bring in the fella. The officers laughed again and went about their business. Pet, the junior secretary, looked worried even as she tried to make me feel better.

'The DS testing you,' she whispered. 'He do it to everybody.' Then she muttered under her breath, 'One of these days *they* going get somebody killed.'

She huffed to her side of the desk and began sorting papers.

All I had was a description of the man from an officer who knew him. They called him Travis, nicknamed Dog Ears. Dog Ears was a badjohn – the type that carried a machete so honed he could shave with it. Travis was the kind who frightened people's daughters into the bush and had his way with them. Eighteen counts of sexual assault, five outright rapes, including a boy. Twelve instances of grievous bodily harm – an arresting officer being one of them. Forty-five years old – twenty-seven of which he'd spent in jail.

My time in the job had already taught me that every badjohn was fucked up. There wasn't a village on the island that didn't have one, and they all had the same history: parents who didn't give a damn about them, and left them almost from infancy to fight up with life on their own. Some little child in them was screaming and bleeding, and they really didn't give a shit about anybody because they had nothing much to live for. Deep down, a badjohn wanted to die and if that meant killing an officer to make it happen, he wouldn't hesitate to do so.

It was easy to find the house where Travis was holding the woman hostage, along with the man who moved in with her during the five years he'd been in prison. When word reached the office – a cell phone call, number withheld – they were already in there for two days.

All I had to do was follow the noise. On the grass verge, a cluster of agitated women – their protests full of attrition and abuse, rising on the air in waves. They were on the bank of the road above a two-room board house behind which the land plunged down past a thick growth of banana to a deep ravine.

A small wooden platform led up to the door. Travis sat on it whittling the end of a piece of wood into what looked like a stake. No movement or sound in the house. My eyes fell on his ears. Lobes large and fleshy, dangling like a dog's. The danger came off him like smoke. I felt my nostrils flare at the size and the heft of the man. I eased my way through the crowd, my hand protecting my face from the women's windmilling arms.

He knew who I was as soon as he saw me. Travis laughed. The fucker laughed. A wash of indignation flushed my skin.

'They joking! Townboy! Go back an tell them they got to send a whole set-a-man for me. Bring the fucking army, y'unnerstan?'

And he was laughing out loud, like he'd just cracked the sweetest joke in the world.

The women went quiet, their grumbles retreating down their throats. After a while Travis lost interest in me, and the women picked up their protests again.

I stepped back onto the road, made my way down the steep curve to the Catholic church perched on the edge of a high precipice that dropped sharply to the ocean. I stood among the headstones of dead parishioners and looked out at the chain of little islands that progressed in a darkening semicircle past the sleeping volcano we knew as Kick Em Jenny, all the way up to the grey shape of Kara Isle sitting on the ocean like a petrified whale. Chilman was born there. I wondered if that little island – crisp and dry as a biscuit even in the rain season, and encircled by a murderous cross-tide – had anything to do with the perverse way his mind worked.

I emptied my head of everything and stood there listening to the breakers destroying themselves against the rocks below, while a hard sea-wind pushed against my body. Two incoming boats ploughed the heavy waters, heading for the frothing bay below.

I left the churchyard and walked down to the beach. There was a dry-goods store backing the shore with, a rumshop beside it – its door propped open with a rod. Inside, four men perched on tall stools with their elbows on the counter.

I walked in.

The shopkeeper sat on a chair with his belly between his knees, his mouth making circles around a matchstick. I dropped a fifty dollar bill on the counter and pointed at a bottle of Jack Iron rum. The man got up, took down a bottle and slid it along the counter.

'Five glasses,' I said. The eyes of the men switched to my face and stayed there.

I looked around and smiled. 'Straight or chaser?'

The smallest reached for a glass. The man furthest along the counter shot out a hand and blocked him.

That one was bone thin, his face so drawn I could see the detailed outlines of his skull. His eyes reminded me of Chilman's. He even sounded like the DS.

'You not a tourist; you don't look stupid enough to throw away

26

your money on people you don't know, and you not from round here, so why you offering?'

'Y'all want the rum or not?' I said.

'You didn't answer me, fella – why you offering?'

The little man who'd reached for the glass cut in. 'Oh Gor, Shadow. How you so? The fella jus feel like offerin.'

I took out my ID and dropped it on the counter. 'I here to arrest Travis.'

Their eyes dropped to the ID. Shadow looked up, squinting. 'Is ask you askin we to do it for you?'

'Nuh.'

'What you want with us then?

'I can't do it on my own.'

'Where all them other police fellas that come with you?'

'I on my own.'

Shadow blinked at me. 'You got a gun?

I lifted my shoulders and dropped them. The man rubbed his head, squinted at me again. A chuckle bubbled out of him, 'If I was you, I would go back to San Andrews and tell all your police friends they playing de arse to send youngfella like you to pick up Travis. Whapm dey don like you? They want you dead?'

I left the bottle on the counter and walked out on the beach. A man sat on the sand, a fish-pot between his knees; three youths, legs crossed at the ankles leaned against the trunk of the only sea-grape tree. Directly in front of me, the raw Atlantic fretted and chafed against the sand, the water darker than I remembered it from the view over the precipice I'd just left.

The prow of an incoming twenty-footer jigged and yawed on the heaving water. The men on the beach moved forward, breasting the waves. Wordlessly, they formed a line along both sides of the craft, steadied it and hauled it up on the sand. They eased it on its side and began to empty the boat: five giant mahi-mahi, a sheaf of barracudas, a bluefin tuna. They left the oars and gaffs for last and were careful with the gillnet, which they laid against the tree trunk. Fifteen minutes exactly and they were done – the fish hauled onto a giant, rough-hewn wood-stand, the oars and utensils lying in a hollow in the sand.

The men from the rumshop had followed me to the beach, the

bottle of Jack Iron – half-empty now – cradled like a baby in the crooked arm of the smallest man. Shadow came to stand at my elbow. A half-smile creased his lips. 'Like yuh give up befo you start, man!' He turned to the others, 'Like the police-fella forget Travis and come to arrest the sea instead.' His laugh was a hiss – a tight release of air through his teeth. 'Lissen, officer, we not sweatin over Dog Ears, yunno. Dog Ears boat done sink arready, an de fucker don't even know it. Them woman up dere just wastin time.'

'I got an idea,' I said.

'Wozzat?'

I told him.

He hesitated, surveying the beach as if seeking some kind of answer there.

'You sure?' he said.

'I sure.'

He scratched his head. 'If it don't work is trouble. Anyway is your blood. I won't be hanging around.'

He was interested enough to gather his friends around him. They called over the three youths who'd been throwing sidelong glances at me from the time I stepped onto the beach. He told them to listen to what I had to say.

They were quiet boys, lean-limbed and muscular with their hair clean-shaven at the sides, the top ruffled with the beginnings of designer lox. It was important, I said, that they stand behind the women who, I hoped, would still be throwing words at Travis. They passed quick glances at each other and sauntered off.

When we got there, Dog Ears looked alert and twitchy. He'd laid a harpoon gun beside his foot, the machete across his lap, his chin pushed forward, the pale brown eyes flaring up at us.

'The officer here to arrest you, Dog Ears, so you better give up yourself.'

Shadow's voice had taken on a new tone, his body stiff as a cockerel's, his voice hoarse with venom. And I knew that magga-bone and rum-sodden as he looked, Shadow was not the kind of fella to run from anyone, once he was stirred up.

Before I left the office, Chilman told me that, in his day, sea folks had no time for police. These people who wrestled with the ocean to make a living handed out their own justice in swift and secretive ways. When a fella amongst them did some unforgivable thing against their own, they took him out to sea and left him to the sharks. I had no doubt that they still had it in them.

I felt the small adjustments of the men, their hands urging the women backwards, exposing me.

Travis saw what I was carrying, drove himself to his feet. A fast turn of his thick body and his hand was lifting the harpoon gun. I felt the shuffling confusion of the men beside me. They heaved themselves backward as I leapt and threw the net.

Travis fought the gillnet with grunts and thrusts of his blade, and a scalding string of words. But I was on him before he could free himself, my left arm locked around his throat, my right knee driving into his tailbone, my forehead slamming into the back of his head. I felt him shudder, felt myself dragged down by his weight. It was then that the others threw themselves on him.

I pulled away, dizzy with exhaustion. I took out my phone and called the office. Pet picked up.

'Digson here,' I said. 'I got 'im. Like I done tell y'all, I need transport to bring him in.'

Pet was so quiet I thought we'd lost the line.

'Pet you there?'

'Where's Caran?' she said.

'Who?'

'Caran not there?'

'Who's...'

I felt a nudge at my elbow, looked around to see a broad-faced man, brown and solid as a mahogany tree in green khaki. Two men stood beside him; like him they'd laid their rifles across an arm with the muzzle pointing skyward.

The man took the phone from me. 'Caran here, Miss Pet.'

I could hear Pet's voice coming high and fast.

'I didn go no way, Miss Pet. I had my piece on Travis all de time. Nothing would've happen to the fella. Remember y'all tell me last-minute. Not so? Is instructions that I follow. Okay I pass 'im over to you.'

When I took back the phone, Pet had rung off.

'I was covering you,' he said, lifting his chin at the window of the house next door, his voice indignant as if he were still arguing with Pet. He turned honey-coloured eyes on me. 'Maan, you move fast. I never see nothing like it.'

He jerked his head in the direction of the trussed-up man. 'Lemme deal with that.'

With a small convulsion of his shoulder, Caran flipped the rifle round, his fingers slipping smoothly through the trigger guard. He slid down the mud bank and stood over the fallen man.

It looked as if all of Leapers' Town had come out. Quiet. Watching with a kind of detached curiosity – some of them with phones against their ears.

The man holding the bottle of Jack Iron winked at me. 'I could get accustom to this, yunno. I could give up chasin fish and start fishin fellas.' He pointed at the net. 'Same equipment not so?'

Shadow had come to stand beside me. He was flicking his tongue across his lips. 'Leave im with us; we'll do the rest.'

'What's the rest?'

Shadow slid sly eyes at the sea. 'As far as we see, govment wasting food on Dog Ears in jail. We could fix dat for yuh.'

'Them days done,' I said.

'Who say?'

'I say.'

He threw me a sour look, 'We had plans fuh him, yunno, and y'all come and spoil it.'

'Criminal intent we call that. You want me to arrest you for criminal intent?'

'Yuh have to catch me first.' He sucked his teeth and slipped away.

## 6

According to Chilman's secretary, police departments used to keep their own records, but the hurricane of 2004 changed all that. They moved everything to the old colonial fort above San Andrews.

The search to find out what happened to my mother would have to begin there.

Fort Rupert squatted on a hill above the hospital, as if presiding over the island's illnesses. In the upheavals of '83, a whole government had died within its colossal stone walls, and there remained the abiding memory of terrified school children leaping from its ramparts to die at its feet.

The archives were housed in a building that hugged the fort's north-eastern slope. I showed my ID to the officer at the desk. He leaned forward from his kiosk and poked a biro at the corridor. 'Right at the end,' he said.

A quiet room, shadowy under a single tungsten bulb. Box folders with their labels faded and unreadable sat on strutted aluminium shelves that seemed barely able to withstand the weight. Inside the boxes were folders; within the files, police reports – some handwritten, some typed. Many of them were templates with questions that officers were required to fill in. I scanned the contents: various kinds of assault, criminal damage, GBH, praedial larceny, minor public order offences…

The murder files were stored in red box-folders at the back of the room. They became fatter and fatter year on year. The victims, if not women, were men in rumshop brawls, the occasional stabbing at a fete, or a brother warring with another over land. The weapon of choice almost always a machete.

Of the disturbances – the ones that involved guns – there was nothing. The 'Sky Red' uprisings of '51; the demonstrations and killings of '74 and '83; the Rape Riot of '99. Nothing. It was as if the island's history of blood and confrontation had no place on paper.

But I was hoping that somewhere inside these folders a diligent or careless policeman might at least have scrawled a note with some reference to the incident.

Each evening after work I climbed the steep hill to the archives, entered the quiet dusk of the little room and pulled a stool. Sometimes I spent a whole night paging through the files, while the town emptied itself of outer-parish workers in a bedlam of horns and chuntering minibuses. At 2 am, the duty officer jangled his keys and pulled the door, reminding me as usual to let myself out at the back of the building – if I was going home that night. He never once asked me what I was searching for.

I enjoyed the quiet, when San Andrews became a different place, with the sea beating against the esplanade, and the buildings echoing the scrape of footsteps on the asphalt. Men catcalled and young women laughed. On the court below, basketball players pounded the concrete, their rubber shoes yelping on the hard surface. It was as if the residents of San Andrews came out only at night to repossess their town.

I'd replaced the files, was heading for the back door when I heard the crunch of gravel outside. The footsteps halted; the latch shook. Warm air and the smell of tar drifted in.

The rattle of a cleared throat, and I knew immediately it was DS Chilman. He made his way up the narrow steps, emerged in the corridor, swaying.

The DS considered me with lowering eyes. 'Dead-end, Digson,' he coughed. 'I telling you right now is a *dead* dead-end you heading toward.'

Chilman leaned forward, holding out something in his hand.

'Wozzat, Sir?' I felt awkward and embarrassed at his drunkenness.

He shook the bag. 'You don't want it? I come all the way to bring this for you.'

He stuffed the paper bag in my hand. It was warm and yielding – a roti.

'What's up, Sir?'

'What's up.' He made a circle with an arm, rolled his eyes at the ceiling 'He asking me what's up. I'll tell you what's up, Digger: you searching for a pinhead in a jungle, that's what. You looking for what not here. That's why I bring you ah-ah fish roti. because…' He steadied himself with a hand against the wall. 'Because you, Missa Digson, need to feed that hole in here.'

He tapped his head, stumbled forward. I reached out to steady him. The DS slapped my hand.

'You think she dead? Nuh! She alive and kicking inside there.' He levelled a finger against his temple. 'Aaall the fuckin time. And she never going be dead until you, you, you, Mikey Digson find a way to kill she. Until we… kill… all… ov em. And that, youngfella, is… yunno is…' – this time he tapped his forehead – 'im-posss-ible. I ever tell you about Nathan?'

'You didn't tell me. Nuh.'

But there wasn't an officer in the force who hadn't heard of the ghost that DS Chilman was chasing.

Nathan – a young man whose mother came to the office a couple of years ago and reported him missing. She was sure he hadn't left the island. In fact, she knew in her bones that something had happened to her nineteen-year-old son. She'd managed to infect the DS with that certainty. From what I heard, he'd visited Nathan's mother many times, interviewed friends who knew the youth. Even with no evidence of a crime, the DS remained convinced.

'You didn hear about Nathan, but you hear about The Runner right?'

'The Runner happened last month, Sir.'

'And you remember what happen last month?'

'Is a different kinda case, Sir.'

Throughout the past month, newspapers carried the photo of a Scandinavian woman smiling out at us: blond, about thirty, a black Alsatian at her side. She'd left her residence in the Drylands to take a run with her dog. We found the animal by the side of the road with a broken right hind-leg. The woman had disappeared.

The Justice Minister took over, made his office the operational headquarters, then called out every retired policeman to join the search. A press statement left the Ministry of Justice every couple of hours until, three days later, a man walked into South San Andrews station and gave himself up.

'So, you telling me that Nathan not people too?' Chilman's eyes were steady on my face. He'd spoken quietly, dangerously. I needed to be careful with my words, not for his sake but for mine. I opened my palms at him, then gestured at the door.

'You pushing me out?'

'Nuh, Sir, I was about to leave.'

He fumbled with the handle of the door and let out himself before me.

'Yuh going about it wrong, youngfella,' he said. 'You not seeing what your mother was seeing.' He slammed the door in my face.

I stepped out, followed the unsteady shape under the street lamps until it disappeared down the hill.

I could have put down Chilman's words to drunkenness, but his drinking never really clouded his mind. We'd all learned that the hard way. I picked up something else in the old fella's tone. It was as if he were speaking from some personal grievance. And it was not just about the fact that his case had been taken away from him by the Justice Minister when that white woman disappeared.

*Look where your mother was looking…*

What the arse he mean by that!


When I came in next day, Chilman didn't look up from his conversation with Pet and Lisa, which was unusual. I hung around my desk, placing myself in his line of vision. The DS finished passing instructions to the two secretaries and cocked his head at Malan.

'Go pick up the fella now. Digger, you go with him.' He made a quick sideways movement towards his office. A couple of strides and I was beside him.

'Sir, just a quick clarification.'

'About?'

I dropped my voice, 'What you said last night.'

'Last night?' He looked totally confused.

'In the archives, Sir.'

'The archives! Which archives? Where?'

'Around two o'clock, Sir. You bring me a roti... and...'

'Roti! Dunno what you talking about, youngfella. Go on, Malan waiting on you.'

At the door, I threw him a hateful glare.

Chilman winked at me, then waved. 'Enjoy each other, I partnering y'all from now on.'

Malan adjusted his seat, jerked his head at the building.

'You like that fella?'

'Not sure,' I said.

'I sure.' Malan gunned the engine and shot off. 'That sonuvabitch don't like me. I dunno why he force me to take this job. The ole bull can't stand the best bone in me. Is like I do him something. I was gettin on perfect before he interfere with me.' Malan sounded aggrieved.

Chilman had conscripted him six months before he picked on me. In his short time in San Andrews CID, Malan had already developed a reputation throughout the island. Chilman had arrested him on Grand Beach with a shopping bag of skunk and a knife in every pocket. He gave Malan a choice: join San Andrews CID or face 14 years in jail and an unlimited fine for directing, organising, buying and selling a Class B drug.

It was our first outing together. Our job was to bring in a youth named Switch who'd been distressing his parish with a spate of break-ins, burglaries and praedial larcenies. The latest, an arson attack on his uncle's house, almost burnt the family in their beds.

It should have taken us forty-five minutes to get to Falaise. Two and a half hours later, we were still on the road because Malan's thing was women. As soon as he glimpsed a swaying arse ahead, he stopped the jeep in the middle of the road and started a conversation. If the woman ignored him, he sucked his teeth, revved the engine and drove off. He hung out for a couple of minutes at the rumshops, had brief conversations with the bartenders before driving on.

"A fella like you could make a killing, Digger. How much ooman you got?"

35

'We should be there by now,' I said.

'Relax, man. I not in a hurry and I sure Switch not in no hurry either. Chilman assign you a piece yet?'

'You expecting a gunfight?'

Malan chuckled. 'You think that's the only thing gun good for? I'll show you something when we reach.'

At the entrance of the parish, Malan stopped again. An old woman sat under a frayed straw hat at the gap of a small wooden house, with a tray of mangoes on her lap.

Malan braked, left the vehicle and crossed the road. I followed his hand as he dug into his pockets and pulled out a roll of notes. He unpeeled a few and gave them to the woman. She looked at the money, then quickly up at him. A dry hand reached down beside her foot and handed him a large plastic bag. He cleared the tray of the mangoes, walked back and dumped the bag on the back seat. The smell hit me in the throat.

'You want?'

'They rotten,' I said. 'You can't see that?'

He jerked a thumb backward. 'Too proud to beg. So what the ole queen do? She decide to sell bad mango to kill people.'

A series of hiccups came from him. It took me a while to realise he was laughing. 'Most expensive mango I ever buy and I can't eat one.'

He slowed at a small bridge, grabbed the bag and slung the whole thing over it. 'Okay, I promise I not stopping again.'

Falaise was a beach facing a tiny offshore island around which boats were moored like a multicoloured necklace. A couple of small concrete buildings stood so close to the shoreline they were almost in the sea. A freshly painted dry-goods shop faced the road. On the left, a mud track led up a hill to a nest of houses tightly packed against each other.

I counted nine boys on the culvert ahead, below them a ravine full of muddy water, its banks bordered by wild pine. Three women bent over basins of jacks and coral fish, stirring them with lazy movements of their hands.

Malan pulled the vehicle off the road and we stepped out. He looked up at the houses, the mud track leading up to them, then at his shoes. 'I not dirtying them,' he said.

The conversation on the bridge had died, the boys gone still, their bodies leaning forward. One of them rose to his feet. Malan shook his head and he promptly sat back down.

The fisher-women had straightened their backs, eyes shifting between Malan's face and mine. They eventually stayed on Malan's.

'Watch this,' he said.

Malan eased a hand under his shirt, took out his revolver and laid it on the bonnet of the jeep.

He jerked an arm at the boys on the culvert; they got up immediately and came running towards us, eyes switching from Malan to the revolver. It was not just the coal-blackness of his eyes and his locked-down mouth that made Malan look different now. He exuded the danger of a man capable of anything.

'Any one of you is Switch family?' He said.

Fingers pointed at the tallest amongst them – a bug-eyed youth with a narrow head, and limbs as knobbled as a stick of campeche wood.

Malan stepped towards him. The boy backed away, the big eyes rolling in his head.

'Switch your brother?'

'Nuh, Sir. We cousin, we…'

'Tell im I down here waiting.'

'I don think he…'

'Bring im,' Malan grated. 'I going in this shop. When I come out, he better be here.'

The youth shot off, his thin limbs pumping up the hill, arms windmilling outward. Malan picked up the gun and pushed it down his trouser waist.

'What you drinking, Digson?'

'Something soft,' I said.

I sat on the stool, while Malan brushed at his sleeves. The linen shirt looked as if it had just been ironed.

The woman at the counter passed him a Malta. 'How you, Dregs?

'I easy. You having same thing, Digger?'

The woman slid a bottle across the counter at me.

We were halfway through our drinks when the boy returned.

37

Another stood behind him – in a khaki shirt, mud-caked Roebucks, and jeans cut at the knees. He was panting and sweating, his arms straight down at his side.

'Yessah, Missa Dregs. I'z… I'z Switch.'

Malan barely glanced at him.

'Clean your shoes, then go in the jeep and wait.'

The young man looked at me. I avoided his gaze. He shuffled out of sight.

'That's how you do it?' I said.

Malan sipped his drink, angled his head at me. 'Fear is – erm – eco-nom-ical. It save effort. I hear a whitefella say that once.'

'Let's go,' I said.

He took a long drag before dropping the bottle on the counter.

A bigger crowd had gathered on the culvert. Switch was leaning against the rear door of the vehicle, his face still wet with sweat.

'You didn hear what I say?' Malan began bearing down on the youth. 'I tell you to clean your shoes and get inside the fuckin vehicle.'

By the time I caught up with him, he'd pulled open the door, wrapped a hand around the young man's collar and body-slammed him against the jeep. I heard the *oof* as the breath escaped the youth. Malan dragged him back, was about to slam him face-down on the bonnet when I threw myself between them. I broke most of the momentum with my shoulders. I closed my hand around Malan's wrist.

'Lemme go,' he hissed.

The raised tendons of his arm were switching. I locked eyes with him, and held on.

I angled my head at the people on the road. 'They get your point. Let's go.'

The tension slackened in his arm and he stepped back. I bundled Switch into the vehicle and we drove off.

Malan rubbed his wrist and sidled a glance at me. 'I thought y'was a waster, soft, yunno, but…' he swung the vehicle around the corner, its tyres yelping as it came out of the turn, 'You got some moves. Don't cross me though.'

'I don't like your method.'

'You know a better way?'

'Yeh.'

'Keep it to yourself, then.' A series of hiccups followed. 'Okay, Digger, you learn the book by heart. So what! All that say is that you learn the book by heart. The real world different from a coupla pages in a book. Law book say man not s'pose to murder man. They still go ahead and do it, not so? Fuck the book. I living in the real world. Anyway…' He nudged my shoulder with a fist. 'Me and you goin get on.'

'Who decide?' I said.

'Me.'


When we got back, San Andrews was simmering in the noonday heat, the air brazen with horns. Office workers weaved neatly between the heavy lunchtime traffic.

We were on Church Street. Along the edge of the road ahead of us a busy array of shifting bodies. Almost a head above them, a tall cane-stalk of a woman.

'Digger, yuh see that?' Malan was pointing ahead. He'd pressed his chest against the steering wheel, his chin pushed forward.

'That's Dessie,' I said. 'My account manager.'

'Jeez!' He'd dropped his voice. 'We got woman like that on Camaho?'

Malan tapped his horn. Two enormous eyes turned in our direction, high cheekbones, skin brown as a beer bottle and just as smooth. The easy strut of a gaulin.

Dessie caught sight of me, and suddenly her face radiated.

'Jeez!' Malan said.

'One minute,' I said. He braked so abruptly I almost hit my face against the windshield.

I stretched an arm through the window. Dessie reached out and slipped her fingers between mine.

'When you coming in,' she said, 'to check your mortgage?'

'How's my mortgage?' I said.

'Doing alright,' she laughed, flashed me a beach-white smile and carried on. We sat in the jeep with a raucous line of traffic behind us, watching Dessie step all the way to the bank. As the big glass door slid open, she lifted a hand at me before stepping into the cool.

'Jeez! Digson she yours?'

'She married,' I said.

'That make it more interesting, not so?'

'Not so,' I said. 'You wouldn't understand.'

Malan wouldn't take his eyes off me, not even when he pulled into the court yard, opened the door and let out Switch.

'You goin tell me how you meet she?'

'Nuh.'

## 7

I'd been eight months in the job, made routine arrests when requested, wrote reports that, more and more, Chilman passed over to me. I had a mortgage and was rebuilding my house. I supposed I was doing alright, but sitting in the office, eyeing the old DS, his sleeves rolled up, hands propping up his chin, muttering over the yellow folder that I now knew was the Nathan file, I needed to convince myself I was.

I knew that later Chilman would re-slot the file amongst his 'live' cases, drive down to the Lagoon Road, which bordered the yacht service and drink until he could barely stand. He'd never been thrown by a case except this one. He kept saying this, and even I – after the little time I'd spent in San Andrews CID – could see that he'd not made an inch of progress, and he probably could not.

But what made me any different from the ole fella? I remembered what he said to me in the corridor of the archives. To free myself of my mother, I too had to kill her – commit a kind of matricide. But how do you kill an absence? How do you rid yourself of something you knew you loved and had never had enough of? How do you empty yourself of all that?

Perhaps the old DS drank to drown out Nathan; and me – I read. I read a lot to distract me from myself. In school, I'd learned the word for every type of killing there was so that I could name what happened to the protesting women of 1999. The word I found was democide – the wilful murder of a person, or persons by a power greater than themselves. And the hand that wielded that power was the Commissioner, my father.

I couldn't say I knew him. He was the man my grandmother

sent me to see in my Sunday best when her kitchen garden did not earn enough to buy my things for school. Every couple of months or so I would walk to his gate in Morne Bijoux, shout a greeting to his Dominican wife who was always in the veranda combing her hair. She never answered me. 'That boy here,' she would say, her hand not missing a stroke.

The maid came out, dropped a few dollars in my hand and returned to the house. I would look at the maid with special interest because my mother used to be their maidservant too.

My anger came later.

I stayed in the office until Chilman left his desk, replaced the Nathan folder and left without a word. He probably didn't see me.

*Look where your mother was looking...* I'd chewed on that sentence, rolled it over in my mind until, the night before, I rose from bed, switched on the light and wrote a single word: *guns*. Of course! My mother would have been looking at the guns, or at the men who held them, which in this case amounted to the same thing.

The guns would have come from the armoury. Somebody would have handed them out. If there was one thing an armourer did it was to keep an inventory of the officers to whom weapons were given, as well as a record of their return.

Now I felt a hesitancy – a reluctance to proceed. When I cleared it all up, what would I do? Take it to my father? Throw it in his face? Then what?

But was it about this at all? I already knew who had done it. All my life I had visualised what happened to my mother. What remained to know – to fill the emptiness that DS Chilman seemed to know so much about – was to find out what they had done with her. To locate where she was.

I locked the office door behind me, got into the car I'd just bought and headed for the part of San Andrews we called The Dims.

I relished the fact that I could drive now. After four weeks of wrestling with Chilman's Datsun – a wilful, spiteful chunk of rusting metal – I had little doubt that I could drive anything on earth with wheels – even on the wrecked roads of the island.

At the end of the fourth week, the DS just said. 'You could drive, Digson; go pick up your license tomorrow.'

I got myself a little Toyota that went in whichever direction I turned the steering wheel, and that was good enough for me.

I tapped on the door of the old stone building, turned my face up to the camera and raised my ID to it. I heard the *thwack* of bolts on the steel door in front of me. When it swung open, a square face, yellowed by the tungsten light, pushed out itself at me. The man's head looked as if it were cut from granite

'Yeh?'

I felt a quiver of uneasiness run down my spine.

'DC Digson here.' I passed him my ID. He stared at it, then at my face, held it in his hand as if it were a useless bit of plastic.

'I have to call for clearance,' he said, with a voice that seemed to rise out of his belly.

'Call who?' I said.

He didn't answer me, was about to turn back, when I planted my foot in the crack of the door. 'Hold on,' I said.

He looked down at my foot, then at my face as if to say it was the stupidest thing I could have done. It was. He could have thrown his weight against it and crushed my foot.

'Hold on,' I insisted.

I dialled Chilman. His cell phone rang a couple of times, then the DS's voice came at me through a clatter of background noises.

'What's happenin, Digson?'

'I'm at the armoury, Sir. The fella don't want to let me in.'

'That make a lotta sense to me. What you want 'cross there?'

'You know,' I said.

He cleared his throat and in the pause I heard someone call out his name. 'Pass the fella over.'

I held out the handset to the man. 'Detective Superintendent Chilman want a word with you.'

The man took the phone, glanced at it, then placed it a few millimetres from his ear.

'Uh-huh?' he said.

Chilman rattled something. The man lifted the handset from his ear, squinted at the screen, then pressed it against his head.

'How I know is you I speaking to, Sir?'

Chilman's voice came through again – a string of squawks.

'Yessir,' the man said. 'Nuh Sir – is my job I doing, Sir.'

The man handed me the phone, looked me up and down. 'What this about?

'The Superintendent just told you, not so?'

'Nuh.'

'Where y'all keep the paperwork?'

He shook his head.

'The files, yunno – the shelves with all the files.'

His face relaxed. He made a movement with his hand and let me in.

I followed him up some stairs. He lifted his chin at a room without a door directly facing us.

'I might be all night,' I said to his retreating back.

'Not my problem,' he said, and clomped down the stairs. A door banged shut and the building settled into silence.

It took me four hours. The whole history of conflict of the island was here in the records of the handguns and rifles passed over to policemen over the years: the bolt action 303 Ross rifles of the 1950s replaced a decade later by Lee Enfields, followed by the AK47s of the early 1980s, then the Ruger Mini-14s. Now in our time, the American patrol shooters – M4s and F2000s.

I found what I was looking for in a folder which I thought was empty because it felt so flimsy in my hands: a single scribbled sheet of paper, dated May 3rd, 1999. Even the time was noted: 10.47am. The paper was sectioned into three rough columns: date and time of issue, date and time returned. In a narrower column on the right were the initials of the receiving officer.

Twenty eight Ruger Mini-14 rifles and twelve Smith & Wesson Model 10 revolvers.

At the bottom of the list there was an initial and a signature, BH. I photographed the paper with my cell phone and slotted back the file.

I went downstairs and knocked the door marked OFFICE.

The man came out, his shoulders so broad they almost filled the corridor.

'Where's the armoury?' I said.

'You in it.'

'I mean the guns.'

'What you want to go there for?'

'You come with me. No sweat.'

'I *have* to come with you.'

I followed him to the end of the corridor, turned left and stopped behind him at an iron door; his square head cast an inflated shadow on the wall. It took him a while to unlock it, and I sensed his reluctance in every movement of his hands and shoulders. The big steel door swung open. The sweetish smell of gun oil wrapped itself around my head. The man slid a hand along the wall and a weak yellowish glow lightened the darkness of the room.

There was a crypt-like quality to the space. A palpable quiet. I ignored the reluctance that came over me and walked in.

Rifles were queued on racks against each wall. I'd done my homework and knew most of them by sight and shape. I walked toward the rack of Mini-14s. I counted eighteen.

'Where's the rest?' I said.

The heavy shoulders heaved. 'Them is all.'

'Used to be more,' I said, staring at the dark-brown weapons. I stepped forward, ran a hand along the wooden stocks and closed my eyes – as if by some kind of necromancy they would rouse themselves and speak to me.

'How long you been working here?'

I heard his breathing, heavy and prolonged. 'One year and a coupla months.'

'You from the army, right?'

He said nothing.

'What's the name of the fella who worked here before you?

'Selo.'

'You know his full name?'

'Selo. He done something?'

'How long Selo work here for?'

'How you know I been in the army?'

'I wrong?'

'Nuh. How you know?'

'You wearing army boots and you got a 9mm Browning under your shirt – army issue. How long Selo work here for?'

'Coupla years.'

'And before him?'

'Dunno.'

45

I asked him to let me out.

Outside, I glanced at my phone. There was a missed call from Chilman, and a text message from Dessie. *1-2-c-u.*

I checked my watch. 11.30pm. Dessie only messaged me when her husband, the manager of her bank, was off the island.

I typed a question mark.

*Grinder*, she replied.

I headed for the old cane mill buried in a wilderness of acacia and dandakayo trees in the depths of Morne Delice valley.

Dessie was the teller at the counter when I opened my bank account – the long-limbed girl I used to watch after school as she walked across the Carenage, a full head above her laughing friends.

She was even more striking than I remembered her, as tall and slim as a river-reed.

'Dessie Manille,' I said, because I couldn't help myself. 'I used to adore you once.'

Her shoulders stiffened; she stopped filling in the form and looked me in the eye.

'Why you telling me that now, Flighty?'

'You know my nickname?'

She continued to scribble on the form.

'Who don't know Flighty Mikey? Inter-college sport. Winning all the time, but never staying round to collect the prize. They calling the boy to give him his trophy – next thing you know, he gone.' The chuckles shook her shoulders.

'My Cinderella years,' I said. 'I had somebody to look after.'

She X-ed the bottom of the paper, pushed it forward for me to sign. 'Had lots of girls crazy-sick about you in my school, but…' She dropped the bank book on the counter, nodded stiffly. 'Thank you for choosing to bank with us, Mister Digson. Next, please!'

'Let's talk,' I said.

'I'm married,' she said, lifting her eyes at the queue behind me. 'Next please!'

When I got home, I saw that she'd scribbled her cell phone number on the back of the receipt.

46

I arrived half an hour before her. Dessie parked behind the crumbling wall, got out and picked her way on high heels to my car. She slid into my seat, took my hands and folded them in hers.

She nuzzled into me. I closed my eyes and took in the smell of her. We didn't talk much. We were not lovers. We'd been doing this for months.

We would get to the point where the closeness became almost unbearable and I would promise myself I wouldn't do it again – this tempting of temptation. Dessie was a Presbyterian, her husband a junior leader or something in their church. I sensed no love between them, but something else that I couldn't put my finger on. What I knew for sure was that she was terrified of him.

'Digger, we have to stop this.'

'You say that all the time, Dessie.'

'I mean it.'

'You say that all the time too.'

I felt her breath against my shoulder. 'I want to wake up with a man who look at me like you look at me.' She eased her weight off me. 'You got somebody yet? I mean, serious.'

'Not yet, nuh. Why?'

'You *have* to?'

'Of course – what you take me for?'

The beautiful eyes were glowing. Dessie didn't look mal-treated. There was a quick bright smile for whoever she chose to bless with it. I only saw the fear when she said her husband's name. Luther Caine.

He would kill her if he found out, she told me, with a certainty that chilled me.

I'd seen him with her a couple of times. Like her, Luther Caine was from an old Camaho bloodline that called itself good family. Red-skin people, Caucasian eyes with a blackman's arse and lips – the part of himself he would be hating most, I thought. And no amount of servants, surround lawns, and a massive wedding cake of a house could change that. There would be tennis on Sunday mornings, dinner and cocktails in an expen-sive restaurant in the tourist south on evenings. In short, my father's kinda people.

'What make you stay with him?' I said.

Dessie would not answer me.

'Y'ever hear about the Thanatos urge, Dessie?'

'The?'

'Thanatos urge. Sigmund Freud. Beyond the Pleasure Principle. 1920, I think. You must look it up. You right, we have to stop.'

We watched a late moon rise and fill the valley with cold light.

'After here, I don't want to go back there,' she said.

'Is what prisoners say, when they come outta jail.'

She looked at me, interested. 'Serious?'

'Serious.'

'Digger, you mean it – not meeting up to, y'know… talk?'

I did not answer her. A couple of weeks would pass and we would find ourselves here again in this grey zone of nebulous transgression, a little frightened of ourselves.

For me it was a kind of brinkmanship – a pleasurable defiance; and fear, perhaps, that one day Dessie and I might tip over, fall into each other and spoil it.

It took me a week of sifting through the Civil Service employment records to find the name of the armourer whose initials were at the bottom of the list I retrieved from the armoury. Buckman Hurd. People knew him as Boko. I took the slip of paper with his name to the office at the farthest end of the building that we called The Staple Unit. I figured that the officer there named Cornwall, who collected reports and sorted them, would remember Boko Hurd, and perhaps tell me where to find him.

Cornwall kept to himself. He was Chilman's age – a man under whose weight the floorboards creaked whenever he crossed the office. Mornings, with his eyes on his door ahead of him, Cornwall heaved past us, grumbled a single sour greeting. He spent the rest of the day in his office. I'd checked his initials against the list I copied from the archives, then studied his employment history. He lived in Saint Patrick's parish but had spent most of his working life in San Andrews.

I waited until he closed his door, went over and knocked. Knocked again until I heard a grunt. He looked up at me, his forehead creased, the thick face sullen.

'Yeh?'

'I'm Digson, Sir, I…'

'I know who you is. You one ov Chilman lil boys. What you want?' He threw me a steady appraising look.

'Sir. I figure that Buckman 'Boko' Hurd was the armourer in your time?'

'"Your time!" You saying this is not my time too?'

'Nuh, but I talking about May '99. Y'was posted in San Andrews at the time?'

He'd dropped his folder. I watched his hands – heavy, thick-fingered – rubbing against each other.

'You trying to tell me something?'

'Nuh, Sir. I asking if you know Buckman Hurd and where I could locate him.'

He was looking at me closely, a gaze that made me feel pinned down.

'Why you don' ask the man who bring you in here?'

'Is just one simple question, Sir. I want to know if you remember Boko and if so where I could find him.'

'That's two question, not one and I not goin' answer none of them. Go talk to your boss.'

He turned back to his papers.

I felt dismissed. I swallowed and look down on the bowed head. 'Officer Cornwall, Sir, somebody do you something?'

He erupted from his desk. I pulled back, felt the heat flare up in my head. The door swung open suddenly and Chilman's turkey neck pushed in. What came from him was a sound that grated out of his guts.

'Take my advice, Conman! Keep pushin them useless paper until your pension ready. You ain got long to go.'

Chilman nudged me out of the space with his elbow. I left him there, shoulder against the frame staring down the man.

## 9

DS Chilman suddenly got the separate office he'd been fighting for. It was a long white concrete building that workmen gutted, painted and refurbished in a week. It stood above the open marketplace, separated from it by two streets, with a small courtyard that was fenced in by a five-foot wall. There was no sign on the door, no indication of the work we did inside.

Ms. Maureen chose the change to announce her retirement, said she wouldn't have the pleasure of being with us in our new place. She smiled at us all, then broke down on Chilman's shoulder. The old fella fell into a nasty mood and remained sour for the rest of the day.

Malan, Pet, Lisa and I fought over our preferred spaces while Chilman drew what looked like an octopus on the whiteboard that we'd stuck against the wall.

He shut us up with a loud wet cough and pointed at the creature. 'The brains – an that don't mean the head – is San Andrews CID.'

Each police division was a tentacle feeding us the information we needed to do the job.

Malan raised a finger, 'I don't see no teeth. How we going to bite?'

Chilman laughed. 'Malan, I always suspect you got rabies.' He looked around the office and grinned. I could almost see the ole fella dancing inside his dried-up frame. Chilman slapped the leather bag against his leg and headed for the door.

He tossed the words over his shoulder. 'Prepare y'all self for hard work, because from now on, they going throw everything at us. From children thiefing marble to ole ooman who can't find she fowl cock. Just to make us crash. We got a torrid year ahead, but they dunno that's egg-zackly what I want to knock y'all lazy arse into shape. And after that is the next step.'

And I have to say, I found those words exciting.

## 10

I was two and a half years in the job when DS Chilman asked me for a personal meeting.

'My parish,' he belched. 'Tonight.' He wagged a finger in my face. 'No questions now. Ask all the questions when you come.'

His 'parish' was halfway up the island. My little Toyota struggled through the rain and darkness while I cursed and called him every indecent name I could think of.

I'd never gone to visit Chilman before, but I knew where to find him.

The rumshop was like every other drinking hole on the island – a one-room shed with a single, fly-spotted bulb dangling from the centre of the ceiling. The three wooden benches against the wall looked as if they were built by drunks. The wall itself served as a back rest.

'My temple,' Chilman said, with a wave of his hand. He pointed at a woman with her elbow on the counter. 'The High Priestess. Call her Mary.'

Mary took me in from head to foot, dropped her eyes and continued picking her teeth.

Chilman offered me a shot of Clarks Court rum. I ordered a Coke instead. Mary pretended she didn't hear me. Chilman winked at her and laughed.

'Detective Constable Digson, sit down.' Chilman pushed his glass away from him. 'Talk to me about the case yesterday morning. I want you to describe it. Don't worry about Mary. Ain' got nothing she never hear or see before. Now don't give me all that police shit-talk. Say it as if you talking to one of your pretty lil girlfriends when y'all lay down in bed. Go ahead, I listening.'

'That's what you call me for, all the way up here this time of night, in this weather?' I asked.

'You didn' have to come. Now tell me, youngfella. I listening.'

'Well, we were notified…'

'"Notified" my arse. Remember you talking to your woman. That's how you talk to her? When she invite you to come and lay down, is notify she notify you? Start again, man. I listening.'

'Call came through around six in the morning, Sir. I was on early-shift. I took the call. They found a young man lying on the beach.'

'In what condition?'

'Dead, Sir. But you know all that already.'

'Dead how, Digger?'

'Incision to the throat. Sharp instrument. Tongue pulled out through the, erm – the oesophagus. Unusual, Sir. Only recorded instance in the region is in Trinidad and that was drug-related.'

The image flooded my head. I choked, tried to swallow back the bile. I stood up.

'Give him one, Mary.'

Mary handed me a small glass. I knocked back the drink and gasped. My head lightened, the suffocation eased, replaced by a warm roiling in my stomach.

Chilman pointed at my glass. 'Now you know, youngfella. The font of all forgetfulness. You think we'll find the culprit or for that matter 'prits'?'

'You the boss, Sir. The assessment is yours to make.'

Chilman curled his lips. 'We won't; they gone. Whoever done it not from here. You the one who tell me you believe some crimes is cultural. Is the first thing I remember when I look at that fella on the beach. You know what they call the way they kill dat lil fella? I take the trouble to find out. My granddaughter goggle it on the Internet for me.'

'Google, Sir; not goggle.'

'That's a word?'

'Yes. Necktie they call it, Sir.'

'Okay, so you goggle it too. You see, Digger, y'all think my job is to push y'all around. That's just the entertaining part. Nuh, my job is to see the trouble coming long before it reach. If y'all don't know it yet, we have a new Federation. Where Marryshow fail, the Mexicans and Colombians succeed. Every island in this region integrated now. They tie together more than ever before by trafficking. Drugs. Look at the size of the engines on dem lil fishing boat. You think they chasing after mullet?

'So, Digger! A lil boy got greedy and they kill him in their own style. They didn have the decency to respect we own clumsy island method. And when I see that, you know what I say to myself? I say something change. I say dis island get visited by something different that is not likely to go away. I say to myself "new crimes". Chilman downed his drink, slapped the glass on the wooden table. 'And new crimes require new minds. Dis old dog too sick to learn new tricks. Is no more bootoo and kick-an-cuff-deir-backside-till-dey-confess. Them days done. You think I didn see it coming? Why you think I fight to separate from them slowcoach?' He pushed himself forward. 'Is y'all fight now; I decide to hand in my resignation as soon as y'all come back.'

'Come…?'

Chilman rasped a laugh. 'England for you, Digger. School of erm… what? Forensics – sound like a headache tablet, not so? Well I hope to God it help you solve my last big headache – if I don't resolve it before y'all come back. In my forty years, I close every crime that come to me. In fact, some of them didn come to me; I went out and find them. Is the Nathan case that beat me.'

He was staring at nothing, the red eyes wide, unblinking. He passed a hand across the stubble on his chin and shook his head.

'I want to leave y'all a clean desk but, like I say, you might have to tidy up that one for me. Now lemme give you the details.'

'I know the details, Sir. Everybody knows it.'

'Know it, my arse. You think you know it? Then tell me what you know.'

'I read the file, Sir.'

'And?'

'And nothing.' I was struggling to suppress my irritation. It was clearly a wasted trip. 'A youngfella left the island and he didn tell his mother ba-bye – that's all.'

'He didn leave; he disappear.'

'Technically yes, but I don't see nothing unusual about that. People walk off this island all de time. They jump boat; they stowaway in plane. I hear some of them even swim. If you bother to look you find them hugging lamppost in Toronto or New York, or hiding from the cold in some little matchbox room in England wishing they never left home. And…'

'Digger! First thing Monday morning, a woman leave home and walk all the way from Five Springs to your office. She so damn worried-an-tired, she trembling. She tell you that big, bright Saturday afternoon her son left the house and he never come back. She cryin off her face and swearing on the Bible that her one boychild would never do a thing like that – and you don't see nothing unusual about that? Eh?'

'No, Sir.'

'Digger, you'z a jackass.'

'Sir, you'z my superior, so I can't answer back and tell you to haul y'arse the way I would've liked to.'

Chilman laughed. 'Digger, you so damn smart, it make you stupid.' He leaned into my face and dropped his voice. It was full of steel and gravel. I pulled back from him. Times like these – Chilman with his red eyes and rum-breath – unsettled me.

'All of y'all think I turn chupid over that Nathan youngfella. Chilman Jumbie is what y'all call him. Don't think I don't know. Well, yes, it eatin out my brain. I can't get rid of it.

'Now hear this: soon as the news break about Missa Necktie on the beach, Prime Minister phone the Commissioner. He want him to send out Coast Guard right away. He don't want them to come back, not even to refuel, until they catch Missa Colombian. That make PM look like international crime buster, yuh see. But as far as he concerned, to hell with lil Nathan because Nathan too local. Well lemme tell you something: Nathan more important than all dem Necktie boys y'all pick up on de beach. Even if y'all find one every foreday morning, Nathan still more important.'

Chilman stood up.

'Anyway, England for you. One year intensive immersion – that's what they offering courtesy of She Majesty Govament. Remember to take a coat. The Ole Queen might be generous but

56

the weather not so welcomin. Some of the natives not so friendly either.'

Chilman laughed, drained his glass and slapped it on the counter. 'By the way, don't think I favour you. Malan off to America to learn everything about guns. Canada will train the rest.

'Y'all coming back to a different Department, youngfella. No replacement for me. In other words no Superintendent. Just a small core ov you in San Andrews CID, but, like I say before, you call on the other services as and when you need them. Malan will run the office, but you, Forensics, going to be your own department at the service of all the regional Forces on the island. Malan doesn't like the restrictions at all. He want full control. But knowing you, Digson... anyway, just call it an experiment that got to work because y'all ain't have no choice.'

With a quick impatient gesture, Chilman tottered out onto the road.

He shouted his last words from his doorway, just as the thick arms of his wife reached out to ease him into his house.

'At least, y'all could point at Missa Necktie grave and say, he there! You should know what I talking about. In fact a jackass like you should feel it too.'


I was scheduled for the late plane to London with a short stopover in Tobago, then a direct flight across the Atlantic.

My phone vibrated; I picked up.

'Digger?'

'Dessie!'

'You'll keep in touch?'

I'd never heard her sound like that before.

'Dessie, you been crying and I know is not because I going away. What he done you?'

She didn't answer.

'Dessie, you awright?'

'Promise you will keep in touch,' she whispered.

'Dunno, Dessie, I...'

A muffled scramble broke through my words, then Dessie's voice. 'Yesss, Luther! I'm in the toiiilet!'

The phone cut off abruptly.

Chilman resigned the week before I returned, and it struck me how long the year abroad felt. When I walked into the office, Nathan's file lay in the middle of my desk with 'DC Digson' scrawled on it in the old man's wild and hostile hand.

So, he didn't solve it after all and that made sense. As far as I could see, it was all inside his head.

I filed it away, or tried to. Like I'd tried to file away Dessie in my mind, who from time to time texted me question marks.

The old DS gave me reminders every month, by way of a 'friendly' phone call, wanting to know how things going with me and the lil Nathan fella. For a couple of months I dodged his calls. Then one afternoon I returned from my lunch break and found the old man at my desk, his head swivelling on his scrawny neck like an evil turkey's, as he took in the new arrangement of desks and chairs, and the fresh paintwork Malan had insisted on.

Malan sat in his office, tense, sour-faced, his shoulders pulled back, chin pushed out – glaring at Chilman. The old DS was pretending not to notice, not until he stood and locked gazes with Malan. A tic of a smile creased Chilman's lips. He waved a hand before walking out the door.

'Follow me,' he said to me.

'Nuh, Sir,' I said.

He curled his lips; threw me one of those nasty sideways looks. 'Digson, you too?'

'I call that provocation, Sir.'

The old DS raised his voice. 'Provocation my arse! Is a promise I calling in. Is almost two years now since I send y'all off on scholarship that I work my arse off to get for y'all. I left a matter in y'all hands. Y'all promise to follow it up, gimme the benefit of the doubt – but naah, y'all take me for jackass. Y'all decide to bury it. Bury it arse! Well as far as I concern; my job not finish until we address the case. Until that happm, I still got my work to do.'

Malan had come to his door, his face tight with a dark malevolence. Chilman turned around to face him, his eyes narrowed down and so rum-shot they looked reptilian.

'Jus try it,' the old man growled, the veins at the side of his neck prominent and pulsing. 'You take another step, Malan Greaves, and you won't leave this office on two feet. Just try it.'

It was Chilman's tone that did something to Malan. He shuttered down his face, turned around and walked back to his desk.

With his hand on the door, the old fella sidled another look at me. 'You let me down, Digson. Is help you want? If is help you want, just tell me.'

For a moment, he looked forlorn and desperate. Then Chilman raised his shoulders and dropped them, addressing the air above my head. 'So is help they want. Okay, is help I going to give them.' He stepped out the door and pulled it hard behind him.

Chilman's disappointment – that last look of his especially – had scooped a hollow in my guts. It struck me that I was part of the old man's plan long before he met me. That trick of memory I pulled when I closed my eyes and pointed out the killers of that school boy in San Andrews must have raised his hopes. And because I did not fulfil his expectations, and didn't look as if I was in a rush to do so, Chilman decided on desperate measures.

Monday morning, exactly two months after he slammed the office door and left his rage behind, we settled down as usual to our desks. We were listening to Malan's update about a case in the north-west of the island. A vegetable farmer had caught the thief who'd been raiding his garden for months. It had been a week since he'd been holding the young man hostage in his house with the aid of several pot-hounds. He fed the youth and brought him out each morning to till his land as repayment. The Northwest police decided not to intervene until the young man had forked and hoed two acres, at which point they would go in and rescue him from the farmer. The officers in that area had obviously adopted Chilman's attitude to crime.

Malan, Pet and Lisa were chuckling at the story when the door opened. I looked up, found myself squinting at a yellow dress with bright sunflowers strewn all over it. I raised my eyes and saw a smooth round face shaded by a little hat that was slightly paler than the dress. And the oddity of the image struck me because the woman couldn't have been much older than I was.

'Missa Chilman send me,' she said.

Malan actually blinked. 'You have a case to report?'

'Nuh.'

'You have a complaint?'

'Nuh.'

'You want something investigated?'

'Nuh. Like I just tell you, Missa Chilman send me to help y'all.'

'Sorry, Miss Lady, Chilman don't work here no more. I run the department now.'

'I know. Missa Chilman retire after forty years.'

'So what he send you here for? S'matter of fact, you sure Chilman send you?'

Despite the air-conditioning, there was a film of sweat on the woman's upper lip. Pet, now Department Secretary, got up in a rush and hurried to the toilet.

'Take a seat Miss, erm…'

'K. Stanislaus. Fank you.' Miss Stanislaus walked to the interview desk, sat down and brought her knees together.

Malan remained standing. 'Now tell me again, Miss erm…'

Miss Stanislaus raised bright brown eyes at him. 'Missa Chilman send me to help out with the Nathan case.'

'Oh!' That was from me. The woman's presence suddenly made sense.

I was on the way to the office that morning when my phone buzzed

It was Chilman.

'Get her in, like I got you in.' He literally coughed the words into the phone. Then he rang off.

I called back straightaway. He didn't pick up.

'Malan,' I said, 'I think…'

Malan swung his head in my direction. His eyes flashed a

threat. Right now he would be deaf to anything I said to him. He'd already made up his mind about this woman's presence in our office. She was another of Chilman's provocations.

I could almost see the old DS raising a dry-stick finger in the air and grinning: *Fellas, y'all can't resolve the Nathan case, so I send a lil woman covered from head to toe in yellow to show y'all how to do it.*

'You could go back to Chilman and tell him what I telling you right now. He days with San Andrews CID done. He fish done fry. In fact it ain just fry; it burn, y'unnerstan? Chilman gone; case gone too. Is not we fault he couldn find that Nathan fella who disappear – like that!' Malan snapped a finger in Miss Stanislaus's face.

Lisa, now Malan's PA, turned down her head and began wiping her keyboard.

Miss Stanislaus's eyes were following every twist of Malan's lips, every shift of his clenched eyebrows.

Malan glanced at himself in the glass wall of his office, then back at Miss Stanislaus. 'He send you to join the Department? And you take him serious? You know what it take to become a Detective Constable? It take time, Miss Santa Claus! Time! Y'unnerstan? At least two years as a uniformed officer before even thinking about transferring here for further training. And even then you just a Temporary Detective Constable a Tee-Dee-Cee, y'unnerstan? And I not even mentioning the extra year on the ground with a coupla experienced officers. So! Is not no wash-your-foot-and-come job. You got to have ah education. You got to know procedure. You got to learn inference and deduction. You got to have a brain.'

The woman got up suddenly. I watched her straighten her dress with a quick flick of her hands. Left handed, I concluded, and damn vex. She headed for the door.

I turned to follow her. Malan curled a finger at me. I forced myself to fix my face. The embarrassment was burning up my skin.

'Yeh?' I said.

'Is Chilman who send this joker for true? Next thing you know, he...'

I don't know how she heard him. Malan's voice was barely above a whisper. But as soon as he said those words, Miss Stanislaus closed back the door and turned around to face us.

61

Those eyes were like the twin muzzles of a gun. She began walking towards Malan. Malan's face darkened and I could no longer see the whites of his eyes. It felt as if the temperature in the air-conditioned room dropped further. Pet returned from the toilet and stood with her back against the window that looked out on the Esplanade. I could hear the hum of the photocopier, the surge of voices in the market square. I thought I heard laughter.

People were out there going about their business, not knowing what was about to take place in San Andrews CID. But come tomorrow, the whole island would read it in the papers.

First Malan would break the assaulting arm. I saw him do that once and I still remember the scream from that youngfella on the Anse. Then he would drop her on the concrete floor, and if she survived, he would charge her for assault. It really didn't matter who it was. These things were never personal, he told me. To make a difference in this job a man must mind his reputation. A man had to be heartless. It was the only profession in the world where heartlessness was a virtue. It got you respect. Ain't got no better feeling than stepping off a sidewalk and watching the cars pile up, or hear the silence that your entrance cause in a room full of drinking men. Heartlessness is the only way to get that.

Just when I was about to throw myself between them, Miss Stanislaus stopped.

She looked Malan up and down with a daub of a smile across her lips. Apart from that little smile, her face was as smooth as the surface of Malan's mahogany desk. Through the gap between her body and his, I saw Pet and Lisa leaning against each other. They looked like twins with their mouths half-open.

'Missa Malan,' she said, 'what fool make you feel you so clever? The overseas school you been to?' She glanced at the certificate above his office door. 'Or the woman you make press-up your clothes so neat? You sure was a wife you want or a lil servant-girl? Because accordin to how I work it out, you almos twice dat girlchile age. She got a baby for you, not so? And you plan to give she another one before she catch she breath with this one, just so you could keep she tie down to you.'

Miss Stanislaus's eyes dropped to Malan's hand. 'You married.

But I don' see no ring. You only wear it in your house. Soon as you walk out, you take it off. Too much wimmen out dere who don' need to know. Right?'

Her voice was soft and pleasant, almost musical. I could listen to her all day.

'Hear something else, Missa Malan: I bet that young-girl, who keep you lookin pretty, not working. Mebbe she used to work but you make she leave the job. Is the way you like it. Dat girlchile got to depend on you. You even think you better than she. Dat's why you choose her in the first case.

'You sleep out whenever you want. And de first time she complain about it, what you do to she, eh? Because I bet she don' question you no more.'

Her voice suddenly filled the room. 'An don bother fool yourself thinkin somebody tell me all of this.' She stabbed a finger at the floor. 'I work it out right here. You want me to go on?

'Now I askin you Missa Malan. How come – wid all them years of infrencin and deductin y'all don't find that boychile yet? What you goin say when I find out what happm to him, and it reach de papers dat is just a lil joker who do it, and not you with your pretty shirt, air-condition desk an dat lil gun you got under your armpit? You don think is better if you do like Missa Chilman say?'

Malan shook his head as if he'd just been slapped out of a drunken sleep.

'You was on your way out,' he snapped. 'Not so?'

The office was quiet after that. Pet tidied her already very tidy desk. Lisa studied the paintwork on her nails. Now and again she raised her eyes to rest them on the entrance.

I caught Malan looking at his reflection in the glass. He noticed me staring, glared back and mumbled something. He adjusted the holster under his arm and strode out of the door.

I watched him ease himself into his Mitsubishi and drive off. It was the first time he did not rev the engine and shoot out onto the road in that crazy way of his.

★

Next morning I found Malan pacing the front office, making cut-eye at his phone.

'That phone do you something?' I asked.

'Commissioner call this morning. That woman coming back.' I thought I saw something like terror flash across his face. 'I sure Chilman behind it. S'matter of fact I know it. Lemme finish make a space for she, while I tell you what the Commissioner say.'

Malan had dragged a desk across the room and placed it against the wall at the far end of the front office. I watched him walk around it, adjusting it, stopping every now and again to look over at his door. Then he pulled the felt partition across the floor and turned it in such a way that it blocked a direct line of vision to his office. When Malan finished he looked up – quick and secretive – at the entrance. Satisfied, he strolled over to me, jiggling his keys.

Malan threw an arm across my shoulder. 'Sooo, Digger, you believe half of what that woman say yesterday?'

'Which woman?' I shrugged him off.

'She,' he said, pointing at the desk.

'Ah her!' I scratched my head.

*Not just half of what she say, jackass. And believe me, she ain' start on your pompous lil backside yet.*

'Oh! Miss Stanislaus, you mean? Naaah, man! Is old talk she talking. Is just guess she guessing. She spinning top in mud.'

Malan leaned in close. 'People like she…' He stabbed a finger at the desk again. 'You don't want them to get vex with you in public. They could make a big man feel small.' He snapped a finger in my face. 'Even if everything they sayin about you is lie. And the problem is – a pusson can't arrest them for obstruction because they working in your department.'

Malan retreated to his office and slammed his door.

I rushed the reports I had to do and cleared my desk. I took out a stack of forensic science magazines and organised them according to dates before placing them in folders.

Like Pet and Lisa, I couldn't prevent myself from keeping an eye on the entrance. All I could think of was the colour yellow.

Well, the colour that came in was purple. It was easy to believe that Miss Stanislaus had dyed the outfit overnight.

I straightened up. The woman bowed slightly at the girls and smiled at me. Malan's office door resisted his attempt to open it smoothly, and so spoiled his big-boss entrance.

He looked at Miss Stanislaus; she looked back at him. She smiled; Malan's forehead creased.

He cleared his throat and pointed. 'That desk across there is yours.'

'Fank you,' she said, her eyes resting on his pointing finger. Malan dropped his hand and eased it behind his back.

'Miss Stanislaus,' I said, 'I'm Digger and I'm assigned to you.'

'So – we start today?' she said.

Malan flicked a finger at the cabinet. 'Chilman left a file on the Nathan case. Pet, get the file!'

'Not nerecerry, fank you.' Miss Stanislaus offered each of us a smile.

Malan shook his head. 'Is procedure – you taking up the case, so you have to read the file.'

'It didn help y'all find de boy; not so?' she said.

Miss Stanislaus turned to face me. 'So, Missa Digger – that's your name for true?'

'Michael Digson, but I awright with Digger.'

'You take me to see Nathan mother first?'

'For now, Miss Lady,' Malan cut in. 'But is I decide whether Digger assign to you.'

Out in the car park Miss Stanislaus slid an eye at me and smiled. 'Go ahead, Missa Digger. You been hungry to ask me something. Say what you want to say.'

I cleared my throat. 'Yes, Miss… erm… Stanislaus – Malan – I mean yesterday… you met 'im for the first time and…'

Her chuckle sounded like gurgling water. 'You mean you didn know them tings 'bout im?'

'Well, I been around him long enough to know. But you…'

She chuckled again. 'De shirt – that was the firs thing. I half-guess he's the sorta fella who wear press-up linen shirt every day. Most man don't have the patience with a linen shirt to iron it like dat. And things that man don't have no patience for, they leave woman to fight up with it. Linen shirt – first you got to starch it, then hang it up to dry in a certain way so it don' get wrinkle. Then you got to iron it. Most woman I know don't have de patience for dat. To do dat every day – nuh! Dat mean the woman got no choice.

65

'Missa Malan love-up imself a lot. Always lookin at imself in de glass-mirror. He can't help it. His perfume smell like he shouting at every woman in de world to notice him. He talk to me as if he accustom bossin woman and don't expect no answer-back. Which woman goin take dat for long except some lil girl?' Miss Stanislaus looked at me as if she really wanted to know.

'Then I look at his ring-finger. Ring-finger ring should leave a strong mark if you wear it all the time, den take it off, not so? So how come his finger just have fainty-fainty mark? Besides…' Miss Stanislaus dropped a hand into her bag, pulled out a bunch of tissues.

'Besides?' I said.

'He's a Camaho man.'

The way she said 'Camaho man' she could have been talking about mangoes or breadfruits.

Her eyes were on me. I saw the challenge and decided not to meet it yet.

'Okay, Miss Lady.' I gunned the engine. 'We heading for Nathan mother house.'

The house stood behind a row of blossoming acacia trees. Each wall was a different colour: bright blue, yellow, red and white. The roof was a dazzling green. Five bamboo poles rose high above it, each bearing flags whose colours matched the house exactly.

A bony dog lay curled up at the foot of the steps. It barely lifted an eye at us. A thin woman who sat on the yellow veranda was watching us approach, with the same indifference as the dog.

'Dog don't bark?' Miss Stanislaus said.

'Only night-time,' the woman replied. She rose to her feet as we climbed the steps and entered the veranda. A faint aura of soft candle, camphor and ground spice surrounded her.

'I'z Iona,' she said.

Miss Stanislaus fanned herself and smiled at her. 'Missa Digger from The Department. Chilman Department – yunno? I come along with him for company. I'z Miss K Stanislaus. We come here about the boy.'

I cleared my throat. 'Just trying to tie up some matters, Miss

Iona, about Nathan's... erm, absence. I take it that you haven't heard from him, or about him since?'

Miss Stanislaus glanced at me. An expression that I could not decipher crossed her face. 'Is awright for Missa Digger to look inside Nathan room?'

Iona fumbled with her headwrap and pointed through the open door at the furthest room.

There was something solicitous about Miss Stanislaus now. She dipped into her bag, pulled out a small packet and handed it to the woman. They both looked up as if surprised to find me there. I headed for the room, feeling dismissed.

Nathan's room smelled different from the rest of the house – slightly perfumed. On one side there was a narrow bed covered with a floral sheet over which a mosquito net was hanging. I noted three pillows with matching pillow cases.

A magnifying mirror sat on a little wooden cabinet to the right of the glass window. In front of it a small tub of cocoa butter, a stick of Brut deodorant, another of Old Spice, a pack of Ambi skin-toning soap, a tiny pair of scissors.

There was a large flat can of Kiwi shoe polish perched on the edge of the narrow table. Hanging on a nail from the door, a brown satchel – all leather and brass buckles. I unhitched the bag, brought it to the window and ran through every pocket: a small bottle of Ponds hand lotion, a heavy nail clipper, a pair of tweezers, a small packet of unopened tissues. A bundle of neatly folded receipts.

I committed it all to memory. Later I would make my notes.

Outside, the women raised their voices. They sounded amused about something.

I poked out my head and lifted a finger at Miss Stanislaus. She got up quickly and came in with Iona close behind.

'Done,' I said. 'You ready to go?'

Miss Stanislaus narrowed her eyes at me.

'Seeing as Missa Digger done, and we still got a lil time, I could see Missa Nathan clothes?'

Iona reached under the bed and dragged out a large suitcase. She released the catch and threw back the soft canvas cover. Miss Stanislaus lowered herself in front of the case, her chin propped up by the heel of her hand. After a while, she reached out a plump brown finger and poked a shirt, as if she did not want to disturb it. 'Nice,' she said. That was all she said before rising to her feet and turning to Iona.

'Sorry to ask you. Where he keep his undergarments?' The woman opened the door of the cabinet. Miss Stanislaus leaned forward and looked in. Again she poked a finger.

'Like I tell you, he used to be a decent boy,' Iona said.

Miss Stanislaus nodded vigorously, then pointed a finger at the tin of polish. 'He wasn't the one who put dat dere. Not so?'

Iona looked confused at first, then her eyes widened. 'No-no-no. I mean, yes. He ask me to buy it for him. I lef it there for im to see it when he come in.'

Miss Stanislaus fingered the buckles of the leather satchel before taking it down, lifting the flap and peering into it. She pulled out the wad of receipts and inspected it.

'An dis?' she said, replacing the satchel, then lifting her chin at it.

'The bag?' Miss Iona sucked in a lungful of air and lowered her head. 'That's what make me worry from de start. You never see im without it. Missa Simday give im it. They used to be good friends.'

'He got a friend name Sameday?'

'Simday,' she said. 'He from Canada. He a teacher. Been livin on the islan long time.' Iona spoke as if we ought to know who Simday was. 'Missa Simday was convince something wrong. He'd ha gone to the police, if I didn go myself.'

'What make im so sure?'

Miss Iona shrugged. 'He know Nathan. They friends. When things really rough for me, Simday help me out.'

Iona turned up her face at the bag. Her eyes were streaming. Her shoulders shook with the effort to hold herself together.

I felt the stirrings of a misgiving that I hadn't felt before. Perhaps it was the same thing Chilman felt when this woman walked into his office and told him about her missing boy. Grief is grief, regardless of its source. Dead or alive, this woman's son was missing. She hadn't heard from him for more than three years. Either way, Nathan was lost to her.

I imagined her sitting in her veranda at night, on her plastic stool, looking out onto the road with the terrible anxiety that now distorted her face. I understood that; I'd had my share of waiting too.

My mind drifted back to the eleven months I spent in England, in that place of high white walls and numerous black-framed windows we referred to as 'The Lab'. There, they taught us a language meant to rid us of all feelings. Everything was procedure. You walked into a crime scene, secured it from every possible contamination, including yourself. Then you ran a fine-tooth comb through it, which could last for weeks because – short of a confession – evidence was everything.

My instructor told us that a time would come when we would take it all for granted. Unravelling a crime would be just a job like an electrician's – a wire breaks, you do your best to fix it. No difference. There isn't a village or a city in the world, he said, where murder doesn't happen. It was all about not feeling.

I turned away from Iona. Miss Stanislaus glanced at me. Her hand paused over the mouth of her purse, then she snapped it shut.

'You got a photo of Nathan?' I asked, 'One... before... erm...'

'Me and Missa Digger leavin now,' Miss Stanislaus said. 'See y'all next Sunday.'


Back on the road I started the car and sat with the engine running. The stretch of asphalt ahead was bright white in the afternoon sun. Heat waves shimmered above it. I switched on the aircon. Miss Stanislaus reached out and switched it off.

That surprised and irritated me.

'Nuffing wrong with sweating,' she said. 'What you find out?'

'About what?'

'Nathan.'

I cleared my throat. 'Well, he very neat and tidy for a fella.'

'For a fella,' she echoed, chuckling.

'How else you want me to say it?'

'Go ahead, Missa Digger. I listening.'

'He think a lot of himself: nice clothes, two sticks of deodor-ant; tweezers – how many fellas have tweezers by their mirror?

Mirror take up pride of place near the window so he could check out them pimples proper. Dictionary of Correct English Usage is the only book in his room. That make me think that he don't feel he cut out for no small-island life. Ambitious, I believe. He can't afford a concrete house, but he make the one he live in the prettiest in the village. Skin-toning cream and skin-bleaching soap. What kinda fella use that? He prefer to be a white man perhaps – a local Yankee who believe he born in the wrong place.'

'You ask for a photo of Nathan. Why?'

I shrugged, 'Procedure.'

'In all dis time y'all never ask for a picture of the boy?' She was staring at me hard.

'I wasn't handling the case.'

'Why you want a photo now?'

'A pusson want to know what he's like; not so?'

'But you jus done tell me what he's like.'

'Like I said, Miss Lady, is procedure.'

She looked out the window, her attention drawn to a flock of white egrets above the blue-grey hills in the distance. 'No wonder y'all never find Nathan.'

'Ever cross your mind he might've run off to Trinidad and said to hell with everybody?'

'What make you think so – dis?' She dropped the receipts on the dashboard.

I looked at the slips of paper, then at her, her hands resting quiet on the clasp of her bag.

'Yes,' I said. 'All of them in Trinidad currency and each one got a different date roughly four weeks apart.'

'And dat mean?'

'The youngfella accustom travelling to and from Trinidad, average once a month. Had a lil business buying women stuff: shoes, handbags, cosmetics – you saw the stuff in the suitcase – and selling for a profit here.' I pointed at the last receipt. 'Last time Nathan was in Trinidad was August fifth, three years nine months ago. Maybe the last time he went to Trinidad he decided to stay.'

Miss Stanislaus dropped the receipts in her bag. 'Or, Missa Digger, mebbe somebody in Trinidad make de purchase for Nathan, then post the goods along with the receipt. People do that all the time too. What I sayin is, you dunno for sure if Nathan went to Trinidad.'

She pulled a tissue from her bag and fanned herself. 'Missa Digger, you kin tell me why we still here sittin in your car by de govament road?'

I didn't trust Malan's smile when we got back to the office. He had laid out a jug of cold mauby on a tray. The glass was sitting on a napkin. A decanter of ice stood beside it. Lisa told me afterwards that Malan went out and bought the tray and glass himself.

He hardly waited for Miss Stanislaus to sit before placing the tray in front of her.

She nodded her thanks and turned to him. 'Missa Malan, we have to report to you; not so?'

Malan drew up a chair in front of us.

'Yes, talk it through first. Digger will write the report later.'

Malan had switched modes. There was no pretence here. When it came to this business, Malan was a different animal altogether.

The week I returned from England, I found one of Chilman's handwritten notes to the Commissioner explaining, in his usual staccato sentences, why Malan had to be the person to run the office.

*Not stupid. Loves the job. Mind works in leaps. Will break the law to catch the lawless. Loyal to nothing and no-one but the department.*

Maureen, Chilman's secretary of thirty years – who knew him better than his wife – would have translated it all into Civil Service language.

I described our visit to Miss Iona as briefly as I could. When I finished, Miss Stanislaus tapped her bag. The afternoon light through the window highlighted the fine mesh of her eyebrows and her purple lipstick. Side-lit, she looked neither old nor young; male nor female – just a glowing face in which the only thing that held you was the brown glitter of her eyes.

'I don't mind people tellin lie, Missa Malan,' she said. 'Lyin not the crime. The crime is whatever the lie is hidin. Miss Iona not lyin, she jus not tellin de truth. She know Nathan never left de islan, but she dunno where he is. She want us to find im; but she frighten to know what we goin to find.'

'She told you that?' Malan queried.

Miss Stanislaus shook her head. 'Nuh. Is the way she talk bout him. Like he not with us no more. H'*was* a good boy; *he use to* like to look neat an clean. *Use to* love to dress up. And yunno, I believe what she believe. Nathan somewhere here.' She gestured as if Nathan was hiding in the room. 'How I so sure? Well, it was that lil leather bag where he keep his costlymetics that the Canadian teacher-friend give him. That bag always pack-up with Nathan hand-cream and comb and finger-clippers. The way I unnerstand it, if Nathan never leave for work widout his comb and clippers, ain' got no way he goin leave Camaho widout them either. Besides, that night he dress in short-pants and sandals. Soft-foot fella like Nathan in short-pants an sandals, I don't think he going nowhere far.'

Malan was staring at some point beyond the window while Miss Stanislaus spoke. I knew that gaze. He was memorising every word. In a few months he would still be able to quote her down to the pauses in her sentences. And if he had to remind her of those words, it would usually be in reproach or retribution.

Malan sprang to his feet. 'Okay, people, if y'all don know it yet, we have a case.'

He strode into his office. I heard the clatter of keys. My heart stepped up tempo.

He came back with a small box, sat down, placed it on Miss Stanislaus's desk and opened it in front of her.

The gun looked stark against the red bed of velvet. It was the smallest we had – a Ruger. Malan loved that little revolver, boasting that he'd walked through many inter-island airports with it and never got detected. On his off-duty days he wore it in a specially designed holster just above his crotch. Mercifully, I thought, he wasn't showing off the holster too.

'This, Miss Lady, is ah LCR.' He hefted the weapon and ran a finger along the muzzle. 'Thirteen and a half ounces – less than a pound ov sugar. Six-an-a-half-inches of polymer and aluminium. Thirty-eight calibre. Five rounds.'

Malan settled the little gun in his palm with the snout pointing at his chest. 'The kind of bullet it pack is called a Plus P.' He flicked a wrist and emptied the chamber. The five bullets lay like bright metallic eggs in the other hand. 'You can't go wrong with this after we finish training you.' He laid the weapon in front of Miss Stanislaus. Of course, she wasn't meant to take it. Not yet. It was simply Malan's way of calling a truce between them.

I watched Miss Stanislaus trace with darting eyes the rubber-ised handgrip, the curve up to the rear sight, then the short pig-snout of the barrel. Her eyes halted on the silver trigger. 'Won't be nerecerry, fank you.' She pressed her back into the chair.

The smile left Malan's face. I could see that he was hurt. That gun was the best peace-offering he could make, and Miss Stanislaus had turned him down.

I think she realised it. She picked up the weapon with a wad of tissue, held it well away from her before resting it on the desk.

She was more enthusiastic about the cell phone he handed her. 'Standard issue,' he said. 'Walkie-talkie went out with Chilman and all dem ole fellas. So,' he turned to Miss Stanislaus, 'that mean you got to see Iona again and when you see her next time…'

'I go to church with her,' Miss Stanislaus said.

'I was goin to say you get heavy with the woman. That's what I was going to say!'

Miss Stanislaus stood up. 'I goin join dat church ov hers.'

'Join!' Malan looked at me. 'That Iona woman is a Fire Baptist, not so?'

I said nothing.

Malan turned to Miss Stanislaus. 'Miss Lady, is protection; you sure you want nothing to do with dis gun?'

'Like I done tell you, Missa Malan, is not nerecerry.'

They locked eyes for what seemed like forever. The afternoon sun cut a bright decisive path across the floor between them.

It was Malan who broke the silence. He smiled that twisted little smile of his, 'You got no choice, Miss Lady. Is what the job require.'

Miss Stanislaus dragged out a tissue from her bag then snapped it shut. 'Nuh!'

74

'I'll train her,' I said. I took the gun, laid it in the case, eased it into my top drawer and locked it. Miss Stanislaus twisted her mouth and shook her head at me.

What Miss Stanislaus didn't tell us was that Nathan had adopted his mother's religion. What I didn't tell anyone in the office was that I knew all about Fire Baptists.

In that complex hierarchy of Deacons and Mothers and Teachers; of Shepherds and Nurses and Captains; Surveyors and Healers and Watchmen, my grandmother who mothered me, was a Prover. She was a discerner of truth. A decipherer of souls.

She was the one who rooted out the false believers from the committed, sifted through their visions, their dreams and revelations and decided which were to be believed, and what were pure invented lies. And when the spirit seized The Flock and threw them thrashing on the earth, my granny picked out the pretenders from the truly possessed.

My old woman was a demon hunter, I told Miss Stanislaus. She was a chastiser of stray souls, and I, along with everyone else, was terrified of her.

Nathan was a Pointer, Miss Stanislaus said, did I know what a Pointer was?

'The Sealer of Hands, Miss Stanislaus. Most times it is a woman who got that job. But sometimes you have a fella. He shepherd the mourners on the Mourning Ground.'

She was dangling on my every word, so I decided to take my time.

'Mourning Ground is a form of cleansing, although I don't see what clean about lying on cold earth with a stone for a pillow. Pointers look after the Mourners cuz they stay there between seven and twenty-one days. Without food. My granny call that fasting; me – I call it starving. You want me to tell you about the

Candle Service, the Flower Service and the Pilgrimage my Granny used to drag me to when I was a lil boy?'

'No, fank you.' Miss Stanislaus laughed.

We left for the church early Sunday morning. It was one of those days when the sunburnt hills in the far distance looked just a hop and a skip away.

Miss Iona, she said, would present her as a friend who wanted to convert. I was to be Miss Stanislaus's 'mister'.

The church was hidden away in a place called Pwin. I saw the flags first, high on bamboo poles, fretting in the wind. The car struggled to get to it on the narrow dirt road, gouged as it was by years of rain and neglect.

I pointed past the old Volvo car in the yard, at the windowless concrete hut that sat just behind a larger wooden building. 'The Mourning Ground. The calabash of flowers by the doorway tell you that.'

They'd built The Children of the Unicorn Spiritual Baptist Church at the edge of the swamp where the rivers that ran through the valleys of Old Hope and Morne Delice met the sea and died. The odours of incense and melting candle-wax were as familiar to me as those of my own bedroom.

A flock of women surrounded Miss Stanislaus, their heads tied in red and blue and yellow scarves, their white dresses flaring off their narrow hips as they shuffled around her, chirping like night-time crickets. To look at these people holding her hands and smiling, a person would think they were first cousins or newly discovered family. Women, I thought, they all the same. Dunno what they see in one another.

I watched the two Watchmen watching me while the women fussed around Miss Stanislaus. The Watchmen held their knotted whips against their legs. I held the gaze of the younger with the pointed beard. He winked at me and smiled. The other – clean-shaven, bald as a polished stone – was staring at Miss Stanislaus. With her frilly white dress and cream handbag she stood out among the other women like an egg in a calabash of stones. I imagined her becoming like them: thin as a sliver of dried bamboo, her lovely brown eyes gone dark and dreamy by seasons of prostration in that little concrete hut. I felt – for the first time – a quiver of dread and possessiveness for this woman who confounded everything I knew about Camahoan women.

There were children in the churchyard too, all standing in a corner of the narrow, stone-packed space, staring at Miss Stanislaus with the honest curiosity of children. When Miss Stanislaus waved at them, they became an agitated little flock of twisted shirts and skirts, and wide uncertain smiles.

A tall man walked out of the long wooden building – a big brass bell in one hand, in the other, a heavy leather-covered Bible that had clearly suffered many preacherly beatings. There was not a person on the island who had not heard of Deacon Bello, Healer and Diviner, whom politicians visited in secret to have their misfortunes fixed and their excesses remain undiscovered. Miss Stanislaus turned to him and bowed. But for the slight lifting of his eyebrows he might not have seen her.

Miss Stanislaus eased herself away from the women and walked over to the children. She lifted a little girl and caressed the child's small face. 'I got a lil one pretty just like you. What's your name?'

Clucking like a delighted hen, she picked up another. 'And who this one belong to? Cuz you sooo sweet I want to take you home.'

'Dat's Millie baby,' one of the women told her.

A young girl just outside the group nodded shyly at her and quickly lowered her eyes.

Miss Stanislaus pointed at another. 'And dat lil man? He belong to Miss Millie too?'

'Dat's Amos,' the girl replied. 'His mother not here. She lef' him with us and gone off to Trinidad.'

I could not keep my eyes off the boy they called Amos. His mouth was soft and fluid, his lips glossed over with spittle. Big, watery eyes that never settled on anything for long. I couldn't help wishing he had a grandmother who would steer him to a place of quietness.

Miss Stanislaus must have seen the agitation in Amos too. She rested a hand on the boy's head and looked into his eyes; then she kissed him on his forehead.

One of the women took Miss Stanislaus's hand. 'Come meet The Mother.' They urged her towards the back of the building.

Deacon Bello was still in the doorway of the church, sleeves rolled up to his elbow. A large wrap of fabric sat on his head like a multicoloured hornet's nest.

I've heard women speak of Bello in a tone that would unsettle any man they lived with. There was a sheen to him. A person got the impression of limitlessness when they looked into those large dark eyes of his. He was wearing his robe – blue like an Easter sea. His body filled it out completely. The famous staff with which, they said, he beat the hell out of the demons that attacked his flock, was leaning against the doorway. He'd angled his head in such a way that it looked as if he were inspecting the flags at the top of the poles. I wasn't fooled. I could see by the whites of his eyes that they were fixed on me.

I lowered my head and genuflected the way my grandmother taught me all those years ago.

A rich voice – thick and dark like molasses – reached me. 'You a Believer?'

'My granny was,' I said.

'I know she?' With a quick convulsion of the hand, he opened the giant Bible.

'No,' I said.

'How come?' Bello hadn't raised his voice but I heard the challenge in it. There was not a Fire Baptist family on this island that Bello wouldn't know, or know of.

'She gone to glory,' I said. 'Long time.'

'What kill she?'

'All flesh is dust,' I replied.

Bello flashed bright white teeth at me, turned and disappeared through the gaping doorway.

The Mother emerged from the back of the building, her hands dripping with soapsuds. Quick, dark-brown eyes took in everything. She was broader than her husband and held herself like royalty, gliding over the rough yard in a white headwrap and a flowing dress to match. Miss Stanislaus looked like a little dressed-up doll beside her.

'Next Wednesday, then?' Miss Stanislaus said.

'Take your time,' The Mother said, her voice as deep-chested as a man's. It seemed to shift the air around us. 'Like I done tell you, these things take time.'

One of the women cast a fast glance at The Mother, raised her hand as if to say something, then dropped it.

'Wednesday fine wiv me, Mother Bello.' Miss Stanislaus patted her handbag and strolled over to me.

'She don't like you,' I whispered, surprised by the satisfaction I got from saying that.

Miss Stanislaus blinked at me, then looked away. Her fingers were restless on the clasp of her purse.

She was silent on the way back, except for one moment when she turned from the window. 'Missa Digger, what they teach you about murder in dat furrin-sick school in Englan?'

'Lots of things,' I said. 'What you want to know?'

She shrugged. She was still fidgeting with the clasp of her purse. Sweat was beading her forehead, but she did not pull out her tissue.

I thought over the question for a while. 'I s'pose, if there's one thing I came away with is the fact that a killer kill according to a pattern. Is like they can't help themselves, even the clever ones – same or similar technique all the time: a blow to the head, asphyxiation, poisoning, ritual murder – same procedure. As if a different part of the brain take over and insist they do it the same way every time. Similar victims too. Habit or perhaps something deeper than that. That's what betray them in the end.'

'What kinda pusson kill, Missa Digger?'

'Any kinda pusson. Make the reason strong enough and anybody can. If they got the means.'

Miss Stanislaus folded her arms and looked out of the window. 'Don think I could. Not me.'

'You say you got a girlchile?' I said.

She nodded.

'Okay – that gun that Malan offer you. Let's say you got it in your handbag and you know how to use it. You walk into your house and find some fella with his hand around your baby-girl

80

throat. You goin stand up there with that gun in your pretty little handbag and watch him strangle your child?'

She grunted as if I'd hit her in the stomach.

'What turn your mind to all this talk 'bout killing now?'

'I only ask, Missa Digger. You the one dat talkin.'

It was all over the news by the time we set out for the office on Monday morning.

They'd found a young man's body – or what remained of it – in Easterhall.

Malan had phoned the stations and told them that San Andrews CID had apprehended a man of Canadian origin who, he had reasonable grounds to believe, was connected with the body that had been uncovered. Miss Stanislaus called me from her cell phone. She sounded so confused I offered to pick her up.

We didn't speak. She was in a light-brown cotton dress and did not have her handbag. I imagined her jumping out of bed, slipping on her rubber sandals and rushing out of the house. She looked as if she was about to cry. I wondered if it was from the same betrayal I felt – that Malan was advertising his victory before he told us anything; or whether it was because he'd beaten both of us to it.

She switched off the radio. I switched it back on. She switched it off again.

When we walked in, Malan was at the interview desk. Pet and Lisa were answering calls and passing notes to him.

I lifted a chair, dropped it in front of him and sat down. 'Tell us what's happening, because we ain't hear nothing yet from you and you gone out there broadcasting it.'

Miss Stanislaus retreated to her desk and sat there quietly. I could feel her bright brown eyes on us.

Malan spread his fingers in my face. 'Had to act fast, man. Time was running out.'

'Don't gimme no ole talk, Malan, because right now…'

Malan shot to his feet. 'Watch your mouth, Digger. Gimme some respect, y'unnerstan? Gimme some respect because…'

'Because what? You'll get me fired? You think you could run this office on your own?'

'Digger! If…'

'If what, Malan? You point your finger in my face again, I report you for assault. And I have everybody in this office here to back me up. In fact you'll have to shoot me right here, because I not takin no abuse from you. Save it for your woman.'

That caught him by surprise. To tell the truth I caught myself by surprise. I didn't know how upset I was until I started speaking.

I wondered if I would have challenged him at all if I hadn't seen Miss Stanislaus do so the first time she met him. It was as if the woman's presence magnified all the things I did not like about Malan.

Malan sat back. He looked chastised. I felt better. 'So what happen?' I pressed.

It turned out that after our visit to Iona's house, Malan began chasing a lead he said we gave him – Nathan's Canadian friend, Simday.

'Well, from inquiries I make in the Post Office where Nathan used to work, everybody talk about that whitefella who pick him up most evenings and drive him home. S'matter o' fact, some of them girls believe that water more than flour between them. Straightforward when you think ov it.'

The boast was creeping back into his voice.

'Yesterday evening, while y'all enjoyin y'all prayers, I gather some fellas from Rapid Response and went up to that lil house by the sea. I raid the place and drag the culprit down to the station. I had twelve men ripping up the floorboards, searchin the yard and vicinity. About eleven o' clock last night we got a result.

That Simday-teacher-fella-from-Canada admit to everything except the murder. Then he start begging to call his embassy in Barbados.'

I stood up. 'So you ain' charge him yet?'

'If you listen to the news, or read this…' Malan pushed a pile of newspapers towards me, 'you'll see *A man has been arrested*. We don't name im yet. A lil bit more pressure and we'll get the confession out ov him.'

'Where he is?' Miss Stanislaus was already at the door. She was looking at Malan over her shoulder.

'South East Main Station,' Malan mumbled. 'Hold on, I'll come with you.'

'Nuh!' Miss Stanislaus slammed the door behind her.

Malan rubbed his head. 'People got the fella; not so? That's not what everybody want? Forget about de approach, man; people resolve de case.'

'You secure the scene?' I asked.

'Course, man. What you take me for? I got a couple police fellas up there. They waiting for you.'

'Not now,' I said.

'I not askin you, Digson. Is a order I givin.'

'Order me round midnight. Maybe later. Like you know, I work better when is dark.'

Malan jabbed a finger at the papers. 'People out there waiting for explanations.'

'Let them wait,' I said and kicked the door close behind me.

Chilman called my number. He did not even greet me. 'Digger! Tell that *jackass*, Malan Greaves, he going about it wrong. Is not no pappyshow and is not about he. Keep me briefed.' He coughed in my ear, then hung up.

I left home at 12.45am.

Miss Stanislaus was waiting for me at the roadside.

'Why so late?' she asked.

'Or why so early,' I replied. 'Depends on how you look at it. You talk to the Simday fella?'

'Yes.'

I waited for more from her but she pushed back the seat, folded her arms and closed her eyes.

When we arrived, the policemen were in their jeeps smoking and talking among themselves. They barely acknowledged our arrival.

Easterhall was the little sun-scorched peninsula in the south-east of the island where the foreigners preferred to live, protected by dogs as big as bulls. The walls surrounding their houses were so high they cast shadows on the soulless concrete mansions they protected, regardless of the time of day.

This rocky coastal outcrop, exposed to the assault of boiling seas and thrashing winds, was where men brought the wives and girlfriends of other men, wrestled with them in the sweaty darkness of their cars, leaving fluttering bits of tissue and crushed condoms among the parched mint grass.

It was a place of secrets, and a silence that prevailed despite the thundering of the sea and wind. I've always wondered why foreigners were so drawn to Easterhall.

I glanced up at the sky. A cold white moon against a flat black sky. A bright scattering of stars.

I followed one of the policemen through the stunted manchineel and sea almonds. Miss Stanislaus stayed close behind.

The officer stopped before a shallow excavation, grunted something and headed back towards the road. I directed my regulation searchlight at the pile of bones – long stripped of the cartilage, ligaments and tissues that held them together.

The team that Malan sent before me would have taken photographs before and after digging. I would collect samples for the lab in Trinidad and do the measurements. But I was here for something else.

My gift was reading bones. It was a talent I almost did not discover. During my year abroad, I could never make sense of the bodies of the victims they laid out under strip lights on those long stainless steel tables. I used to stand amid the other students feeling helpless and diminished as they prodded and poked cadavers, and whispered to each other.

I failed the osteology exam twice; would be forced to return home embarrassed if I did not succeed in my third attempt. One Friday evening a fuse blew somewhere in the building and the weak emergency lights came on. One of the students pulled out an LED torch and I happened to glance over his shoulder. Suddenly that single, frigid beam was like a connection to my brain.

I told the other students everything they missed and what I thought it meant: the shattered radius and ulna of the left arm, the slightly larger trapezius, deltoids, brachii and pectorals of that arm. Left handed, I concluded.

I imagined the dead man raising that arm to fend off a blow from something blunt and heavy. A small sledgehammer perhaps, aimed at the head. And given the location and the nature of the lesion on the parietal region of the head, he'd probably seen the blow coming and tried to duck. The instructor looked at me for a long while. Then he shook my hand.

Here in Easterhall, the desolation of the place – the blackness of the dripping precipices shouldering back the ocean, the stunted, hunched-down vegetation – made me want to finish as quickly as I could and head home to my bed.

I switched off the searchlight, slipped on a pair of Neoprene gloves and pulled out my LED. I stooped before the bones and directed the narrow finger of light.

I began to speak my thoughts.

'Bones have their own language, Miss Stanislaus. They say a lot about the person who owned them.'

I pointed at the mastoid process. 'See how it stand out? See how the angle of the jawline sharp and how the pelvis narrow? That telling me these bones belong to a fella. The tailbone telling me the same thing too. Look how it angle forward. Shallow pelvic basin – you see? A woman would have a lot more room down there to hold a baby. You also got the size and thickness of them bones. So everything here shouting loud and clear that these bones belong to a male.'

But that, I told her, was not enough. I wanted something more from these remains. I wanted to know what happened in the last moments of Nathan's life – for I had no doubt that it was he; no doubt at all that the lab in Trinidad would prove me right.

I ran my light along the limbs for fractures. People use their arms to protect themselves, and if they have any fight in them, they kick out or try to run. That is instinctive. That is life looking after itself.

I did an inventory of the subsided rib cage. The mess underneath was the business of the lab.

I took some pictures, then some samples. I turned over the skull: smashed frontal bone, cracked maxilla, fractured mandible.

I went on like this while the world around me faded to a hum and I fed my mind with details. It was all I could do; all that was required for now. What I had before me was a mess – more than three year's worth of what nematodes and the soil in its slow reclaiming had already erased.

I had to work like this until, somewhere in the recesses of my mind, these observations rearranged themselves and delivered a pattern, or better still, a story – or some crucial part of one. Problem was, it didn't always happen, or sometimes it happened too late.

I stood up. 'Nothing above the ordinary,' I smiled. 'Broken parietal bone.' I pointed at the back of the head. 'Fractures on the forehead when that Simday fella throw him in. Some trauma to the arms and spine. Smashed occipital bone. As you see yourself, we find Nathan face down.'

That reminded me of something else. 'In some parts of the

world, Miss Stanislaus, if you want to disrespect the dead, that is what you do. You bury the body face down.'

As far as I was concerned my job was done. When I got to the office I would file my report, draw the appropriate conclusions and leave the rest to Malan and the law.

The sky was brightening in the east. There was no sign of movement in or around the jeeps. I didn't blame the officers for grabbing a chance to catch a nap.

I glanced at my watch. Five o'clock. I had spent four hours over Nathan's bones. It struck me that Miss Stanislaus had been standing there for just as long.

I took her arm. 'Let's get out of here. This is no place for humans. And by the way, Nathan wasn't wearing no sandals; the fella was barefoot. S'matter of fact he didn't have no clothes.'

'No undergarment either?' Miss Stanislaus sounded shocked.

'S'far as I could tell he didn't have undergarments.'

'Missa Digger,' she said, 'you ever wonder why Missa Chilman make finding Nathan so important?'

'All the time. Why?'

'I tell you when the time come. Or p'raps you could work it out yourself?'

Before she got out of the car, Miss Stanislaus looked at me. 'You member you tell me that some kind ov killin cult… erm…?'

'Cultural,' I said. 'A mad idea I have. For example, here on this island: let's say a man meet his woman makin fancy noise under another man: he go berserk, he take a cutlass an do something terrible. He don't think knife or stone or piece ov wood, even if they right in front of him. He reach for what he using all his life – from the time he small – for clearing, cutting, cleaning… everything. He reach for a cutlass. Then he give up himself or run in the bush and hide. All we have to do is drag him out or go to his place and pick him up. Look at overseas… Look at the things they do to children. You think that could happm here? You think…'

'What's cultural about dis one?'

'Ask me that tomorrow. Right now I can't think. My mind full up. I tired.'

'Dat's why you talkin so much nonsense?' She patted her bag and started to get out.

As soon Miss Stanislaus pulled her door shut, I took out my phone and texted Dessie.

*12cu*.

It was the first time that I'd asked to see her. It had always been the other way round.

We hadn't met up since my return from the UK, although we kept in touch with brief exchanges – mainly question marks and exclamations. The desperation I'd detected in her voice all those months ago resurfaced from time to time, however far back in my mind I'd tried to push it. Dessima Caine had her own life, not so? Whatever her trouble was, she had family and the money to get her out of it, or through it.

I waited for an answering *ping*, then realised I was probably one of the few people on the island who was awake at this hour in the morning.

I drove home but could not sleep; stretched myself out on the sofa and listened to the village stirring – the splash of water followed by the giddy shrieks of children, the smell of burning charcoal and kerosene, cooked provisions and fried bakes, women's voices harassing their kids to get ready for school.

I went to my little cabinet in the corner of the kitchen, poured raw rum, cane syrup, freshly squeezed lime juice into a glass. Stirred. Dropped in a couple of ice cubes.

I fed a CD into the player on the kitchen worktop. I sipped, laid back and closed my eyes. John Coltrane's *Crescent* took me back to Beach Bum Bar, and a woman who called herself Alana Joi sitting on the lee-side of a rock at the northern end of Grand Beach. She was looking out to sea towards America where, she said, all the hurt had been.

She wore a pleated cotton dress, a coloured headband printed with what I later learned were Adinkra symbols. A small, smoothly groomed Afro. Leather sandals. A book in her lap entitled *The Bluest Eye*.

Earlier, at the end of my shift, she'd called me over to her table, pointed at a Camaho cocktail on the menu. 'What's in it?'

'Three measures of Bacardi, one Cinzano, one fresh orange juice and a suggestion of cinnamon.'

'You gat time?'

'For?'

'To sit and talk? Just talk.'

I guessed her age to be about twenty-five. Her face had the smoothness of a doll's, except for the very fine lines radiating from the corners of bright, honest eyes towards her temples. Not magga-bone thin, but with a flimsy delicacy that made me feel I could easily lift her up and run with her in my arms.

'I'm about to go home, Miss. Besides, staff not allowed to do that on the premises.'

'Do what?'

'Sit with clients.'

'We walk, then?'

The sensation of her was all that remained with me now: the smell of essential oil on her skin, the press of her head against my chest as she settled between my knees, stared out at the sea and began talking in that sleepy, exhausted drawl of hers about the lover she'd escaped from.

'I'm like Trane,' she chuckled. 'Trane *knows* pain.'

She reached into the folds of her dress and pulled out a music player – a small, flat silver thing that looked like jewellery in her palm. She woke the screen with a circular movement of her thumb and turned to plug the headphones into my ears.

'Oh! Not *that* one!' She moved to change the music, but I'd already heard the opening notes, felt them sinking into me, already felt the sudden expanding and release. I held her wrist. At the end of the music I let go.

'You were hurting me,' she said, massaging her wrist. 'But…' She rose to her feet and dusted her dress. 'I didn't want to spoil it for you.' She stood looking down at me. A soft chuckle escaped her. 'And that's – that's my problem, right there – Digger is it?'

In the twilight, with her back against the water, I could not see her face clearly. 'You won't forget me, will you?' she said.

I remembered the flush of sadness that came over me when she said that.

I don't remember what I said, or if I said anything at all. Lately, I felt that same sadness whenever I thought of Dessie.

## 16

For one full week after Malan uncovered Nathan in Easterhall, he sparred with journalists like a shadow-boxer. I didn't tell him what Chilman said; I just sat back and watched him. The fella couldn't get enough of looking at himself on the little television he brought into the office. Miss Stanislaus came in, sat at her desk and glared at him from under lowered lashes.

The days she did not come in, she phoned and said she was spending time with the Sisters of The Children of the Unicorn Spiritual Baptist Church in Pwin.

'That's what Chilman send she here for? To dance around flagpole and clap she hand?' Malan wanted to know. 'S'matter of fact, the case done finish, so we have to consider the implications, 'specially since she can't find it in sheself to celebrate what the Department achieve.'

Lisa coughed, excused herself and began shuffling her papers.

Malan didn't push it further. I suspected he wasn't looking forward to another call from Chilman through the Commissioner.

The atmosphere of the office changed in small ways, although it was noticeable enough to make Malan less relaxed. Pet and Lisa began turning up to work in lovely floral dresses and matching shoes. Pet even procured a handbag, inside of which she peeked and poked her fingers as if tending to some delicate living creature. Me, I bought myself a set of five ties, ranging from bright yellow to magenta. I wore a different colour every day.

Malan muttered something about 'the wrong time of the year for carnival', and his office becoming a Mas Band. We pretended we didn't hear him.

Miss Stanislaus was on her way out and I suppose that Pet and Lisa knew it too. Malan wouldn't have to push her.

I imagined her walking into the office any day soon to tell us to haul our hifalutin, low-fartin arses. And if the girls and I were lucky, she would finish off Malan with a more in-depth exposé of all the shameful things about himself that he didn't want the world to know. I was missing her already.

She phoned me late one evening. 'Missa Digger, you busy?'

'I just about to head home. Tell me…'

'You kin, erm, take a pusson to Fort Jeudy – I mean, if you got de time?'

Her voice was strangely distant, as if she were holding the handset some distance from her mouth.

'Fort Jeudy, you say, Miss Stanislaus?'

'Uh-huh.'

Fort Jeudy was a wide inlet of dark-water that spilled off from the Atlantic and settled in a deep lagoon shut in by mangroves. The dirt road to it ended at a small, partly-hidden, grey-sand beach.

'Missa Digger?'

'Yes, Miss Stanislaus.'

'Take de ting from your desk-drawer and bring it wiv you.'

'You mean, the, erm…'

'Uh-huh.'


She was silent all the way. From time to time, I felt her eyes on me, but when I turned my head she was always staring directly ahead. We had swung into the dirt road when she broke the silence.

'Yuh girlfriends,' she said, 'you ever tell dem where you going?'

'Girlfriends?'

'You got two, not so?'

'What make you think so, Miss erm…'

'I not no fool, Missa Digger. I got ears to hear, and I not blind. Mebbe they want you to make up your mind; not so? Mebbe them tired of you jumpin round?'

I'd stopped the car on the slight incline that led down to the beach. I found myself tapping the steering wheel and looking straight ahead at the gulls squabbling over the water. In the

decaying light, the little islands in the near distance were silhouettes frilled at their base by dimly glinting breakers.

'That's what you call me here for?' I said.

'What you think I call you here for?' Her eyes were on my face,
her mouth lifted in a half-smile.

'You tell me,' I threw back.

'I want you…' She fumbled in the bag I'd brought and took out
the Ruger, 'to show me how it work.'

'You change your mind about guns?'

'Change my mind? Nuh! I didn make it up till…'

'Till?'

'Till today.' She opened the door and stepped out of the car,
leaving behind a pleasant, lemony trace of her perfume.

I made her watch me first; then I stood behind her, curved my
arms around her shoulders and lightly cupped her hands in mine,
partly taking the weight of the gun while I talked her through the
motions. Then I stepped aside and studied her face as she lined up
the pistol and pulled the trigger.

I knew it well – the emotion that comes when a trainee raises
a weapon and fires it for the first time: the shiver of wonderment,
the stupor even, as it dawns on them that they've just crossed a
boundary – that by aiming that gun and firing at some imagined
person, they've been nudged a little closer to killing another
human, and the likelihood of doing so is far greater than before.

I didn't see this in Miss Stanislaus's expression. I detected it in
her posture, the pause after that first shot, the way she lowered her
head and refused to look in my direction.

On the way back we did not speak. I was conscious of her
presence in the vehicle beside me, and of some new dimension to
our relationship.

I brought the car to a halt outside the row of croton and
hibiscus plants that stood between her house and the road.

'The wimmen in the office missing you,' I said. 'They wondering when you coming in.'

Miss Stanislaus opened the door and slid off the seat. When she
was outside she poked in her head. 'Missa Digger, I miss you lil
bit too. A pusson didn mean to upset you. But seein as I start, I
might as well finish. Go wiv de girlfrien that give you de most hell

93

– that is my advice. You not always goin to like it, but she'll make you into a better fella. Even if you kinda nice already.' She squeezed my shoulder, withdrew her head and closed the door. I listened to her chuckling all the way up to her door.

## 17

I couldn't figure out what I said or did that could give Miss Stanislaus the slightest indication of what was going on in my mind. I felt the unease I thought I'd detected in Malan when she turned her attention on him.

A full month after I'd messaged Dessie, she replied to my text saying she would call. The few times she did – often very late at night and very briefly – there was trouble in her voice. And yet, whenever I saw her at the bank, she was radiant. Except that one time when she covered my money with her hand, leaned forward and whispered, 'You like me, Digger? For myself I mean. You don't think I have no substance, right?'

Before I could reply, she smiled at the woman on the yellow line behind me, and was herself again.

It brought back to mind the hastily truncated call she'd made when I was about to take the plane to London. And there was that Sunday night a few months after I'd returned when a call woke me. I heard soft sobbing, like that of an exhausted child, and I knew straightaway that it was Dessie. Then I heard the phone clatter to the floor, followed by a man's voice – flat, toneless, close, almost casual – as if he'd picked up the phone and was addressing me.

'Shut up and get up.'

Dessie stopped crying abruptly, then the phone went dead.

A couple of days later, I met Lonnie on the road.

I was on my way home after handling the first real murder case fully assigned to me.

They'd found the body of an Indian girl floating in the river that ran through a village named Les Terres. It was the rainy season and the river had dug her up from its bank and deposited her in the marshland where it met the sea. My friend, Caran from North Division, had pulled her out along with a cardboard suitcase of her belongings. When I got there, first stage maggots had not begun to do their work, but bombo flies had already lain eggs on the body. I estimated that the victim was exposed for less than twenty-four hours.

The water had partly dissolved her cardboard suitcase when they pulled it out, along with a crumpled heap of brightly coloured clothing, a pair of white pretend-leather shoes, a plastic hand-mirror and matching brush – the type Syrian and East Indian salesmen sold to plantation villages inland. A small tangle of gold-plated chains and bracelets lay on top her clothes. The girl was no more than sixteen, flimsy as a stick insect. Her slightly misshapen mouth and forehead suggested inbreeding.

The red silt in her clothing led us a couple of miles up-river, past the cool gloom of an old cocoa plantation where the earth thickened into rust-red clay because of the iron that infused it. We found the remains of an excavation on the river bank about two hundred yards below the village. Despite the heavy rains of the past few days, the teeth marks of the fork were still visible at the edges of the hole.

'We need to find the fork, then ask who it belong to,' I told Caran. 'They poor people; the fella won't get rid of it.'

'What make you think is a fella?' Caran asked.

'You ever hear a woman kill another woman here?'

Caran shook his head.

I looked up at the toss of corrugated iron and bamboo constructions tacked against the hillside. Women worked in sloping kitchen gardens. Children moved in and out of smoking outside-kitchens, their voices high and sharp as bird-calls.

I pointed at the kids. 'Most of them inbred: cousin breeding cousin, grandfather makin great grandchild with granddaughter. This whole village dying, and the women always the first to know it. I tell you something, Caran. When women most likely to conceive they avoid their fathers. They cut down on the time they interact with daddy and talk to mammy more. They don't even realise they doing it. Yunno why that is?'

Caran shot me a sideways look. 'Even if I know, Digger, you still goin tell me.'

'Is a precaution against making unhealthy children. Nobody need to tell a woman incest not healthy. Is in her bones. Call it instinct. So! As far as I work out, is either that girlchile was runnin off with a blackfella down there in the valley – in which case, as far as her people concerned, she better off with a dog. Or she refuse the cousin they forcing on her. Or maybe she got impregnated by the father and he can't take the embarrassment. I betting on the blackfella explanation. Forget about the fork; I got an idea.'

We climbed the mud path to the village. Children, slim as egrets, flocked the open space. I called out the adults and asked them to stand behind the children.

'I got a story,' I said. 'Girl – fifteen or sixteen, same size as this young lady there.' I pointed at one of the girls. 'Poopa catch her coupla times talking to one of them blackfellas down the valley. That give him grief, y'unnerstan? He make it plain he don't like it, but girlchile not listening. She behave like if she rather dead. And yunno, she really rather dead for true. So a coupla days ago – late Tuesday or early Wednesday gone – Poopa say he taking her somewhere else on the island. He say he find a job for her in San Andrews with a cousin who own a shop, or mebbe an uncle or auntie living somewhere on the island. He say things hard, so is better for everybody. So he pack her lil green dress with the white buttons and collar, her nice white shoes with the gold buckles on the side, the bracelets and the chain her mother give her and they take it along with them in the cardboard suitcase.

'And oh! He say she not coming back for a while. Well,' I stopped and scanned the faces. 'Poopa didn lie when he say she not coming back.' I swung an arm in the direction of the swollen river down below. 'We find her body in the river-mouth this morning.'

I heard a whimper to the right of me, turned to face the child at the edge of the ragged circle – broad-faced, a rust-coloured head of hair, fingers splayed over her mouth, big eyes brimming.

'What's your sister' name?' I said.

The girl raised wide uncertain eyes at the woman standing by her. I watched the men, lips locked-down, faces inscrutable as the hills that leaned over their houses.

97

'What's your daughter's name?' I asked the woman.

'Leyla', the little girl answered and she couldn't hold it in any more. She doubled over bawling.

'Where's he?' I said. The woman raised a hand towards the upper reaches of the plantation.

Caran shifted the rifle on his shoulder. 'Tell him to come down to the station and give imself up.'

We turned to leave.

Caran cleared his throat and spat. 'Tell him if we have to come looking for him tomorrow, he might end up like his daughter. Or he could save me the trouble and kill imself.'

'You didn't have to say them words,' I said to Caran.

We were clear of the red-mud path and on the track that would take us back to Les Terres town.

'Dem coolie hate us, Digger. They think we shit, and look at how dey live. Look what he done to his own daughter.' Caran adjusted his rifle on his shoulders and glared up at the hills.

On the way home, I couldn't take my mind off Leyla. Somewhere in my family there was a runaway daughter too – an East Indian girl-maroon who'd taken flight. She was there in my grandmother's slim and agile frame, her grace of hands and feet. That runaway girl had passed on traces of herself to me; she'd given me her lashes and her eyes, the hairs on my head and lower stomach that every woman I'd ever been with commented on.

I was still thinking about Leyla when I saw the woman ahead of me, ambling along the grass verge, her hair pulled out, a red comb in her hand. It was as if someone had opened a door inside me and let in a strong, warm wind. I stopped the car.

She turned her head, took me in for what felt like a century. Dark, dark eyes. Clean-skinned.

'What you want?' she said.

'Where you going?' I said.

'Not far.'

'That's far enough for me.' I opened the door. 'I offerin you a ride.'

'Nuh,' she said and kept on walking.

'I don't do this all the time, y'unnerstan?' My little boy's voice embarrassed me. 'I see you and I stop. I don't even know why I stop. I just stop. Is a ride I offering you, nothing else. You want a ride or not?'

'Nuh.'

I fumbled under the dashboard for my notepad. 'Okay, I give you my number. You take it? Take it, please. You don't even have to call me. Just take it.'

'Then why you givin me your number?'

'Well it might cross your mind, yunno – to jus gimme a call one day. Soon? Just to say "Hello, is me the nice girl you meet on the road last time."'

She shook her head, grinned. Teeth white as sun-bleached coral.

'Please,' I said.

She hung there as if bothered by something, then she looked down at me, a quick dark flash of eyes that took in my face, my hands, the rest of me, my face again.

'Where you live?'

'San Andrews.'

'Who you live with?'

'Nobody. Is me alone. You want to come and check?'

'Nuh.' She was studying my face again, as if she were trying to read between the folds of my brain.

'What you find?' I said.

'What you mean?'

'You looking at me kinda hard, so I ask you what you find?'

She flashed her teeth again. 'Mebbe next time.'

'Next time where?'

'Round here.' She made a gesture that took in the trees, the sea, the world.

'When?' I said.

'Whenever.'

'Make it evening,' I said. 'Who I should ask for when I come?'

'Me,' she said over her shoulder, and kept on walking.

'No name?'

'Nuh.'

I drove home in a daze. Woke up, wishing I could hurry the day forward.

Marais was fifteen and a half miles from San Andrews, the shortest route a rough drive through the mountains, then down the other side.

Damn fool! I not doing it! No woman in the world worth that kinda hard work. That's what happen when you just see a dead girl and meet a lovely living one on the gov'ment road straight afterwards. Never mind she nice.

I would get into my vehicle, decide I was going home, only to find myself driving across the island.

I patrolled that road every evening after work for two weeks with a picture of the woman in my head. The Walking Girl, I named her; every evening after I came home with no result, I chastised myself for being a jackass.

The Friday of the second week, I saw her sitting on a root that overlooked the road – red-strapped sandals, a plain sea-green dress flaring at her ankles.

I pulled up.

She eased herself off the root, stepped down beside the car, opened the door and sat beside me.

'You know how much time I drive this road in the past coupla weeks?' I said.

'Fourteen,' she said. 'Twice yesterday.'

I shifted on the seat to face her.

She twisted her mouth in one of those woman-smiles – sly and satisfied. 'I wasn hidin; you jus didn't see me.'

She dropped a hand on my knee, turned and held my gaze. 'How else I know for sure you not tryin to play the arse with me?' She arranged her dress and looked out the window of the car. 'Besides, it make a pusson want a lil bit stronger, yunno. You taking me with you?'

'For good?' I said.

'Nuh, I back in my house tomorrow.'

'Jeez!' I said. 'Jeez!' because it struck me that, just so, our courtship was over.

I sat with Lonnie on my step and we talked through the chill of an Old Hope night. At eighteen, Lonnie had built her own concrete bungalow from the fruits and vegetables she traded in Trinidad. She had her own car too, and owed no-one a cent. She said little about her childhood, although somewhere among the shadows of her past I detected the presence of a man.

Close to morning, she drew up her knees and folded her arms around them and began rocking back and forth. She gave me a long, sideways look.

'I have to tell you something.'

'Tell me, then.'

'You wouldn like it.'

'Your past won't bother me, Lonnie.'

'You wouldn know until I tell you.'

'Go ahead, then.'

She gave me a smile that wasn't a smile at all. She stopped the rocking, slid me another sideways look. 'I'll tell you when I ready.'

She pressed her head against my shoulder and said we should go inside.

In the morning, she squeezed herself into the chair I sat on. 'I want people to see us together. Everybody.'

'Easy,' I said. 'Next coupla weeks suit you?'

She selected my clothes – a soft white shirt patterned with gold crosshatches that felt as if I had nothing on. She'd bought me a pair of cream, tightfitting denims; black convos with white soles and laces. And when Lonnie had finished dressing me to please herself, she handed me a bottle of aftershave and said that tonight she wanted me to smell like that for her.

She was dressed in a shimmering something that looked as if a layer of silver liquid was clinging to her skin.

We stepped out, silenced the group of boys sitting on the culvert by the roadside in the moonlight. I fed a pirated cd of DJ Terror – Bounty Killer – Dance Hall Mix into the player, nodded and bounced all the way down south.

We got there after midnight. BeeGee's Night Club was heaving. On the beach behind the building, fellas drifted like washed-up sea-creatures.

I heard my name, looked around to see Caran – in a loose multicoloured shirt, the short sleeves rolled up to his deltoids – a white cap turned back to front on his head. A full-fleshed woman with permed hair and eyes as black as Malan's was standing beside him. Despite the pretty party shirt Caran still had the aura of a soldier. I hurried over to them with Lonnie. He dropped an arm on my shoulder and turned to the woman – 'Digger in the flesh,' he said. 'Digger meet my breaker. She name Mary.'

Mary laughed, held out her hand and offered me a beautiful gap-toothed smile. 'Boy, I tired hear 'bout you from Caran. When you coming to my house?'

I opened my palms and grinned. 'Right now if yuh want.'

'Not tonight,' she laughed.

Caran was holding Lonnie's hand in his. 'Digger, this is your queen?'

I lowered my head and raised my brows at Lonnie. Lonnie's face was glowing when she nodded and took my hand.

'Enjoy y'all self,' Caran said. 'We heading home early. Urgent bizness.' He cocked his chin at Mary and winked. She slapped him on the shoulder. I watched them walk away laughing.

Inside, Ajamu was finishing off a hot and celebratory song. Tallpree's voice, like a goat's on steroids, slammed through. The building pulsed and rocked.

Lonnie laid the hand of ownership on my arm, and as we wove through the women air-drying themselves outside, she slipped her fingers under my shirt and tightened them on the erector muscles of my lower back.

We waded through the disco lights, ducked and sidestepped a forest of bump-n-grinding backsides until we found our own little pool of darkness in a corner of the hall.

And we danced, Lonnie and I – her forehead resting against my sternum, me flushed with wonder at my luck, and how easily and sweetly this woman's body folded into mine.

We danced until the DJ simmered down the tempo with the easygoing strains of Gregory Isaacs's 'Bumping And Boring'.

But then Lonnie was barely moving. Her body grew stiff, her fingers limp in my hand.

'You want a drink?'

She shook her head, flapped her wrist in front of her face. 'Too hot in here. I want to go outside.'

I turned for the door, glimpsed Malan, his back leaning against the counter, his elbows on the bar, a sad-faced girl in a light-green dress standing by his side. I lifted a finger at him. He nodded twice, turned to the girl and said something.

I felt Lonnie's impatient finger on my back. I pushed my way out, she following.

She headed past me for the beach. I watched the stiffness of her head and shoulders. I caught up with her sitting under a sea-grape tree, face resting on her drawn-up knees.

'What spook you, Lonnie?' I said. 'Because sure as hell…'

She took my hand and tugged me down beside her. I leaned into her face, tried to hold her eyes. Lonnie looked away. 'What?' she said.

'You tell me.'

'Digger, I jus' getting to know you and I full-full-full ov love for you already. Becuz,' she sniffed and wiped her eyes, 'you make a pusson feel they worth someting.'

'That what making you cry now?'

She sprung to her feet, dusted herself, then passed a vigorous hand on the seat of my trousers. 'Let's go for a drive.'

We drove in silence through Coburn Valley, then up the hills of Morne Bijoux, till we got to the highest fort above San Andrews.

From Fort Frederick, all of the Drylands lay before us. San Andrews was directly below, steeped in the amber glare of its streetlights – the waters of the Carenage a black void except for the places where it became a shifting mirror for the lights of the town. Ahead was Salt Point, and the blaze of the airport whose runway thrust straight towards the sea, defined by a parallel string of white lights.

I felt dizzy and dry-mouthed, knocked off my stride by the suddenness of Lonnie's mood-swing.

She dropped her hand on my lap, shifted her body towards me, her face tense and intent.

I closed my eyes, took a breath and dropped my hand on hers.

'Lonnie, I promise that you safe with me. I been in this job long enough to know that when it comes to what I going to ask you, a lotta wimmen don't have the luxury of telling the truth, because the truth could cost them their life. So, they either say nothing or they lie. I don't want you to lie for me. That's going to spoil everything.'

I turned to face her. 'You either got something with Malan, or you had something with him. Y'all body language tell me that. Truth or lie?'

She eased back on the seat and stared out of the window.

'Okay, here's the important question: anything going on between you and Malan now? I have to ask because I work with the fella. And besides, I just want to know.'

She shook her head.

'You sure?'

She shook her head again, emphatically.

'That's good enough for me,' I said. 'Let's go home.'

I was at the photocopier next morning. Malan strolled over smiling.

'Didn know you could dance, Digson.'

'Now you know.'

'How's the Guinness?'

'Guinness is a drink.'

'I jus want to tell you no sweat, Digger – that's all.'

'About?'

He sucked his teeth, 'C'mon fella, I know she talk 'bout me.'

'Nuh, I the one that talk about you.'

'All I want to say is no sweat, y'unnerstand. I…'

I tapped him on the shoulder. 'Something wrong with this conversation, Malan. You talk as if you done something to me. You didn't.'

'So, we awright, then?'

'Why not? Like I say, something wrong with this conversation.'

Pet had her eyes on us. Malan must have noticed because he swung round on his heels and walked back to his office.

## 18

I'd come back from England with the resolve to abandon the case around my mother. Allow it to lie and die.

After a winter of watching TV in a foreign country, it struck me that if DS Chilman thought we had a problem with missing people, I should show him the figures for the British.

With ten million CCTV cameras watching every movement of its citizens night and day, two hundred and fifty thousand of them still went missing every year. By my calculations that meant about one person every three minutes.

A thousand bodies lay in mortuaries across the country, many of them for years. Nobody knew them or came to claim them. What if I told Chilman that the British were better at tracing cars than locating missing people?

I'd watched interviews with parents who'd dedicated the best part of their lifetime to looking for a missing child. I saw what it had done to them, how forensic they'd become in their interpretations of the details. How consumed – the same vacancy in their eyes that I observed in Iona; the same hanging on to the belongings of the missing – clothes that would no longer fit, bedrooms that remained untouched from the day the loved one left. These people had projected their lives into the absent dead, while outside the window of my flat above Peckham Road, people went to work, huddled in bus-stops, plugged themselves into Walkmans, argued, made love and laughed.

So, I'd decided to bury the questions about my mother and live. But who was I fooling? In a different country, three thousand miles from home, I mistook distance for detachment; made myself believe I'd dropped it – until Miss Stanislaus arrived and we had our breakthrough with the Nathan case.

I returned to the list of officers who would have worked with Boko Hurd, or would at least have known him. I'd checked the registry records for deaths dating back from the present to 1999. Boko's name was not among them. He had not been issued with a passport in fifteen years. As far as I could tell, Boko Hurd was alive.

I'd shortlisted fourteen former officers. I called their numbers. One was living with his daughter in Florida, another had moved to Trinidad, five had passed away. The next three fell silent for a long while, then began batting away my questions by aggressing me with their own. Exactly like Cornwall did.

I got lucky with the eleventh. His name was Pablo John. He asked me to repeat my name, apologised for his hearing, then told me how to find his house.

His wife led me through a small forest of blossoming okra plants to a slope of land where an old man was weeding sweet potatoes. He was over six foot tall without an ounce of fat on him. He had what looked like a little girl's cloth hat perched on his head. He was rubbing his lower back and gesturing for me to come closer. 'Can't hear like I used to. Cricket ball, yunno – a bouncer. Fella bowl a compo, hit me right here.' He stuck the cutlass in the soil and tapped the right side of his face. 'These past coupla months, after all them years, I start feeling it. That's not one helluva thing?'

You can tell a decent person anywhere – something in their bearing and the openness of their face, I suppose.

'Come siddown an lemme see how I could help you. The Rape Riot, you say?'

'May 3rd, 1999.'

'I 'member the day. I was up here. They post me here for seventeen years. In fact is here I meet my wife and is here she anchor me.'

'I know,' I said.

'You one of the affected?'

His words melted something in my stomach. I took a breath and nodded. 'Yessir, I one of the affected.'

'My advice is to leave it.'

'I can't.'

106

He passed a hand across his face, considered a while, then nodded. 'Go ahead, youngfella; I'll do my best.'

He did not know whether Boko Hurd was dead or alive and was not interested either way.

'He give police a bad name,' the old man said.

'That's one way of looking at it,' I said.

He frowned – a genuine look of puzzlement in his eyes.

'Somebody had to give the orders,' I said. 'Somebody above him. There is always a line of command.'

'Yes.'

'And the Commissioner…'

He lifted a staying hand and shook his head.

'Nuh, Sonny – what you don't understand is that in them days, the line of command didn always end up where you expect it to. The order didn't come from the force. I could swear to that.'

He held my gaze. 'Ain' got one officer I know who wasn't asking questions after the Rape Riot. Not one. And if that order did come from our superiors, we would've known. Even I used to know what go on inside the Governor General house – the Governor General, yunno! Far less! Because police talk among themselves.'

'I dug up the list of the men deployed that day – the initials that is. As far as I surmised, they were all officers, including Boko Hurd, the armourer at the time.'

He nodded dreamily. 'You right about Boko, he was on the payroll. He come in and out ov any station on the island as if he own it. Used to boast h'was protected, and he was.'

He frowned and threw me a direct curious gaze. 'You say you sure about the others?'

I told him I had no hard evidence.

He nodded. Boko Hurd, he said, was one of a group of thirty men from different parishes who answered only to the man who believed he owned the island in those days.

Boko did not just look after the weapons, he went out of his way to use them. He was good with guns, carried a stainless steel Czech-machined CZ-75 pistol, gifted to him on a training trip to Chile. He used to boast that he never wasted a shot.

It was his idea, during the troubles of '74, to commandeer two truckloads of bottled Coca Cola, stand them in the hot sun, then throw them into the crowd of protesting school children.

'Ever seen a glass bottle of hot Coca Cola explode?' the old man said. 'Same as a grenade. Is Pinochet police that teach im that.'

He raised the hat and fanned his face, the gray eyebrows twitching as if they had a life of their own.

'The Rape Riot...'

'Boko wouldn ha' missed it for nothing. Not even if you tie him down. Yuh see, Boko got a chance to shoot. In fact, the fella never stop talking about the Rape Riot afterwards, for months. Even after they try to kill im. Coupla days after the riot, somebody run a van straight at him in front San Andrews Station. Revenge, yunno.'

'So he got away?'

The old man nodded. 'Almost lost a leg, though. A good doctor save it. Boko didn walk straight after that.'

'You said he talked a lot about it afterwards. Remember what he said?'

The old man shrugged, 'Crazy talk – that's all I remember. Boko talk crazy after that. The only thing that stay with me was what them fellas say he called them wimmen. It didn' make no sense to me.'

'Tell me, Sir.'

'Chalk.'

'Chalk?'

'Yes, chalk. I never forget that.'

I stood up, dusted the seat of my trousers. 'Sorry, Missa John, but I have to ask you, I take it that you were not present at the riot?'

He shook his head. 'I was in the hospital with my wife. The trouble happen same day that my first child born. Rape Riot Day is my first daughter' birthday. That's why I can't forget it.'

I took the breakneck mountain road up the Grand Etang Hills. The first time Chilman made me drive up it with his car, I came out of it dizzy. At the peak I pulled into a small gravelled area that sloped down to the depths of the dripping rain forest, now ill-defined and ghostly in the rolling mists.

A strong wind pushed against the car and even with all the windows closed, the chill still crept in.

I wrote a summary of what Pablo John told me. I drew asterisks beside the things I thought significant. And gradually, in this place of strangeness and discomfort, as I reread my notes I felt better. The old man might have given me a way to find Boko after all, not by what he said about the armourer, but by what he told me about himself and the cricket ball that struck him.

His was the story of every ageing person I knew. The body remembers. The knocks and traumas of youth are written there and resurface with old age. And Boko with his shattered leg…

I went straight to the hospital.

The nurse in Admin looked at me with red-rimmed eyes. She went to a shelf of folders and ran an index along their spines. 'Say the name again?'

'Buckman Hurd. Bad left leg. He come for check-up, sometimes, not so?'

'You know his address?'

'That's what I come to find out,' I said.

'Got a lotta people on this island with bad leg, yunno.' She found something in what she said amusing, because she was chuckling.

'We could narrow it down lil bit,' I said. 'He's 68, male; besides, is a left leg we looking for.'

'You funny,' she chuckled. 'This should be him, then.' She pulled a folder, dropped it on the desk, began leafing through the file. 'You want his history?'

'I know enough already. Just where he live will do.'

'Last consultation June 6th – that make it…'

'Nine weeks two days,' I said. 'Where he live?' She looked up at me quickly before turning back to the pages.

'Woman by the name of Edna Greene bring him in every couple of months or so. We have her down as his carer.' She straightened up. 'He live in Drylands South. The housing scheme.'

'Thanks, Miss, erm…'

'Carol.'

'Miss Carol, you should get some sleep.'

I gave her my best smile and walked out.

## 19

Boko Hurd lived in the only social housing scheme on the island. Before I was born, Drylands South was the island's idea of pulling itself into the modern age. There was an abandoned open-air cinema with its rotten billboard still standing after forty years, its car park now a pasture for grazing sheep and cattle. It backed the two-lane highway – half a mile of asphalt that was four times the width of the average island road; pot-holed now, but wide and straight enough for drivers to convince themselves it was a runway. The Traffic Department had a special file that kept a running total of the numbers killed on it each year.

There was an old sugar mill that used to be a disco at the roundabout; and the beer factory, of course, overlooking the two-lane road, with shiny steel chimneys that filled the air with the smell of hops and malted barley.

I walked through rows of concrete bungalows, so drastically modified over the years it was impossible to tell that they used to be identical.

I knew by now that Boko's was a blue house and the veranda was painted deep red.

The rusty wrought-iron gate leaned away from its top hinge. The pole that supported it was covered in creeping vines.

I climbed the four steps and tapped the side of the open door. There came the abrupt clang of metal against metal. The smell of stewed chicken and steamed provisions. The slow shuffle of feet.

A woman with a crumpled face and round, indolent eyes leaned out the door, wiping wet hands on a flowered cotton apron. Behind her was a little colour television, flickering with the red and blue of the CNN Newsroom.

'Yes?'

'I'm DC Digson. I'm looking for Boko.'

The hands paused from drying themselves.

'You could tell me what it about?'

'A coupla questions – that's all.'

I saw the hesitation – as if she were debating with herself. 'I don' think Boko could have no conversation with nobody, you know.'

'How come?'

She wiped her hands and shrugged. 'Okay, lemme see if I could make him get up.'

Inside, I heard soft words – the woman's growing louder from time to time, then dropping.

She was holding his hand when she came back. He could barely walk. The old body was curved forward from the waist, his mouth partly open. The woman drew a rusting iron chair and sat him at the door-mouth.

I stared into a grey face. Flared nostrils sprouting wiry hairs. His stare was focused on nothing in particular.

'See what I mean?' she said. I glanced at the sagging blinds, the old wooden chairs inside, the uneven partition with nothing on it but a calendar dating back ten years.

'Y'all family?' I said.

'Famly don't know nothing 'bout him now.' I detected a mild defensiveness in her tone.

'You got children?'

'I got children, but I won't bring them here now.' She turned back to the kitchen.

Fair enough, I thought. She would not bring her children here until he died, but as repayment for looking after him, she would keep the house.

'Boko,' I leaned forward. 'My name is Michael Digson. Coupla questions I want to ask you. You hearing me? My mother' name was Lorna Digson. On Monday 3rd May 1999, twenty-eight officers including yourself went down to the Carenage to break up a demonstration. It ended up with y'all shooting nine people, six bodies were recovered, three disappeared, including my mother.' I drew breath and leaned back. 'All I want to know is what y'all do with the bodies. And why y'all left the rest and took those three?'

His hands remained curled in his lap like the feet of a dead bird. The dark lips moved. He tried to speak, or I thought he did. What came out were little puffs of air.

I sat with him for half an hour – me leaning so close to his face, I could smell the sourness of his breath.

'Chalk,' I whispered. 'Why you call them chalk?'

Boko kept on staring. Talking to a stone would have been better, I would know at least that the stone was dead.

'You won't find nothing in there. Doctor Spence at the hospital tell me the name for it. Start with a Zed or something.'

'Alzheimer's,' I said. I did not realise the woman had returned.

She shrugged. 'I don' remember; I could offer you some lime juice?'

'Nuh,' I said to her retreating back. I leaned forward, placed my mouth against his ear. 'Boko, lemme tell you about the worm you got in your brain and the best way to get rid ov it.'

Back on the path I looked back at him. 'Best way,' I said.

I thought I saw the limp hands twitch.

I stepped onto the sidewalk – a narrow strip of grass that petered out at the junction. I strode past my car, walked the two miles to Grand Beach. A regiment of hotels bordered it. Blinding white by day, the beach was now a stretch of muted beige and silver in the twilight, empty but for a pair of footprints along the wet edge of the shore.

I sat and faced the ocean; scooped up handfuls of sand, watched the pale grit slip between my fingers.

Who had I been fooling? Chilman's words returned and settled in my brain. *What make you change your mind – desperation or the temptation to find out what happen to your mother?* I said nothing then. Perhaps I did not want to face it. But even then, something in me must have known that this chasing after my mother's ghost was, in Chilman's words, *a dead dead-end*.

A couple of children appeared at the southern end of the beach, picking their way along the stone jetty with the exaggerated steps of egrets, their shapes like stick-drawings against the sky. A tussle, shrieks, the rapid flail of limbs before their feet left the stones and their naked bodies hit the water.

I stripped down to my underwear, folded my clothes around my watch and shoes and took to the water running. Allowed myself to float and drift until I'd emptied my head of thoughts, and told myself that I felt nothing.

That night, I wrestled with dreams of rifles bleeding into dirty drains. Limp hands scrawling the part-written names of women on the road, then wiping them away.

I got up to a cool grey morning, hushed trees in the valley down below, the musk of rotting vegetation and drying concrete.

Chalk. I bought some in San Andrews. I held a stick in the palm of my hand and closed my fingers around it. It crumbled so easily.

## 20

Miss Stanislaus called the day after I saw Boko Hurd. Malan tried to press his ear against my phone. I pushed him off.

'What she up to, Digger?'

'Getting baptised,' I told him. 'Day after tomorrow.'

'Easter Sunday? Lord ha Mercy, is like she fall in deep. That's all she say?'

'More or less,' I said, and busied myself doing nothing useful. Lisa and Pet complained that the office felt half-dead.

'Feels rather off-colour, doesn't it?' I said in my best pretend English accent. They fell about the office laughing because Malan didn't get the joke.

'Digger,' he said. 'I want to know why that woman phoning you to tell you that she gettin baptised this Sunday when she so dam vex with you an me.'

'She more vex with you than with me,' I said. 'She just say she makin progress there.'

'Vex is vex,' Malan threw back. He snapped up his keys and strode out of the office.

'I don't give a damn,' I shouted at his back. 'She's your headache, not mine.'

I couldn't get Malan's question out of my mind. In the dimming evening, I sat on my step, closed my eyes and tried to shut out the grate and shout of boys scootering on the road below.

I recalled Miss Stanislaus's words. 'Hello, is me.'

'I know,' I'd said.

'Keep yuh phone charge-up tomorrow cuz I gettin baptise.' I heard the background hum of women and children in the yard, then The Mother's bass-drum voice urging Miss Stanislaus to join them. Miss Stanislaus had muttered something and hung up.

I phoned Malan. 'You know that call Miss Stanislaus made to me in the office?'

'Yeh?'

'She didn say my name.'

I heard Malan chuckle. 'Digger, I not interested in you and that woman love life. That's what you call me for?'

'Malan, I serious. Tell me one time you hear Miss Stanislaus address me and *not* say 'Missa Digger', first sentence.'

'Digger, hear this…'

'*Lissen,* Malan! I believe she didn't want people around her to know who sh'was talking to. Then she instruct me to keep my phone charged tomorrow *because* she getting baptised. Conversation didn't even finish before she cut me off.'

'Eh-heh, and besides she didn call you, doo-doo darlin.'

Malan was silent for a while. When he spoke again, his tone had changed. 'Is clear, Digger. The woman want you on standby. I told you something was funny 'bout that call, not so? Phone she now; then call me back.' Malan hung up.

I phoned Miss Stanislaus. After my ninth attempt, I gave up and left a message.

Easter Sunday morning I found myself heading for the office. My standard issue, which I only took out of its case to heft and polish from time to time, was strapped under my armpit.

I wasn't surprised to find Malan at the office either. He barely looked at me when I walked in.

He pushed himself back in his chair, clasped his hands over his stomach and closed his eyes.

The town was quiet. I heard footsteps on the road outside, closed my eyes and tried to work out whether it was a man or woman by the drag of their feet on the asphalt and the pace at which they walked. I decided it was a woman. That done, I tried to work out her age.

The clock towers on Church Street sounded seven-thirty. They struck again at eight and with every stroke of the bells, Malan cocked his head.

I almost missed the call. My phone was on vibrate.

I snatched the handset, glanced at the screen, and brought it to my ear. 'Miss Stanislaus?'

'Come! Come now, Missa Digger.' Something flipped inside my guts. The voice sounded terrified. It was the kind of voice you heard once and never forgot. It brought me to my feet.

'Mother Bello! Where you callin from?'

'I have ter… Co…ome… Missa…' Her voice rose to a shriek. Then the phone went dead.

'What's happenin.' I felt Malan's breath on my neck.

I fiddled with the keypad, calmed myself and called back. The call went straight to voicemail.

'Bello wife,' I shouted. 'Calling from Miss Stanislaus phone. Sound like serious trouble.'

I bolted out the door and headed for my car.

Malan's voice was a whiplash in my ears. 'Leave that tortoise, Digger. We taking mine!'

I swung towards his jeep, pulled open the door and slipped in behind the wheel. Malan dragged me out.

I barely managed to get in on the other side before he was off.

'Where!' he shouted, above the snarling engine.

'Dunno,' I said. 'She didn have time to tell me. She sound frighten like hell.'

Malan slammed on the brake. The vehicle bucked and swerved. His mouth twisted in a snarl. 'Where, Digger?'

'She didn say, man!'

'Digger where the hell we going!' The ferocity in his voice jolted something in my head. A memory. It arrived with my grandmother's voice. *Where the Sweet meet the Salt. Like in John-de-Baptist time. Ain got no other place for baptisin in de Spirit.*

'Where the river meet the sea,' I said. 'That's all I know.'

Malan revved the engine and brought a fist down on the steering wheel. 'Make sense, Digger. You wastin time.'

This was Malan at his worst: dangerous, murderous, and unrea-sonable. This was Malan the nightmare of every small-time crook and criminal on the island.

In my mind, I scrolled through the rivers that ended in the sea. There were seven of them. Five were at the far north of the island.

116

I ruled them out. The nearest was at the busy western exit of San Andrews – dirty, smelly and slow-flowing with the detritus from settlements in Temple valley, and in full view of the public. I ruled that out too. The seventh was ten miles east.

'Sadie Bay,' I shouted. 'Take the Eastern Main.'

'Belt up!' he snapped. The vehicle shot forward. 'You better be sure. You send me on the wrong road, is hell to pay.'

The Eastern Main Road wound itself around the edges of the island like the reckless scrawl of a child. Malan drove with the seat pushed back forty-five degrees; the only animation was in his rapid footwork on the pedals and his spinning hands. We were all horns and screeching tyres. I caught flashes of alarmed faces outside, the smeared colours of houses, vehicles and streaming vegetation.

I willed the Mitsubishi on, counting the bends as we took them in a howl of tires under Malan's lightning hands. With his foot still flat down on the pedal we swung into the sandy side-road to Sadie Bay.

Malan reached into the glove compartment, took out his SIG-Sauer and laid it in his lap. He threw a sideways glance at me. 'You got your piece?'

I nodded.

'Take it out.'

'Might not be necessary.'

He slammed on the brake. The jeep skidded and humped till it was sideways on the road. 'What you say?'

I raised my chin at the row of coconut trees in the distance.

'You wasting time. We don't have time. Drive the vehicle!'

We arrived in a cloud of sand and blaring horn. Then we were out and running along the river bank towards the sea.

There was a huddle of women under a large sea-grape tree halfway up the beach. Malan went straight for them, the gun pointed at their faces.

'Where she is?' he shouted. 'Y'all don't tell me now, I shoot every one ov you! Where she is?'

I swerved onto the sand, sprinting over three pairs of footprints that led to the far end of the bay. Then I saw them, crouched beneath an overhang of elephant grass.

I bore down on them gun in hand, my head hot with hate. The Mother – her whole body heaving with sobs – was sitting on the sand beside Miss Stanislaus. The two women, like the rest of the group further up the beach, were dressed in loose white gowns.

A ceremonial headwrap was bobbing on the water.

Miss Stanislaus lifted her head and coughed. Her face was swollen. Traces of blood patterned the torn fabric of her gown. I lowered myself beside her and tried to ease her to her feet as gently as I could, but she wouldn't let me. I wanted to pull her to my chest and hug her. I wanted to cry.

'Where's Bello? If Malan find him first, he'll shoot him on the spot.' I said.

Miss Stanislaus raised her head. 'He try to drown me.' She broke out in a fit of coughing, then drew in a lungful of air. 'It take all ov dem to get im off me. Tell me I bring trouble to his church. I corrupt his congregation and he goin to make me pay.'

Miss Stanislaus stopped abruptly and looked into my face with streaming eyes.

The Mother was weeping too. She kept fluttering her hands and making those heavy, deep-chested grunts.

I took off my shirt and laid it across Miss Stanislaus's shoulders.

Malan came running; he threw a fire-and-brimstone look at The Mother then at the overhang of vegetation at the end of the bay. He glared at me. 'You let im get away?'

'He didn,' Miss Stanislaus said. She raised her head at the mounds of sand directly behind us.

Malan and I locked gazes. His mouth was half-open, his brows pulled together. I followed him up the sandy incline and there was Bello, white-robed, his great body splayed face-down in a sand-trough.

'How?' Malan said, his voice hushed. 'Digger, how?'

'She shot im,' I said. 'She… woy, Man! She shot the fella.'

Malan rolled his eyes towards Miss Stanislaus and The Mother. His lips were working. He shook his head. 'How?'

I lifted my shoulders and dropped them. 'The gun you give her – what else?'

Malan looked lost for a long while. Then he drew a breath and snapped himself out of his daze. 'We got some tidying up to do. Make the necessary calls, Digger. Lemme instruct them people cross there what to say and if them cross my word, I implicate their arse too – right down to de chilren.'

'Ain got no children here,' I said.

I stood there staring down at the body, hollow-headed, my mouth dried out. Aware of the heaviness of my own heartbeat.

Malan loped off towards the group under the grape tree. I watched the muzzle of his gun taking them all in together, then each one in turn.

When he returned, I had finished making my call to the Ambulance Unit in San Andrews.

'Malan, I need to check this out,' I said, pointing at the body. 'Before the ambulance get here.'

'You not blind; you done see what go down arready.'

'Is procedure.'

'Fuck procedure; we ain got time. What you lookin at is trouble and right now I tryin to fix it, y'unnerstan?'

He was glaring at me, his chest heaving. Malan swung around and levelled a finger at Mother Bello. 'Go join your people. Let them tell you what I tell them. And make sure every one ov y'all go along with what I say. This is not no cover-up, y'unnerstan? Is a proper orderin of de facts of this incident–' he stabbed a finger in the direction of Bello's body – 'as me, in my capacity as Chief Officer of San Andrews CID, decide to order them; y'hear me?'

He turned to Miss Stanislaus, reached down and eased her to her feet.

'The weapon,' he said. 'Where it is?'

Miss Stanislaus pointed at her bag on the sand. Malan got out the Ruger, reached under his shirt and tucked it in his waist.

We took Miss Stanislaus's weight on our shoulders and guided her to the jeep.

Malan still looked stricken. He glanced at me, moved his lips around the words before he spoke. 'Hospital.' He threw me the keys. 'I goin sit in the back with her.'

In a quiet voice, to no-one in particular, he said, 'This thing not finish yet. It not finish becuz I not satisfy. I not!'

## 21

Miss Stanislaus's body was a plump curve against the door. She'd pressed her head on the glass of the window, her fists closed tight on my shirt, which was around her shoulders.

'Tell me how it happen, again.'

It was the third time Malan had asked the question on the way back to San Andrews.

Miss Stanislaus repeated the sequence of events on the beach: Bello dragging her into the sea to drown her, his wife and the others fighting to hold him back, she leaving the water in a panic with Bello chasing after her.

'That is when you say you shoot im?' Malan queried.

Miss Stanislaus gazed out of the window and said nothing.

Malan tried to catch my eyes in the rear-view mirror. I pretended not to notice.

'Okay,' he said rubbing his face. 'I want you to go through the whole thing again step by step.'

'Ease up, Malan! Give the woman a chance!'

We were on the white road down into San Andrews. The town was at its usual Sunday ease. The concrete houses on either side of The Avenue sat back from the verge in a green display of neat front lawns and trimmed bougainvillea hedges. We drove through the smells of spiced rice, steamed vegetables and rich meat sauces.

As we entered San Andrews, the clock tower on Church Street measured out the hour with lazy, resonant gongs. Eleven o'clock.

On top of Market Hill, Malan tapped me on the shoulder. 'Go get your vehicle, Digson. I'll take her to the hospital.'

Malan adjusted himself behind me, leaned forward, and placed his lips against my ear. 'That's an order.'

120

In the rear-view mirror, I saw Miss Stanislaus stir, her bright eyes switching quickly to Malan's face, then mine.

'Is Sunday,' I said. 'S'far as I concerned, I off duty; I not taking orders right now.'

I thought I saw Miss Stanislaus nod but I wasn't sure. It could have been the fast-changing play of light from the window on her face.

Malan leaned back, his whole body rigid with dissatisfaction.

I, too, was dissatisfied with Miss Stanislaus's account. My head was swarming with uncertainties because, from the moment I saw Deacon Bello on the sand with a bullet through his shoulder, I knew that his death could not have happened as Miss Stanislaus described it. And if it did, this woman could not be the person she'd led us to believe she was.

I knew Malan wanted to have her on his own to drill her. He would use every trick he knew to catch her out, even if it meant stopping the vehicle in the middle of the road or at the hospital gate and pointing his Sig Sauer in her face. And from the little I knew about Miss Stanislaus, she would not allow that kind of liberty from any man.

## 22

Up here, the air was a mixture of sea-salt and the heady antiseptic emanations from the old colony hospital. There was something else – for me at least. It was part of the smell, yet separate from it. Almost like a memory of blood.

As soon as we stepped out of the car, a very short woman in a pale green uniform came out of the building signposted *Accident and Emergency*. She looked up at us from under the stiff, white peak of a nurse's cap, miraculously stuck halfway down her forehead. Her eyes halted on Miss Stanislaus's face, travelled over the bloodied shirt draped around her shoulders. She eye-balled me in my vest, then the welts and lacerations on Miss Stanislaus's legs and arms and suddenly Malan and I were staring into two very hostile eyes. 'Which one ov you done this to her?'

'We police officers,' Malan said. 'We…'

'That make it worse then!' The woman swivelled her eyes at me, 'What you done to her?'

I spread my palms in self-defence. The woman placed a hand on Miss Stanislaus's shoulder and manoeuvred her away from us.

'Miss Lady? You wamme call the real police?'

Miss Stanislaus muttered something I did not hear. The nurse soured her face, turned on her heels and guided Miss Stanislaus through the doorway.

Malan looked stunned. He threw his weight against the car.

I thought I heard Miss Stanislaus's voice, soft and girlish, punctuated by the nurse's deeper, animated tones.

Then brisk footsteps returning along the corridor.

The nurse pushed out her head, raised her chin as if she were talking to the air. 'She under observation.'

Malan frowned at her. 'What's that s'pose to mean?'

'We keepin her in.'

'When she coming out?

'We'll notify her next-of-kin – as and when.'

'We the people you got to notify, y'unnerstan?'

'Well, if that is so,' the woman glared at us, 'nobody goin get notify.' She slammed the door behind her. I followed the padding of her footsteps as she moved deeper into the building.

A string of obscenities rolled off Malan's tongue.

'Digger,' he turned to me, his forehead bunched. 'Hospital people *s'pose* to behave like that in de presence of de law?'

I shrugged, swallowing on a chuckle. 'Mebbe is procedure? Anyway, where's your heart, man. You don't see the condition Miss Stanislaus in?'

Malan strolled over to the horizontal bars of metal piping that served as a barrier against the drop to the sea-slicked rocks below. I drifted after him.

'She don't realise that I could put her lyin arse in jail: she, Bello's wife, the whole damn church. I could put all their arse in jail and throw away the key! You want to bet me?'

He leaned forward abruptly. The bones of his face looked sharper, his jawline more pronounced. Again, it struck me how anger transformed him.

'Digson, you part of this?'

'Part of what?' I snapped. I held his gaze until he looked away.

'Because yuh see, a situation might arise when I have to explain to *people* that Miss Santa Claus was forced on my department by Chilman – that sonuvabitch – to undermine my authority. You was witness to how she insult me in my office. Now she insultin my brains. Like I ain' got no training. Like I can't visualise a fuckin scene. Like I dunno when people tryin to gimme bullshit. Is like Chilman send she to make a pappyshow of me. *Again*!'

Malan was frothing with rage. That one word threw me back to an afternoon in the office when we were eight months in the job and still shadowing experienced officers in various departments around the island. Malan was on a six-week placement in Customs at the international airport. He'd stopped a foreigner who owned one of the offshore islands in the south and insisted on searching his luggage. The man called him a *con*. Malan understood the insult and threw back, 'Same to you.' The French-man slapped him in the face.

The news reached Chilman and he sent a car to pick up Malan. When Malan arrived, Chilman sat him down in the middle of the office, drew up another chair and placed himself in front of him.

'So! The whitefella box you in your face; what you do?'

'I tell the boss.'

'And what the boss do?'

'He tell the French-fella he not s'pose to do that.'

'And what the French-fella say?'

'He say I make him vex; then he offer to settle.'

'Settle – how?'

Malan shrugged.

'How!'

'He gimme a coupla hundred dollars.'

Chilman stood up. He gestured Malan to his feet. The DS put all his weight behind the punch, hit Malan so hard Malan fell back and brought down the desk with him. Chilman strode into his office, pulled out his drawer, returned with a wad of notes and dropped them on the floor. 'Coupla hundred dollars,' he grunted. He headed for the door.

At the threshold, the DS raised his fist at us. 'I only hit Malan Greaves with this, fellas. What that Frenchman hit my officer with is completely different. He use the hand of history. If he try it again with any of y'all, you got my permission to shoot him.'

Chilman got into his car, drove off and was away for the rest of the day.

Malan pulled me out of my thoughts. He'd turned his back on me, his voice edgy with resentment.

'She not employed by the Department. She don't have the protection of the job; she therefore liable…'

'And when they ask you how she came by the gun?'

'Believe me, Digger, it wouldn't reach that far.'

'You forgetting one thing,' I said.

'Wozzat?'

'Me.'

'Naaah, man,' Malan forced a chuckle. 'First thing I thought about was you.'

Back in his vehicle, he pressed his back against the seat and started the engine. I stood outside, my hands in my pockets.

'You not coming?'

'Nah,' I said. 'I decide to walk.'

He gunned the engine, swung the jeep around and shot off.

## 23

I dialled Chilman's number five times. My calls went straight to voicemail: *Say someting, or call back, but only if you have to.*

I decided to leave a message. 'DC Digson here. Miss Stanislaus in trouble. Like it or not, I coming to your house tonight because I needing some answers… Sir.'

I had a couple of hours to kill so I showered, laid back on my bed and tried to think my way through the events of the morning. I reviewed everything – from the moment I took the call from Bello's wife on Miss Stanislaus' phone, to finding Deacon Bello dead on the beach.

I imagined myself sitting in front of Miss Stanislaus, as choked as I felt now, still smouldering at the disappointment I was feeling. *I never know you wuz a liar; you fool me good…*

My phone buzzed. 'What's your headache, Digson?'

'Not mine, Sir, yours.'

Chilman coughed in my ear. 'Go on, then, tell me.'

I described the situation. The old man was silent all the way through. When I finished I was breathless. 'You still there, Sir?

'Uh-huh.' Chilman cleared his throat. 'You got to go talk to her, Digger. Go talk to her right now. Find out what really happen. How Malan taking this?'

'Not well.'

'Go talk to her; then call me.'

I glanced at my watch. 'Is past visiting time, Sir.'

'Digson, what wrong with you! You a police officer! Make up a story if you have to. Tell them she'z your woman or something. Find y'arse down there and talk to her. Then call me afterwards.' Chilman steupsed – a dirty wet sound – and switched off.

I stared at the handset. There'd been something in the old man's voice I'd never heard before – the quavering undertones of distress.

On the road to the hospital, I thought about Miss Stanislaus; how, without thinking, Lisa, Pet and I had aligned ourselves with her. When she was in the office the women laughed more often; their conversations were quick-witted and relaxed. And me – I had no words for it – this feeling that my job had become something else as soon as she arrived.

An old security man in grey khaki had a shoulder against the hospital gate. I held out my ID. He unbolted it and stepped back briskly.

I waded through the smells of iodine and benzyl alcohol. On the bottom floor, people in all manner of disrepair were laid out in rows on iron beds. A couple of juvenile nurses drifted in soft-soled shoes along the passageways between the beds. Above the barely audible murmurs of distress, I picked up the keening of a woman – probably in childbirth – somewhere in the ward above.

I intercepted one of the nurses. 'I looking for Miss Stanislaus,' I said. 'I brought her in today, round midday. She's my, erm, next-of-kin.'

The young woman looked at me from head to toe, nudged a ribbon of hot-ironed hair back under her cap and frowned.

'Which ward?'

'Not sure,' I said.

'Her name, again?

'K. Stanislaus.'

'First name?'

'K will do.' I offered her my best smile.

'Hold on.' She spun on her heels and disappeared through a swing-door at the far end of the aisle.

The young nurse returned with the same woman we met when we brought in Miss Stanislaus. Hers was a brisk waddle towards me: busy swinging arms, chest pushed out. I prepared myself for another round of accusations.

'You the one call Missa Digger?'

'I'm the one,' I said.

'Is your modder give you that name?'

I felt a blood-rush in my head. 'How my mother become your business, now?'

'De nice lady check out. She say you goin work out where she gone?' Her eyes were luminous with curiosity.

'Who picked her up?'

'Two woman in a hire-car.'

'How you know it was a hire-car?'

'It had "for hire" mark on it.' She muttered something under her breath and waddled off.

I shouted thanks at her back and hurried out.

I drove through Grand Beach Valley, up the Eastern Main, turned into the thick greenish gloom of a mud track that was half-hidden by an overhang of flamboyant trees – a rocking, punishing drive against which my little Toyota protested with every dip and swerve.

The flags of the church rose out of the vegetation like a row of outlandish flowers. I glimpsed two figures trailing behind the car, each balancing a hefty log on his shoulder – the Watchmen of the flock.

Miss Stanislaus was sitting in the yard in a blue dress that flowed down to her ankles. She was balancing an enamel plate on her right knee and a mango in her left hand. A little girl stood on the other side of her, her head a mass of curls and ribbons.

The yard was full of children – I counted eleven – most of them gathered around a noisy game of hopscotch. The little boy we knew as Amos sat on a log with a toddler between his knees. A hive of women's voices rose up from behind the church.

Miss Stanislaus did not look up, not even when the girl beside her went still and stared at me. She kept on slicing the mango with fussy, delicate movements of her hand.

I lowered myself on the stone beside her.

Miss Stanislaus held out the plate of fruit to the child. The little girl sighed a prolonged thank you – more a movement of her lips than sound – and began a dainty walk towards the back of the church.

I couldn't help smiling. 'She even walk like you,' I said.

'Daphne.' Miss Stanislaus reached for the blue handbag beside her foot. She drew out some tissues and wiped her fingers. It was then that she turned those eyes on me. My heart flipped over. I couldn't say exactly why, except that no one had ever looked at me like that before.

'Missa Digger, you here to talk, not so?'

'Yes.'

'Go 'head.'

'Miss Stanislaus, I want to know what really happened in Sadie Bay. I want the truth.' I found it difficult to go on.

Miss Stanislaus was staring straight ahead, one hand nesting inside the other. The welts along her arms and legs had darkened into purple ridges. She exuded the mild astringency of ointments, which I supposed the women had rubbed on her.

'Missa Digger you upset…'

'Uh-huh.'

'I could ask you why?'

I closed my eyes, forcing back the agitation. 'Miss Stanislaus, let me tell you why your story don't make sense. You say that Bello dragged you in the water and tried to drown you, right? Then Bello' wife, The Mother, and some of the other wimmen pull him off you. You got out of the water and started running away from him. He caught up with you and started to beat you up. So you had to shoot him to save yourself. Right?'

Miss Stanislaus shifted her weight, said nothing.

'Well, first, you got no reason to believe Bello want to drown you, so why you carrying that gun in the middle of your baptism? On which part of your person you hide it so he didn't see you got that gun?

'Okay! Okay! Let's pretend you manage to hide the gun on some part of your body. Even so, I still got a problem with your story because you say you got out of the water and started running with Bello chasing after you. *That* is when you shot him. You notice how Malan kept stopping you and coming back to that part?

'That's because Malan and I know you only see them kinda fancy action in movies: to pull out a gun from wherever you hiding it *while running*, turn around *while running*, aim and fire *while running* and still get a perfect shot. Nuh! Make matters worse, is only a coupla weeks since I show you how to use that gun.'

I realised I'd raised my voice. The children had stopped their game of hopscotch. They stood in a nervous knot at the far side of the yard, their eyes on us. I forced a smile in their direction and sat back.

Miss Stanislaus raised her chin at the children. Her words came soft and quick from the side of her mouth. 'Look at all dem chilren, Missa Digger, and tell me what you notice.'

I shrugged. 'Children!'

'Watch the lil boy 'cross there, wearin khaki pants, the happy-jumpin long-hair girlchile who was playin lil while ago. And that one there – de lil baby Amos holdin in front ov im. Watch de face an mouth an eye.' She slid a glance at me. 'You don't notice nothing 'bout them children?'

'They just children,' I said. 'That's not what I here to talk about.'

'You right, Missa Digger, they children; they Bello children. All ov dem. Same shape head, same face-bone, same teeth and eye. Same big-bone body. None of them belong to Bello wife, but Bello blood so strong in dem, it pushing outta dem skin.' Miss Stanislaus kissed her teeth. 'So, Missa Bone Reader, with all your foreign-sick eddication, how come you never notice that?'

She said it quietly, earnestly – as if she really wanted to know. Still, I felt the sting of her reproach.

'Make it worse, Missa Digger, every one ov them lil children got a different modder. Mek it even more worse, all dem children modder not older dan fourteen or fifteen when dem have dem chile.'

Miss Stanislaus spoke softly, urgently, with her lids lowered, so that I could not see her eyes.

'That start me wonderin about all them woman here. What could make that happm to all dem likkle girlchile in dis church and nobody make a stink about it? It bring me back to Nathan. You wamme tell you why?'

I said nothing; I was still staring at the children.

'Nathan was a Pointer in de church. And like you know, a Pointer look after dem Mourners on the Mournin Ground. Dat mean Nathan witness everything that go on inside dat lil concrete house.

'I believe that Nathan see how Bello pick-an-choose whatever girlchile he fancy and do as he please with them. And it mus ha been so damn easy, Missa Digger…' – Miss Stanislaus raised appalled eyes at me – 'because, after seven or fourteen or twenty-one days of starving on dat Mourning Ground, I askin you, where a woman goin get de strength or sense to fight off a bull like the Deacon? Eh? He been doin it for years. Most ov those lil girls hardly know what happm to dem until they with child.

'I believe that Nathan see all dat and he confuse. He couldn make no sense of a man of God who condemn *him* for what he is and that same man doin a lot worse tings right in front of him. And it look to me that Bello wife couldn stop im eider because…' Miss Stanislaus plucked a tissue and patted her face. 'She know if she complain, she good as dead.

'Something else been bothering me, Missa Digger. Remember first time I come here with you, they tell me Amos mother run off to Trinidad? They tell me she left a coupla months before Nathan disappear. I don't believe Miss Alice run off nowhere. I got reason to believe somefing happen to her.'

The Mother appeared from behind the building. She floated across the stones with an open coconut in her hand. I studied her face, the broad serenity of it, as if her husband hadn't died this morning, shot by the woman sitting beside me. The Mother caught me staring and a small change came over her demeanour. She held out the coconut to Miss Stanislaus.

'Drink,' she said. 'Good for the blood.'

Miss Stanislaus smiled at her. 'Me an Missa Digger jus' decide to take some breeze. Mebbe when we come back?'

Miss Stanislaus rose carefully – as if testing the reliability of her limbs. I reached out to help her to her feet. She took my hand. 'Come wiv me.'

'Couple hours ago you shoot her husband,' I said. 'Now she offering you a drink.'

Miss Stanislaus's footsteps slowed, but she did not look back.

We were on the mud track heading deeper into the mangrove.

She raised an arm at an incline to the right of us. 'Up there,' she said.

A flat boulder capped the hill. It overlooked the swamp beyond which were the whispering waters of the inlet where sharks and barracudas came in on the evening tide to feed on dead and rotting things.

Miss Stanislaus sat, then patted the space beside her. I shook my head and made a point of looking at my watch.

'Somebody been talking to you,' I said. 'Who?'

'I work out most ov it myself.'

'About the children belonging to Bello, yes. But the information about Nathan and Miss Alice – that had to come from somebody. I asking who it is. I asking for clarity, that's what I want right now.'

'Missa Digger, I can't tell you because…'

'Okay, Miss Lady! Keep it to yourself. Choke on it till it kill you. Lemme tell you what I think: y'all sign and seal Bello' death warrant before y'all got to Sadie Bay. I dunno if you put them up to it, or the other way around. But there is not one woman in that church who didn't know what was going to happen.'

She sat perfectly still, her head cocked in the air.

'Miss Stanislaus, no matter how loud you shout that Bello jump them little girls and breed them… it don't explain or justify what happened in Sadie Bay this morning. Now, for the Alice person you mentioned – the one that run away.'

'She didn't run away.' Miss Stanislaus shoved a hand into her purse and pulled out a cell phone. It was covered with a white rubber case, a glittering marijuana leaf embossed on the back. She dropped it in the hammock of her dress. 'Couple days ago one of the Sisters give this to me.'

'Which Sister?'

Miss Stanislaus shook her head.

'Miss Stanislaus, if you don't start talking to me straight, I walk out of here and leave you in your shit.'

'Missa Digger!'

'Don't "Missa Digger" me! You either talk to me or you don't. I asking you again, what's the Sister' name!'

She turned bright defiant eyes on me, then softened. 'The – The Modder. She gimme this phone quiet as if she know all along why I there. Phone was wrap up in a grocery bag. I take it, but I was careless. Lil Amos see it. "Dat's mammy phone," he say. Bello almost run out de church. He stan-up in front de door long time, like if he tendin to God business, then he walk back inside.'

Miss Stanislaus blinked at me, 'You should see how frighten de Modder look when Bello come out de church, because she hear Amos words too.' She bounced the phone in her hand as if she were hefting it. 'Commonsense tell me dat same way Nathan wouldn leave his bag behind, ain got no way Miss Alice going leave dis phone. I see how young people love-up dis ting. Dey dress it up an feed it with every penny they got. Sometimes the way they hold it and look at it, a pusson believe they praying to the ting. Miss Alice might run off and leave she one boychile, but she not goin leave she phone.'

I held out my hand. Miss Stanislaus hesitated. Then she passed it over. The handset wouldn't switch on. "I'll check it out," I said.

She nodded absent-mindedly. 'Missa Digger, I believe Nathan did know dat Bello kill dat girl; he might've even seen it.'

'All the evidence pointed to Nathan boyfriend, Simday.'

She sucked her teeth. 'Why Simday goin hide Nathan body just a lil way from his house? He got a car; he got a boat. Why he didn take Nathan to the ocean where nobody goin find him? Where's the sense in buryin him nex door?'

She rose to her feet. 'Bello kill im while he kneelin down to pray for forgiveness.'

'Forgiveness for what?'

'For he an Missa Simday secret. Bello know dat secret too. Is why he take Nathan up dere an drop im near Simday house. He figure if anybody ever find Nathan, de whitefella get de blame. And that's eggzackly what y'all do.

'Besides, Missa Digger,' she dabbed at her face, 'if I wrong about Bello killin Nathan, is your fault.'

The woman was almost pouting with the accusation. 'People kill de same way – that's what you say. You tell me they can't help it because is habit. That's what come in mind this morning when I see how Bello baptise people. He don't turn your face up to the sky an push you back in the water to baptise you, like all dem other preacher in the worl does do. Nuh! He grab your neck and push your face in first. Dat's what happen to Nathan. Only, the

133

concrete floor ov dat church is not no water. Dat's why Nathan face mash up. Like you tell me, it was habit.'

Miss Stanislaus looked perfectly at ease and very sure of herself.

'What I wondering now, Miss Stanislaus, is why you didn't say all of this to Malan? It might've…'

'He didn giv me a chance to talk,' she snapped. 'He was too busy tryin to force word outta me. And no fowl-cock ov a man goin manage dat, y'unnerstan?'

The evening sun had begun to lose its sting. There was a hint of copper on the water down below. It had been a long day and I was tired.

'None of that explains what happen on the beach,' I said. 'And I know for sure that I can't help you if I dunno what really happen in Sadie Bay this morning.'

What I didn't tell her was that come tomorrow, Monday, when the island emerged from its weekend stupor, rumours of Deacon Bello's death would break. Tongues would amplify the story. The newspapers would begin digging. There were men in government who visited Bello for their bush-bath, their secret potions of voodoo-luck and remedies for impotence. They would be asking questions. Malan and the Commissioner would always put the Department first. Not even Chilman could protect Miss Stanislaus.

I brought my face close to hers. 'Which is true, Miss Stanislaus: that you honestly can't tell me, or you won't because you just don't give a damn about the consequences?'

Miss Stanislaus fixed me with a level, moist-eyed stare. 'Is de wimmen dat I don't want no more trouble for. They go through nuff already. Is time for all ov dis to stop, y'unnerstan? An even if Bello got to dead a couple more times to make tings right, I not goin turn my back on them. Dat's all I have to say.'

On the way back Miss Stanislaus walked a step ahead of me. I was aware of the shift of her shoulders, the padding of her sandals on the damp earth, her fingers tensed around the mouth of her handbag.

She halted at the beginning of the stone-path that led up to the churchyard. For a moment she searched my face, then Miss

Stanislaus raised her hand. I felt the soft grate of her knuckles against my jawline.

'Miss Stanislaus, I thinking about your daughter.'

'My girlchile goin be awright, Missa Digger. Is I that bring she up. I *know* she going be awright.' Her eyes were sparking when she said it, and there was murder in her tone.

She turned abruptly and began walking up the path.

I watched The Mother, Iona and another – slim and supple as a bamboo shoot – come to stand beside her. They'd lowered their heads and had their backs to me. All four dressed in blue and so tightly huddled, I could barely distinguish Miss Stanislaus from the other three.

Somewhere at the back of my mind, just beyond reach – was something Miss Stanislaus had just said – a nagging little dissonance in the way she'd strung together her words. I closed my eyes, trying to locate it. I decided to leave it alone.

I was out of the tunnel of flamboyant trees, turning onto the main road when the words came: *If Bello have to dead a couple more times...* I stepped on the brakes so abruptly, I almost wrecked my car.

## 24

I called DS Chilman and told him I would see him around eight-thirty.

'Why so late?'

'Late by whose standards, Sir?'

'Okay, Digson, so you in a bad mood. Make it eight.' Chilman hung up.

I phoned the mortuary. 'Lucille, DC Digson here. Daryl in tonight?'

'Hold on – yes, he is. You want to leave a message?'

'Nuh. Around what time he starting work?

'The usual – from seven.'

'Thanks Lucille, how you?'

'I good. Missa Digger, I pregnant. When you coming home to tell my mother about me and you?'

'Wha?'

Lucille burst out laughing. 'Eh-heh! I thought you say nothing could surprise you.' Another belly-laugh and the weekend receptionist at Otter's Sanctuary hung up.

Dusk had begun to powder the Kalivini hills when I swung my car towards San Andrews. A bluish light seeped from a sky choked with strato-cumulus clouds. I took the quiet road south to the mortuary in San Andrews – a sprawling white concrete building that followed the incline of the steepest hill in the town. Otter's Sanctuary was owned by brothers whose family name was synonymous with the thriving business of death. It was always open. I tapped my keys against the metal grid of the gate.

My agitation was not just because Miss Stanislaus was involved and I could not bear thinking about the consequences. Fact was I'd failed.

I was about to do what I should've done the moment I saw Deacon Bello lying in the sand at Sadie Bay. Despite Malan's temper, despite the shock of an action I least expected from Miss Stanislaus, I should have secured the scene, examined Bello's body in detail, collected whatever evidence there was and taken as much time over it as I needed to make sense of his murder. I would never allow myself to be pushed by anyone again – not even by DS Chilman – to abandon the work I was meant to do.

I tapped my keys harder on the gate. A young man trotted out of the building wearing yellow elbow-length Neoprene gloves. Big serious eyes.

'Missa Digger, you workin tonight?'

'Daryl,' I said, 'anybody else in there with you?'

He nodded, 'Seven ov us. Anodder one comin in tonight. She pass away dis mornin.'

That made me laugh.

He unlocked the gate. 'Somebody you come to check out?'

'Deacon Bello.' I said. I waited for his reaction and sure enough Daryl stopped. He looked startled.

'You mean Bello the…'

'Yeh!' I said. 'How come you dunno that?'

'I check in less than five minutes ago. Peter tell me we got seven residents – that's all.'

I followed Daryl into a corridor past a large reception built along the lines of a chapel. Blue fluorescent lights bathed the space. The chemical sweetness in the air flared my nostrils. Already my skin began to prickle with the cold.

Daryl went to a small desk in the corner and took up a green folder. He flipped it open and ran a finger down the first page. 'He come in this afternoon. Eighteen minutes past one… Missa Digger, I could ask you a question?'

'Another time, Daryl.' I winked at him and smiled. 'How's the family?'

'They awright. Rack Five, third shelf down.' He glanced at the paper again before replacing it. Daryl took me through to a white storage unit and pulled open the heavy door. Bello was one rung up from the lowest shelf. I could see the sense in that. He was a heavy man. Less work to manoeuvre him in and out.

Daryl handed me a pair of gloves. I dropped a hand on his shoulder. 'You learning fast,' I said. I'd gotten him the job four months ago.

They'd pushed in Bello feet first, his toes facing the ceiling of course. That meant not much disturbance on my part. I took out my LED, lifted the drape that covered him and lay flat on the floor directly under the body. I scrolled the beam along its full length, then more slowly from the nape of the neck, up toward the head, stopping at the bloody contusion at the junction of the jawline and the ear. Daryl watched me closely as I took some swabs and placed them in small canisters of formalin.

I stood up and allowed myself to breathe. The beginnings of an idea had begun to take shape in my mind.

Tomorrow, the old English pathologist we nicknamed, Rumcake would do a more thorough examination. Me – I needed answers now. The bullet had entered Bello's left shoulder blade at an angle, exiting through the shoulder muscle. I kept my torch on the wound for a long time.

'Missa Digger… I could ask you a question?'

With the fluorescent lights directly overhead, Daryl's was a blue-sculpted face.

'Daryl,' I said. 'You want to be a good mortician?'

He flapped a wrist and grunted.

'Well, Starboy, a mortician is like a lawyer or mebbe a doctor. They don't ask questions, yunno, unless is necessary. They just do their job.'

Daryl didn't look convinced. My example didn't convince me either, but it would have to do.

'How's your father, Daryl?'

'He awright.'

'And yuh mother?'

'She awright too.' He was still working his lips around the question he knew I was sidestepping.

'Tell them I say hello.' I dropped the gloves in the bin. 'Another thing – nobody don't have to know that I been here, y'unnerstan?'

'Awright,' he said.

138

At the gate Daryl threw me a worried look. I took out the cell phone I'd taken from Miss Stanislaus. I'd plugged it into the charger in my car on the way down. The handset had come alive but it was passworded.

'Daryl, I got reason to believe you know how to break into these?'

He stared at the phone, than rested wary eyes on my face. I thought he was going to deny it, but he took the handset from me.

'What's it not doin?'

'I can't get past the password.'

'You want the password off?'

'Uh-huh.'

'Pick it up tomorrow.' He pocketed the phone.

'How you do that?'

'Root it, then secure shell, then back-door.'

'That a new language?'

Daryl ignored the question, jerked his head in the direction of the building. 'Missa Digger, what happm? Ah mean…'

'Next coupla days the whole island will be asking that, Daryl. Is why I looking for answers now.'

He sucked his teeth, grunted his exasperation.

I left him standing at the gate.


A soft drizzle was glossing the tarmac when I turned onto the West Coast Road.

I realised I hadn't eaten since morning.

I stopped off at Beau Sejour – a small village on the edge of the mangrove swamps where, thirty-one years before, US Marines had left the bodies of five local militia boys burning by the roadside. On my right, a scattering of board houses; above them, the Belvedere Mountain Chain, purple in the draining light.

Women stood behind rows of coal-pots and curtains of rolling smoke, selling anything from stewed lambi, saltfish-cake, fried bakes to blood-pudding and roasted corn.

Beyond them was the black pebble beach with a row of twenty-footer fishing boats bobbing on the water, nets draped along their length. Among them, and barely noticeable, I spotted a couple of grey, pug-nosed crafts, their sterns broad enough for two engines.

I felt eyes on me.

Four young men stood shoulder to shoulder observing me observe the boats. Expensive canvas shoes, heavy watches, American baseball caps turned back-to-front. A Subaru jeep with darkened windows was parked on the grass verge a couple of feet from them.

The tallest of the bunch waved a long muscled arm at me.

'Digger!'

'Mister Digson to you,' I said.

A chuckle rumbled out of him. 'You don' remember me, man?'

'Yep! Lazar Wilkinson. Friday August 5th last year. Queen's Park. Arrested and charged for attempted assault and affray and possession of a lethal weapon. Three months!' I jerked my chin at the sprint-boats. 'I see you got promoted.'

I tossed the rest of the fishcake over the seawall and ambled towards my car. I opened the door, waved at him. 'Catch you later, Lazar. And when I catch you next time, it not going to be three months, it going to be years.'

I heard a burst of laughter from the stalls as I triggered the engine and pulled out. In my rear-view mirror, I glimpsed his contorted face. Two fingers rigid in the air. I pushed out my arm and returned the compliment.

## 25

Chilman was out on the road, waiting – even more of a scarecrow of a man than usual – dressed in loose brown shorts and an old string vest, his toes splayed like ten brown mice in his ancient leather sandals.

'My house, Digson.'

A racket greeted us when we entered the yard – an agitated scattering of dark-winged creatures that sounded inconsolable.

'Wozzat?' I said, my body tensed for a quick sprint back to the road.

'Guinea fowls,' he said. 'Better than dog. Besides, you could eat their arse when they fret you. Keep that in mind, Digson. Is good advice. Mavis, shut them up!'

A thick, heavily braceleted arm shot out of a window, sent a scattering of something pale into the yard. Another bout of alarmed squawking, then almost silence.

'Only thing to quiet them. Food! Same with some people if you ask me.' On the veranda, Chilman pointed at an old canvas chair. 'Sit down and gimme a minute.'

I sat back listening to the contours of a murmured conversation in the house. Chilman's was an unpretentious concrete house on high pillars with a wide veranda. It hung over an incline that dropped down to the sea. A few coconut trees of the short variety fretted the walls with their fronds. From what I could glimpse inside, there were framed photographs of family on the walls, cushioned mahogany chairs, and a table with the usual burden of knitted doilies, plastic flowers and vases. The house smelled of cooking.

When he came out, he had changed his clothes. He dragged a

chair and sat in front of me, the hot red eyes steady on my face. He got up abruptly and switched off the veranda light. Now, only the yellow spill from inside the house lit up the space between us.

'Okay, Digger, talk to me.'

The secret to what was going on in Chilman's mind was in his hands – what they were doing while the rest of him remained unreadable as stone. I'd learned that in my first month of employment under him, and kept it to myself. Now he'd interlaced his fingers and his thumbs were circling each other. Chilman was very, very worried.

I decided not to mince words. 'The woman you sent us to deal with the Nathan case just gone and stir up big shit, Sir.'

'Spare me the attitude, Digson. Debrief me the way I taught you.' The old DS's voice had gone tight and edgy.

I ran through the events of the day, repeating sentences and words whenever he flicked a wrist – part of the language he'd invented for our meetings at the office. 'In brief, Sir,' I concluded, 'it was – to all intents and purposes – an execution.'

I felt Chilman's reaction rather than saw it. Night had rolled in quickly and his guinea fowls had taken to the roof of the house in a clatter of wings and jumbie cries.

'At least,' I said. 'That's how Malan would put it.'

He said nothing for a long time. I could hear the whisper of the skin of his circling thumbs.

'Tell me again – the riddle she give you 'bout killing Bello a couple times.'

'It wasn't a riddle, Sir. In Miss Stanislaus' mind it was a fact. I checked Bello's body at the mortuary before I came here. The point of entry of the bullet was the upper left edge of the shoulder blade, left side of the body. It exited through the shoulder.

'From the angle of travel, she was most likely crouching low when she shot him, one of the shooting positions I taught her. No vital organs hit. Basically a deep wound with some damage to the shoulder joint and muscle – the anterior deltoid to be exact.'

'In other words?'

'In other words this talk about killing Bello coupla times was her way of saying he was already dead when she shot him. My conclusion is that one of the women killed him.'

Chilman was massaging the side of his nose with a finger.

'How, Digson?'

I shrugged. 'Serious trauma to the right side of his head, contusion of the skin directly above the temporal bone. Basically, something hard and heavy knocked him down – most likely a big stone.'

'She told you that?'

'Who told me what?'

'That she didn't kill the deacon?'

'She didn't tell me, but she *said* so.'

'Talk sense, Digson.'

'Is sense I talking, Sir. Miss Stanislaus don't lie. I believe she can't. You got people like that; their brain sort of wired that way. They find lying almost impossible – which is not to say they can't decide to withhold information… if that make sense.'

'Make the point, youngfella.'

It felt like the old days with Chilman guiding me along a no-nonsense line of reasoning. I used to love it and resent it at the same time – this cantankerous sonuvabitch trying to trip me up, tear apart my logic and toss it back in my face.

'Like I say already, Sir, I believe one of the women did it – most likely The Mother. She got the strength to use a very heavy stone. I believe they planned to get rid of him. Miss Stanislaus might have even encouraged them. Whatever they had in mind didn't work out the way they expected. But an opportunity came when Bello tried to drown Miss Stanislaus. They dragged him off her; one of them knocked him down. Miss Stanislaus decide to take the blame by shooting him.'

I looked him in the eye. 'What I want to know, Sir, is why Miss Stanislaus feel she could do a thing like that and get away with it.'

Chilman sucked his teeth. 'Use your brain, Digson. You're an officer, you shoot a man while acting within the auspices of the law. Who going to arrest you – the same police you working for? That's why she take the blame. Problem is, she miscalculate, or misjudge how Malan was going to deal with it.'

He crossed his feet and leaned forward, the salt-and-pepper head bowed slightly. 'Is the kind of thing that she would do. Carrying all that stuff inside her head – all that…'

'All what?'

'Sorry, Digson, Kathleen will have to tell you herself.'

'I want to know what she is to you,' I said. 'I have a right to know.'

Chilman threw me a red-eyed squint. I thought he wasn't going to answer. He rubbed his head, then another slice of silence before he stirred.

'Kathleen is my conscience, Digson. That's what she is. The one I left behind on Kara Isle. Bright! Bright as firefly backside. She just didn't have the chance the others here had. If she had she would be running this island better than the whole pile of them who trying to run it now.'

His voice had retreated down his throat. 'And you right, she don't lie, not even to protect herself. That used to get her into trouble as a child.'

'And you, Sir – how about you and lying?'

I heard Chilman's slow intake of breath. 'I should take exception to that, Digson; but you an investigating officer and you doing your job.'

'What is she to you?' I pressed.

Chilman waved aside the question. 'You want a drink?'

'No, Sir. I want to finish this business and go home.'

The old DS stood up. 'Well, I don't know about you, but I want a drink.'

He was in the house for a while – a series of rattlings and bangings punctuated by the protests of his wife.

He returned with a bottle and a glass, filled the glass with the care of a dispenser, knocked back the alcohol with a quick jerk of his elbow.

Chilman smacked his lips and sighed. 'I tell you something, Digson. Them Trinidadians foolin theyself when they say steelpan is the only thing that we, West-Indies-Man, invent. Is a lie. Is not we invent rum too? Before steelpan! It won't surprise me if the fella who invent pan had a couple of shots inside him when the steel pan idea come.' He chuckled at his own joke, wagged a finger in my face. 'We got to make Kathleen official. She got to be an officer before all this shit break out.'

Chilman slid the glass and bottle under his chair.

'Malan wouldn't...'

'Fuck Malan. Sorry about the language, Digson, but you fretting me. Malan could've done the paperwork, employ the woman as instructed, *weeks ago*, and this would've been no problem. But that womaniser hate my arse so much, he decide anything that come from me not good. Even if I the one who pick up his arse from off the beach selling black sage to tourist and telling them is special marijuana. I give him a job and look – is that decision I make that cutting my arse right now. Digson, you ever wonder about my employment policy?'

'All the time, Sir.'

'I tell you something: a lil over thirty years ago, we had some young fellas running this island. Shit go down in the end, but I learn one thing from them: to make things happen you got to create your own bureaucracy. Else you'll wait till hen lay cricket ball and cock grow teeth before you get a result.

'Now,' Chilman settled back, 'Word of that preacherman death going to hit the island tomorrow. Y'all either have to ride it out or pre-empt it. I in favour of pre-emption – that's a word, Digson? So, first thing tomorrow, press statement from the Department with all the allegations – all of them – against Bello. Don't make it sound like speculation, make it sound like fact.'

'You, erm, involving the Commissioner again?'

'I always involve him. How you think you got your job? S'matter of fact,' Chilman wagged an index in my face, 'you owe him a conversation. Now, Digson, this is the essence of the story as it going to appear in the news tomorrow:

'An officer attempted to arrest Bello. He resisted and gave said officer good reason to believe the officer's life, and members of his congregation were in danger. Officer had no choice but self-defence. You notice how I word it, no name involved.'

The old DS made a circle in the air above his head. 'And while people out there still in shock, you go out and get hard evidence. You find it fast, Digson, because Camaho people not stupid. Leave them jackass foreigners to believe that. We who live here can't afford to make that mistake.'

'Malan, Sir...'

'I tell you already, fuck Malan. Malan got no choice. He can't

145

say he had nothing to do with it. And if he say he didn't, I will get one of those newspaper people to ask him in public why he allowed a woman who is not an employee of his Department to shoot a preacher with a gun that he himself accustom wearing.

'You think I goin siddown on my arse and watch all my hard work come to nothing because of Malan feelings? A statement will be on his desk tomorrow for him to read out on the radio.'

Chilman filled himself another glass.

'You forgetting one thing, Sir: you retired. Is Malan run things now…'

Chilman chuckled – a soft throaty sound. 'If you really believe that, Digson, you wouldn' be here right now. Anyway,' he scratched his head and raised his brows at me, 'Bello connection with the Nathan case surprise me.'

'Soon'z Miss Stanislaus said it, it made sense,' I said. 'Even though Nathan' mother not convinced the remains we uncovered is Nathan.'

'Iona not wrong, Digger. That could never be the same Nathan she give birth to. H'was clothed in flesh and talking when he left the house. Now, all these years later, all she see is bone. So she right; is not her son; is bone. What the lab say?'

'Report coming from Trinidad at the end of the week.' I said.

Chilman pushed himself off the chair. 'Link all of it to Bello. Create a chain of evidence: Nathan, the business with the lil girls, and the young woman – what's her name again?'

'Alice.'

'And in the meantime, Digson, when newspaper come to ask you questions, blind their arse with science. Use them big words you does show off with to make good people feel ignorant and small. Do that if you have to, because you'll be buying time. I don't believe Kathleen wrong about Miss Alice. Find that girl wherever Bello hide her. You do that and you rest the case. I done talk. I got a coupla calls to make. You sure you don't want a drink?'

'What's she to you, Sir?'

'What's *who* to who?'

'Miss Stanislaus.'

'Use your brain.'

'I want to hear you say it. What's Miss Stanislaus to you?'

He sucked his teeth, mumbled something about 'chupid attitude' and slammed the door behind him.

I made the call before I went to bed. 'Digger here. I just been talking to your father.'

I heard nothing for a while – just the background rise and fall of women's voices, the tik-tok-tinkling of night insects, a fretting child. Then, 'How's he, Missa Digger?'

'Drinking but still thinking, Miss Stanislaus. Is a miracle he still got a brain. You plan to go to the office any time soon?'

'You advise me to go?'

'Nuh. You got good reason to stay home; you still recovering. Next time Malan interrogates you, I want you to tell him you were in shock, you were feeling a little bazodee because of all the confusion. You forgot how things happen. Bello beat you up and drag you in the water. He was trying to drown you. The Mother pulled him off. You run out of the water. When Bello come after you, some of the wimmen hold onto him. The others tried to hold him back. Bello broke away from them and was coming for you again; that's when somebody hit him.' I paused, 'All that happen for true, not so?'

'Uh-huh.'

'Now I want you to add this part: h'was about to get up again, and with him having already made an attempt on your life, you felt you had no choice but to retrieve your gun and shoot him before he could turn on you again. You got that?'

'Nuh.'

'You want me to repeat it?'

'Nuh. Missa Digger, that last part not true.'

I could hear her footsteps and knew that she had retreated from the group.

'I asking you to give yourself a chance, Miss Stanislaus. That's what I doing. I asking you to do that until I clear up matters.'

'Nuh.'

'Miss Stanislaus, what's the difference between lying and holding back the facts?'

'One is a lie.'

'They both doing the same thing in this case.'

'How come, Missa Digger?'

'They both hiding the truth – except you save everybody a lot of grief if you tell Malan what I tell you.'

'Nuh!' I could hear her breathing over the phone. 'Missa Digger?'

'What?'

'Fank you.'

'For what?'

'Is what I feel to say right now. Missa Digger, you like Julie mango? I got one for you.'

'Oh God.'

'Beg yuh pardon?'

'I say "not bad". DS Chilman say to call him.'

'Nuh!'

'You not calling him?'

'Nuh.'

'You saying "nuh" to everything tonight?'

I thought I heard her chuckle. 'Nuh!'

'Miss Stanislaus, don't change your mind about the mango. Tomorrow I come for it.

## 26

I'd never known Pet and Lisa to begin work this early. The sun had just struck the waters of the Carenage and water taxis were bobbing against the sidewalk for the Monday morning work-rush to the government complex in Canteen. The bus terminal had just begun to boil with the thunder of incoming traffic, raucous with the shouts of harassing bus conductors.

My arrival cut short Pet and Lisa's conversation. I jangled my keys at them, dropped into my seat and closed my eyes.

'What wrong, Digger?'

'Lil headache,' I said. 'Not much sleep, yunno.'

'How come?'

'Things a little bit twisted,' I said.

'What tings?' Pet said.

She was sifting through the Friday post. She pulled out a brown A4 envelope, got up, dropped it at my elbow. I nudged it aside and turned around to face them. 'Talk to me, ladies. Something on y'all mind?'

'Digger, how's Miss Stanislaus?'

I dismissed the question with a flick of my head, held their gazes until Pet directed a glance at the window. 'Talk out there say that something happen, yesterday?'

Pet paused for my reply. I offered none.

Lisa raised blue-pencilled eyebrows at me. 'People say the Department kill a big-time preacherman? Is all over San Andrews.'

'When y'all hear that?'

'First thing this morning. Neighbour come round and tell my mother. I wasn listening but I overhear.'

The two were looking at me closely.

'Is true,' I said. I rose to my feet and stretched my limbs. 'Circumstances made it so that we had to defend ourselves.'

'Who's "we"?'

I reined in my irritation. 'I can't get into that right now. I'll talk to y'all later, although I not obliged.'

'Okay,' Lisa said. 'Miss Stanislaus involved?' Concern was etched on their knotted brows. Women! Not giving a damn about us fellas.

'Yes, Bello – the Preacherman – assaulted her. He was going to drown her.'

Lisa raised a hand to her mouth. 'She awright?'

'She'll survive. Miss Stanislaus only look like a dolly, but she tough as gru-gru nut.'

Pet looked up mid-chuckle. Her expression froze. Lisa sat down abruptly and began straightening her keyboard. I heard the rumble of Malan's engine.

When the vehicle stopped, Lisa squinted at the window facing the courtyard, her head jerking sideways like an anxious chicken. She soured her face and sat back. 'Bad weather.'

'More like a hurricane,' Pet said.

It was how they announced Malan's mood. They were never wrong. It didn't matter how laid-back he looked when he arrived. When times were good, one of them would say, 'No rain today.'

Malan grunted a greeting and strode into his office. I raised my brows at Pet and Lisa.

I walked over to Malan's door. I was about to turn the handle and enter when he raised a staying arm. His eyes were on his screen. I watched his changing posture, his narrowed eyes, the stiffening shoulders, the forward thrust of his upper body. The printer in the office woke and spat out a couple of pages. Malan lifted a finger at Lisa. She promptly retrieved the pages and brought them over to him. Malan took them, looked over his shoulder in my direction in a way that sent a current of unease through me.

I retreated to my desk, sat there doing nothing. After a while Malan shouldered open his door, strode across the floor toward me.

'So you went to Chilman house last night to make your report? I thought you was going home to rest?'

I stood up to face him. 'In the light of what happened yesterday, I wanted to get some answers from…'

'Don't waste your breath, Digson. I know what happen.'

The women were quiet. Pet had stopped typing.

'Hear me out, Malan…'

'Why! Where's your loyalty, Digson?' He'd curled his lips around my name. 'You Chilman likkle boy? He running you? How come you driving all the way to his house late Sunday night to make report?'

He shook the sheets of paper in my face. 'You think I didn't see this coming? I far ahead of y'all. News break six o'clock this morning; you know who make that happen? Me!' He strode over to the women, his eyes on me while he spoke. 'Do me a favour, Lisa, call the minister, tell him I on the way.'

He paused at my desk, his voice low and thick with malice. 'I take this personally, Digson and I going get personal too. You watch!'

Malan stepped out of the office, the folder under his arm. His Mitsubishi roared out of the yard in a spray of fine gravel.

I sat back feeling choked. Pet came over and rested a hand on my shoulder.

'Digger, what goin on? I worried and confuse.'

'Me too,' I said, and began sorting through my papers. 'Which minister Malan gone off to see, Lisa?'

Lisa did not answer.

I turned to her, 'You not telling me?'

Lisa shrugged.

'The MJ,' Pet said. 'The Minister of Justice. That's where Malan gone.' She was looking at Lisa hard. Her lips had barely moved.

'Justice Minister,' Lisa echoed. 'Digger, I…'

'Too late,' I said. 'If y'all don't realise what's happening, lemme make it clear. Malan going above the Commissioner's head. He going try to override him. That look to me like suicide.'

'Digger…'

'Can't talk now, Lisa. I got a report to write.'

I sat with the pen in my hand staring at the blank sheets of paper in front of me. For the first time in my career I had to think about how to begin a report. I would need to come up with a language that a legal mind could not twist to their advantage. I decided to offer no analysis, but just a brief chronology of the events in Sadie Bay. I started a couple of times but finally gave up. I turned to the envelope I'd ignored all morning. It was postmarked Trinidad. I ripped it open.

Three A4 sheets of paper: the first two pages were a summative commentary by Ramlogan, the Chief Tech at the lab in Trinidad. The last sheet was a grid layout of numbers attached to an acetate printout with columns and rows that looked like barcodes. The acetate was an extra. Ramlogan wanted to impress me and I was impressed. The Forensic Science Centre routinely did pathology and toxicology work for us, sometimes firearms analysis, but never DNA. This was our first and I felt a quickening inside me.

I scanned the headings:

DATA TABLE OF DNA MARKERS, COMBINED MATERNITY INDEX, PROBABILITY OF MATERNITY.

I halted over the conclusion. Reread it.

*Based on the genetic testing, results obtained by PCR analysis of STR loci, the alleged parent is excluded as the biological mother of the child. The probability of maternity is 0%.*

*Prior probability* = 0.50. COMBINED MATERNITY INDEX: 0

I went to the cooler, filled a glass and drank, strolled over to the photocopier and made duplicates. I returned to my desk and stuffed them in my bag. Found myself muttering at the ceiling, 'Nothing don't make no fuckin sense no more.'

'Y'awright, Digger?' Pet again.

'Headache still there; that's all,' I said.

The phone rang; Lisa picked up. Her tone told me it was Malan. Lisa asked Pet to transfer the call to Malan's office. Lisa did not look at me. I watched her leaning against the desk, her pencil making circles on the paper, the movement broken occasionally by a busy scribble on the pad.

When Lisa came out, her eyes were wide and bright. She

bent down as if she was adjusting the straps of her shoe, but I noted the movement of her lips. I saw Pet's face go dazed and wondering.

Lisa took her lunch bag and offered me a sapodilla. I shook my head. She dropped the fruit on my desk. Pet kept her head down, typing.

My chest felt scooped out, the hollowness extended to my head. Malan returned late morning. I still felt frayed by his earlier insults.

'Staff meeting,' he announced. He dragged a chair to the middle of the space and sat down.

'Take notes,' he said to Lisa.

Malan reached into his folder and pulled out a sheet of paper. It was in his handwriting. He took in all three of us.

'Like y'all already know, this morning the Commissioner called me on my cell phone instructing me to make Miss Kathleen Stanislaus a bona fide member of staff. He told me I got two hours to do the paperwork.'

'I kin handle that,' Lisa offered quickly.

Malan glared at her. Lisa clamped her lips and lowered her eyes. Pet's face had gone cold and wary, her eyes never leaving Malan's face.

'Commissioner also informed me by email to put out a statement informing the public that, yesterday, officers were called to the scene of a disturbance at Sadie Bay.' Malan flapped the printed email in front of him, then began to read it. 'When officers arrived they perceived a threat in the person of Bello Hunt, Deacon of The Children of the Unicorn Spiritual Baptist Church. Deacon Bello was in the process of… of, erm, strangling a member of his congregation. Officers prevailed on him to stop, whereupon Deacon Bello turned on them. Officers had no option but to defend themselves, resulting unfortunately in the death of the Deacon. The public must also be informed that Police are now making inquiries into serious allegations of assault and sexual exploitation against Deacon Bello himself.'

Malan slid the paper into the folder.

'Problem is, people, I know nothing about these allegations. Nobody report them to me, nobody call me to discuss them.'

'I will do that now.' I looked at him directly. 'And I want it noted that this is the first opportunity I have to talk to you about it.'

'You spoke to Chilman before me.'

'Yes. Yesterday evening, I paid him a call for reasons I have no problem explaining to you. Today, Monday, is my first official day of work since the incident. I'm more than happy to report.'

Malan looked at me a long time.

He shrugged, then turned to Pet and Lisa. 'You ladies want to take early lunch-break?'

'But you ask me to take notes,' Lisa protested.

'Nuh,' Pet said bluntly. 'I want to know what go on. Besides, we got we lunch here.'

'Take y'all lunch with y'all then.'

Lisa flounced out, followed by Pet, who made a show of her resentment. Malan smiled briefly at the wall behind me and settled back.

'Shoot,' he said.

'Hm!' I said.

He narrowed his eyes at me.

'Miss Stanislaus checked out of the hospital as soon as we left her. I went to the church to find her. She has good reason to believe that Bello was taking advantage of the girl-children in the church – some as young as fourteen. She figured that one of those girls, Alice, who is alleged to have gone off to Trinidad, like Nathan, is not in Trinidad. She's convinced that Bello did something to her.'

Malan made a gesture as if to push aside my words.

'Digger, you and I know it couldn't happen the way she tell us. You and I couldn't do what she say she done: shoot a pusson with she back half-turn to them when she running to save she life. She think she is Clint Eastwood? Or she taking people for coo-noo-moo-noo?'

'Miss Stanislaus never claimed she shot Bello while running away from him. Remember every time you asked her about the exact moment that she shot Bello, she wouldn't answer you? You the one who concluded that. I believe Miss Stanislaus shot Bello when he was already dead. Miss Stanislaus felt obliged to protect those women, for whatever reason.'

154

'Then why she lie to me?'

'She didn't lie to you; she just didn't tell you the truth.'

'She shoot a man...'

'Who was about to kill her,' I cut in.

'How you know that?'

'She got the marks on her body to prove it.'

'Was a set up, Digger. That make she...'

'Malan, what you got against Miss Stanislaus?'

'I doing my job.'

'You sure?'

'Why you defending her, Digson.'

'She was doing a job we gave her.'

'I didn't. Commissioner instructed me. But she not on staff. I saw to that.'

'How you going to explain the fact that a woman shot a man with a gun owned by San Andrews CID? She didn't thief the gun; you gave it to her.'

Malan showed me all his teeth. 'Is like you and Chilman work it out, not so? Don't fool yourself.'

He tapped the folder. 'The press release that's going out today is the one I got in here. It might make you happy to know, it make no mention of your girlfriend. S'far as people concern, she don't exist.'

I was tempted to tell Malan that I'd found out Miss Stanislaus was Chilman's daughter. I almost said it, then changed my mind.

I dropped my eyes on the folder in his hand. 'No mention of the allegations against Bello, then?'

'I didn know about it till now. Besides, where's the evidence? In the meantime...' Malan opened his folder, took out an envelope and handed it to me. 'You on Restricted Duties, effective from today, and pending...'

I felt my mouth go dry. 'Pending?' I could barely hear my voice.

'Pending whatever going to happen. Is what the minister want and I couldn't make him change his mind. Dunno if you know, but Deacon Bello was his spiritual adviser – that's what them woman fuck with when they got rid of him. Digson, rumour makin ole maas out there and that don't feel good. Is my job to do something about it.'

I got up. I felt tired and hard-done-by, but not angry. 'A politician in post five years,' I said. 'Commissioner always there. What happm when Justice Minister get voted out of office? Who you going to turn to?'

'Easy, Digger; I'll keep the next one sweet.' Malan pushed out a hand. 'I obliged to ask you to hand over your piece.'

A feeling of breathlessness came over me. I unstrapped the Remington and gave it to him. I cleared my throat. 'Another thing, Malan, Miss Stanislaus got good reason to believe that Bello killed Nathan, not Simday.'

'Case close, Digger.'

'Not if we have reasonable grounds to believe otherwise.'

'Like I say, case close. We got the fella who done it.'

'Definitely not. Case just got shot down.' I pointed at the envelope. 'DNA lab report from Trinidad. It says zero percent chance the body we uncovered in Easterhall belong to Nathan. In other words we didn't find Nathan; we found somebody else.'

Malan swept the envelope from my desk, shook out the pages, shuffled through them. I watched his mouth go loose, his nostrils flare.

'Where it say that?'

'Work it out yourself.' I said. 'I gone.'

156

## 27

In the car, I tore open the envelope Malan handed me.

*Complainant:* DC Malan
*Allegation:* Breach of the Standards of Professional Behaviour, Regulation 5, Police (Conduct) Regulations 2009.
*Misdemeanours:*
• Insubordination – wilful flaunting of the orders of a superior in the course of duty.
• Breach of confidentiality – jeopardising the successful outcome of a criminal investigation by divulging information to parties not related to the department.

The letter ended with notification of a pending departmental inquiry, first Monday of the following month – at which the Minister of Justice would be present along with 'concerned parties'.

I was requested to sign the attached form, acknowledging receipt of the letter and to return it within three days.

I tossed it in my glove compartment.

Chilman called me several times. I refused to pick up, although my jitterbugging phone served only to heighten my anxiety.

Later in the evening, he left a voice message. *Digson, check the news.*

An hour later, another call came in. I let it go to voicemail.

*Digger, Pet here. Put on your radio for the nine o'clock news. And oh – Malan release Simday, the fella they say kill Nathan. Call me after.*

I knew Pet had a soft spot for me. In the office, she made me aware of it in quiet, secretive ways, but I pretended not to notice.

At nine I took my little radio, sat at my kitchen worktop and switched it on. Bello's death was the feature story:

> *The death had been reported of Bello Hunt, Deacon of the San Andrews Chapter of the Children of the Unicorn Spiritual Baptist church. Deacon Bello was a well-known Spiritual Baptist leader throughout Camaho. San Andrews CID has released a statement saying that yesterday, Sunday, two officers were called to the scene of a minor disturbance in Sadie Bay which resulted in the death of the Deacon. Minister of Justice, Peter Void, has expressed deep concern over the tragedy and promised a full and detailed investigation. In the meantime, the station has been informed that an officer, whose name was not divulged, has been placed on restricted duties, pending further investigation.*

I switched off the radio.

I saw what was laid out ahead of me as plainly as if Malan and the MJ had sat me down and told me to my face.

Malan had Chilman where he wanted him and I had no doubt that the Commissioner would step back and bide his time. They'd made Miss Stanislaus disappear because her involvement was too awkward to explain. That left me.

Pet phoned; 'You hear it?' Her voice was pitched higher than I'd ever heard it.

'Uh-huh.'

'What you going to do about it, Digger?'

'They didn't say my name,' I said.

'But is you they mean. Any ole jackass will know is you. All they have to do is find out which officer got restricted. And that not hard to do. Digger, why they blamin you?' Pet's voice had become plaintive.

'Because is easier, Pet. Because is not a criminal case any more; is politics.'

'What you going do about it, cuz, far as I see, is fire in their arse they want!'

I said nothing. I heard her breathing at the other end of the line, waiting for something better than my silence.

'You there?' I said after a while. I realised she'd rung off.

Lonnie called. She'd heard the news. 'Digger, you tie up in that?'

'They trying to tie me up in it.'

'Hold on,' she said. 'I coming right now.'

In the gathering dusk, I sat on my step watching Lonnie walk up my half-finished drive.

I felt again a fizzy mix of possessiveness and desire that I'd never before had for another woman. Lonnie lowered herself beside me.

I thought of the times she came to see me at the office when I was on night duty. Lonnie would stretch out on the aluminium beach chair she'd brought in and unfolded beside my desk. She would ask me to tell her about deciphering the language of the dead, to explain my trick of reading bones – which all sounded so much like obeah.

All this talk of death did something to her. At whatever hour in the morning we got home, she wanted sex. Maybe the talk confirmed for her that there was nothing quite like being alive, and the only way to be sure of it was to feel as intensely as our bodies allowed.

Whenever one of my cases broke, Lonnie came to my house, dropped her bag on the floor, rearranged my furniture and kitchen to suit herself and told me she was staying for a while, understanding, perhaps, that I too needed this – to lose myself in her.

Tonight, Lonnie looked distracted. She kept pulling at the hem of her dress, staring at her red strappy shoes.

'I going be alright, Lonnie.'

I wasn't sure she heard me.

I leaned forward and looked into her face. 'Something wrong?'

She'd rested her elbows on the top step, crossed her legs and pressed her back against it.

'Lonnie, what's going down with you right now?'

'Digger, I not awright. Right now I not.' She jerked at the hem

159

of her dress. 'I got to tidy up inside myself before… before…' She switched her eyes at me. 'Why you didn tell me about the bank girl.'

'Bank girl? Which bank girl? Oh – you mean Dessie?'

'That's her name? You didn tell me.'

'No, I didn't tell you. It cross my mind a coupla times, but you right, I didn't tell you. You want me tell you now? I'll tell you everything you want to know. What you want to know? *If* I know a 'bank girl' name, Dessie? Yes! *If* she is my woman? No! *If* I ever lay down anywhere with her? No! *If* I intend to do so? No – especially since I meet you. *When* last I speak to her? Certainly not since I start seeing you. Why? Because I didn't want to give you reason to ask the kinda question you asking now. *If* I intend to talk to her some time in the future? Definitely! Because I know her, and I like her, and something going on in Dessie life that she not talking to nobody about and it bothering me. Bottom-line, you got nothing to worry about.'

I felt breathless after that – breathless and confused.

She stood up quickly and smoothed her dress. 'I know what you going ask me next, Digger and I not going to answer you.'

'Where you get that ole talk from?'

She did not answer me.

The rain drove us inside.

'You hungry? I can cook something.'

She shook her head. 'I got a headache, I want to sleep.'

She went inside the bedroom. For a long time, I sat in the kitchen and listened to the water drumming on the roof.

Come daylight, the world outside was dripping. I steamed sweet potatoes, pum-pum yams and eddoes. I made a bowl of soused saltfish and two cups of hot cocoa. Like me, Lonnie preferred solid food on mornings.

While she picked at the food, I told her about the dead preacher, which she already knew about from the news; my restricted duties, and the trouble I saw ahead. I had two weeks to set things straight, by which time there was going to be a meeting of the men who ran my life at work to decide what to do with me.

'Why you, Digger?'

I shrugged, 'Is kinda complicated.'

She pushed aside her plate, began casting her eyes around the house. I'd been replacing the old board walls with concrete, following the basic design of a dream I carried in my head, of a small clean place full of light and air.

'Your salary, they still…'

'Uh-huh.'

'But they might…'

'It won't get that bad, leas'ways I don think so.' Suddenly I wasn't so sure.

'I have money,' she said.

'I don want your money.' The words left me more brusquely than I intended. I saw the recoil in her eyes. I reached out and placed my hand on hers. 'I don't mean it the way you take it. I upset, that's all. Money not going to be a problem.' I hoped I sounded more certain than I felt.

'Digger, I want a baby.'

I dropped my spoon. 'You…?'

'I want to have a child wiv, wiv you. You don't have to mind it, I…'

'Lonnie, hold on. How come we jump from talking about my trouble at work to making baby? Last night you wouldn't even lemme breathe near you.'

She wouldn't look at me. She was making agitated circles on the table with her fingers.

'Lonnie, what's the problem?'

'I just…' She wiped her eyes and looked away.

'It make more sense to hold on, not so?'

'No,' she said.

'Why not? I keep asking you what's behind all this.' I reached for her hand. Lonnie prised herself from me, rose to her feet and headed for the door.

I got to the main road in time to glimpse the flare of her brake lights as she took the bend and disappeared.

## 28

I retrieved the letter Malan had handed me, signed the attached receipt and slotted it into the supplied envelope. I would drop it off at the post office, then head for Lonnie's place in Marais. I needed to sit with her, find out what the trouble was and settle her mind. Things would work out because they had to. Malan's war was not against me.

Okay, the fella behaving vex-and-ignorant right now, but a man could unnerstan that. He wanted Chilman out of his Department and that made a lotta sense. The island needed my services. So the worse that could happen was a few marks on my record.

I-man would keep my head down, ride out the restricted duties, and chill out till tings cool-off-an-sekkle. Miss Stanislaus was Chilman's problem. Not mine. Definitely.

I felt better as I drove into the choke and heat of San Andrews. The woman at the post office took the envelope and stamped it. She raised her head as if to speak and something in her manner changed.

'What?' I said.

'What, *what*?' she threw back. Wary now. Sullen-faced. 'Tash,' she called, with a casual turning of the head. 'Bring the other stamp for me!'

I walked out of the post office and looked over my shoulder. There were two of them now, side by side, staring at me through the glass door.

I headed for the usual places where I bought my fruits and vegetables. I felt eyes on me; told myself it was just them wimmen in the post office playin the arse. Man just imagining all them bad-eye from people on the street.

But then there were the nudging elbows, the quick turn of

heads in my direction. At the entrance of the market, a man – short and rough as a dehydrated yam – placed himself in front of me and looked me in the face. I felt a tightening in my guts.

Miss Mark told me she didn't have the coconut oil she usually kept for me. I pointed at the bottle against the box on which she sat. That was for a macmere, she said. I looked about me: market women all gone silent, leaning against their stalls, arms making handles on their hips. Staring at me.

'Why y'all lookin at me like that,' I said.

The one with the dark-blue headwrap, dense as a boulder, in front of a giant cocoa-basket of yams and sweet potatoes answered.

'You de police fella that shoot de Reverend, not so? Her voice – resonant like a kata drum – turned heads in my direction.

'Where you get that from?' I said.

The woman pushed a hand behind her back, rummaged a while, then lifted a newspaper above her head.

'Is here! Right here.'

A full length snapshot of me leaning on my car with my phone against my ear.

**ISLAND VOICE EXCLUSIVE!**

*Uncovered: Suspended Officer, Michael Digson.*

The way the woman held the paper, I could not read the strapline.

'You want to lie an tell me is not you that murder the Reverend?' She'd raised her voice, in the manner of the preacher that she surely was.

In all my time of bantering and buying from these market women, I had no reason to interpret the meanings in the colours of their wraps and the way they'd tied them on their heads. Now I realised I was in the middle of a flock of outraged Sisters from various parts of the island.

'Is the seed of retribution you goin suck today. Amen.' I thought it was a curse – a Bible-driven condemnation – until I saw the man several heads in front of me.

I can spot a Watchman anywhere: something in his eyes and an aloofness that cannot be explained by the poor-arse job he did to make a living. I also knew him by the *fouet* he carried in his hand – a whip the exact length of his striking arm; thick as a thumb

163

with protrusions the size and shape of knuckles all along the length of it. A good Watchman understood the human body as well as any doctor; knew all the sites of disablement and pain. A blow – quick and secretive – to a bone, a nerve in the leg, or spine could maim for life. I watched him approach, the long body riding easily on the jostle of the crowd, being carried forward by it, his eyes everywhere but on me.

I shambled through the market crowd until my feet hit the pavement, then sprinted to my car.

Once out of San Andrews, I pulled into a cul-de-sac that overlooked the yacht marina in Canteen. I pressed my neck against the headrest and considered how just two days ago, I would have called for backup. Now I did not have that option.

So! Pet was right. The newspapers had no problems identifying and naming me. I thought of calling her to tell her she was right. I phoned Lonnie instead. She did not pick up. I called a second time, left a message, started my car and drove home.

I spent the day in a stupor, my thoughts swimming with the image of the Watchman in the market bearing down on me, the *fouet* like the rod of reckoning it was, in his right hand. The scene replayed in my mind unbidden.

This was Malan's punishment, not the MJ's. Chilman had given Restricted Duties a whole new meaning when he took over San Andrews CID. It was no longer a matter of leaving an officer desk-bound for a couple of weeks, or 'lending' him at short notice to a policing outpost in some remote part of the island. Restricted Duties became Chilman's version of purgatory.

An officer sent home was meant to be on call every second of his working hours. Calls rarely came, but if one did it was to demand rapid response to something trivial like coming to the office to locate a misplaced file or wash and polish the Governor General's car. The punishment was in the waiting.

I must have been sitting there for hours, because when I looked up, the light in the valley had thickened and the sounds were those of late evening.

I followed the rise of a chicken hawk on the wind above Mont Airy heights – its wings bright in the last of the evening sun.

…Fire in their arse…

Pet's words

Also my grandmother's. I was twelve when I last heard her say them.

A great war had started between certain Sisters of the congregation over a brown-skinned deacon from the north. Full of himself, and thundering words, he disputed my grandmother's position as a Prover.

The day he challenged her, she took down my grandfather's belt. It hung from a fat brass buckle on a nail above her bed-head – a heavy thing of leather slightly darker than the wood against which it rested. It was almost as thick as it was wide, apart from the tail of the strap where the leather flared out. The buckle was an odd thing – a metal that did not dull. Not smoothly curved at the top, it tapered into a pointed tip. My grandmother wore it every day for a month; rehung it on its nail the night after she drove out the Deacon with the curly hair.

I went into my bedroom, took down the strap, returned to my seat and laid it across my lap.

I called Pet.

'What's happenin, Digger?'

'I managing. Sorry about the late call, Pet. You could do me a favour?'

'Uh-huh?'

'Tomorrow, you think you could get to the office before everybody else?'

'Uh-huh.'

'Tell Malan I phone in sick, and I sound really sick. When you find the time, go to Doctor Garth on Market Hill. His surgery opens till seven in the evening. Ask him to write out a sick note for me, Michael Digson. It got to be for two weeks, minimum. No less than that, y'unnerstan? I want you to give it to Malan day after tomorrow – that's Wednesday. You got all that?'

'Uh-huh.'

'Pet, in a coupla days, I'll text you a number. Keep it in your head. Don't give it to Lisa.'

'Yeh,' she said, her voice alert now. 'What you plan to do?'

'I working on it right now,' I said, tossing the rest of my drink over the wall of the veranda.

## 29

The passenger ferry I'd taken – Fish Eagle – approached Kara Isle under a doomsday sky that turned the rough waters of the harbour copper. Shaped like a prancing dog with oversized ears, Chilman's and Miss Stanislaus's birthplace sat north of Camaho.

These were the people at the root of my troubles. For all her directness, Miss Stanislaus felt as elusive as smoke. She was all flesh and warmth with me, but ill-tempered steel with Malan, and I could not help noticing her resentment towards her father. I wanted to understand why, during all the time I knew him, Chilman had never talked about his place of birth and this woman who he'd confessed, only under pressure, was his daughter.

I gave myself twelve hours to find out.

Crosscurrents threw up waves as high as hills at the north-western approach, but it was the only way to get to the harbour. Past the boiling waters, the sea opened up to a curving necklace of islets, coves, hidden beaches and sheltering mangroves that allowed a vessel to travel undetected all the way to the Florida Everglades. In The Force, we knew it as a trafficking backdoor and a getaway gateway for inter-island rum-runners. Chilman had shown no interest in them until the necktie killing.

Like he told us, 'Them pirates was heroes in Francis Drake and Captain Morgan time. But now them Youropeans not profiting from the proceeds, they call it trafficking. They done suck we dry and abandon we arse to fight up on we own, so how them expect West-Indies-man to survive?'

I walked to the guest house named Guest House, situated at a junction called Cross Roads. Eyes in the doorways of tiny fried-fish bars and eateries followed my progress up the curving street.

One of the bars was called The Matchbox and it struck me that folks on Kara Isle named things for what they were. No wonder Miss Stanislaus didn't know how to lie.

When night fell I stepped out of the guest house into a seawind that was clearing the streets of everything that could be shifted or lifted.

I headed for a drinking hole that faced the wooden jetty. I expected it to be named Drinking Hole, but somebody had called it Delna's. I walked into a storm of crashing dominoes and chesty guffaws. A drunken argument between four men was raging at a table near the entrance. I raised my voice, ordered fried fish and breadfruit chips, sat a couple of paces behind them and kept my eyes on my food.

No other place I knew made me more aware of the ocean than Kara Isle – its thundering, blustering vastness – and my insignificance in a world where water ruled.

From somewhere out there, a voice, raised above the wind, jerked me out of my thoughts. The drunks had taken what remained of their argument outside. It was now an incoherent rumble.

I left the half-finished food and stepped outside. The street was empty. The fluorescent spill from food stalls and shop fronts barely gave shape to things. The beach was a dim white curve directly ahead of me.

A weak quarter-moon hung over the heaving water. I narrowed my eyes at the dark outline of boats on the foreshore. I strolled towards the jetty. The catamaran I had taken from San Andrews was rocking ponderously against it. The wooden pier shuddered with the suck and surge of the tide.

I walked out on the jetty towards a wall of sound and spray, with the wind pummelling my face. About two thirds of the way out, I turned around to scan the beach. Stood there until my eyes adjusted to the dark. Then I began to walk back.

I smelt the presence before I saw the man – a mixture of engine oil and rancid fish. He was directly in my path, backlit by the lights from Delna's cafe.

'You lookin fuh someting?' The voice seemed to trundle out of a tunnel.

I felt my nostrils flare, aware now of the size of the man ahead of me. My armpit itched where I would have worn my special issue, and I felt a heavy thump of regret for giving it up so easily to Malan.

I pulled up myself full height and deepened my voice. 'What make you think I want something?'

Still I was no match for him. I could have identified myself as a policeman, but in my shorts, a pair of rubber slippers and an old t-shirt I could barely convince myself that I was an officer.

'You find I look like if I jokin?' He took a couple of steps toward me. It was then that I saw the outline of the gaff against his leg – the dull wink of the big steel hook.

I filled my lungs and raised my voice. 'I dunno what you want from me, fella. I want to know why you standing in my way and threatening me!'

I heard the tumble and shift of bodies on the boat, then a voice from the deck. 'What happenin deh?'

A round head dimly silhouetted against the sky popped over the edge of the jetty.

'Juba? Is you? That's you, Juba?'

A brief silence, followed by the deeper irritated tones of another man. He'd pushed most of his upper body over the railing of the boat. 'Juba, why you don't leave de fella alone. You not tired giving people grief!'

Juba didn't move.

I heard the men consulting. 'That not the fella who come up with us this evening?'

A couple more men leaned over. The same voice, stronger now, more indignant. 'Juba, I goin call de captain – Captain!'

Juba stepped aside. I took my time walking past him, or tried to; felt the brush of something hard and cold against my thigh.

'I watchin you,' he rumbled.

'I watching you watch me,' I threw back – and lengthened my stride.

I hurried back to the guest house, irritable and jumpy. I showered and stretched out on the bed. The scent of the man still clung to my nostrils and I was tempted to shower again. For the first time in my job, I'd been truly spooked by another person. I resented it. I resented Chilman and Miss Stanislaus for dragging me into this shit; for exposing me to enemies who did not know I existed until some Fire Baptist women killed the preacherman who'd made a harem of his church. And I felt betrayed by Malan.

I berated myself for not walking with my belt, which I'd only used once against another person.

That belt! For years I wanted to know what my grandmother did with it to chase away the Deacon who had threatened to remove her from the church. She always sidestepped the question or ignored me, until one day she ordered me to get out of her frikkin face and never ask about no blaasted belt again.

I gave up.

My last year at primary school, I returned home one Friday with a busted lip. She wanted to know what happened. I refused to tell her. The Wednesday of the following week I came back with a limp.

She saw to my injuries, said nothing; went inside the house and brought out a large enamel bowl of soapy water. She unrolled her red headscarf and dropped it in.

After a while, she lifted the cloth and began to wring the water from it. She beckoned me with a finger. I was a couple of feet from her when something struck me so hard in the chest I fell backward. I scrambled to my feet. Another flash of red and I doubled over gasping.

'Get up!' she ordered. She flicked the dripping coil of cloth at me again. It unfolded from her hand in a heavy writhing curve, struck me on the ear and threw me over.

She left me there sobbing, went inside, returned with the belt and dropped it at my feet.

'Leave his face alone,' she said.

After that, Dalo never laid his hands on me again. Eight years later, I saw him in the market square – a sack of charcoal on his shoulder. He was still walking with a limp. From then I wore that belt – double-looped around my waist – whenever my grandmother let me, and the more I used it, the more its nature changed in my hand, until it became like a living thing.

My mind returned to the big man on the jetty and the voice I'd heard that brought me out of Delna's eatery. It was Lazar

Wilkinson's – the young man I'd met in Beau Sejour on my way to Chilman's place.

In different circumstances I would have called Malan and have him come here before daybreak with a unit from Special Forces. I had no doubt that a go-fast boat with twin engines was among the twenty footers out there in the shallows, laden with Vincen Island ganja, or something which, based on Juba's reaction to my presence on the jetty, was worth killing an intruder for.

## 30

The next morning I strolled inland in my shorts, a pair of sandals and a Boston Celtics T-shirt. No need pretending to be native, Kara-islanders knew the names and faces of their own – all six thousand of them.

People ambled past, each giving me a quick once-over without breaking stride, even the children. I smiled at a boy dangling a string of red snappers in his hand. 'Nice catch. You selling?'

He shook his head.

'I'm just passing through. Looking for family. Been away a long time.'

That halted him. 'Who you lookin for?'

'Chilman – they my people.'

The boy cocked his head, accessing no doubt his very own built-in database of family names, their history and connections to each other. I'd never met a person from Kara Isle who could not do that.

'We don't have no more Chilman here. The rest of dem gone 'way. Same like you.' I thought I saw something like reproach in his eyes.

'Thanks, what's your name?'

He shrugged and walked on.

I climbed the only hill on the island they called Top Hill, crowned by a huddle of limestone rocks that overlooked the harbour and the ocean – now so bright in the morning light it hurt the eye to look directly at the water.

My phone buzzed. From Pet: *Done*. I sent her a smiley face.

When I was at the crest of Top Hill, I realised what brought me there. It was a memory of the time I saw Malan shoot a man.

It happened after a hold-up. Bank robbery was a new import from Vincen Island. It started when big business moved from the capital, San Andrews, to the Flatlands in the south.

With a big white beach to die for, a cluster of plush hotels beside it and enough space to put up cinemas and malls, the banks moved most of their business there.

The first time Vincen Island men walked into one of the foreign banks in broad daylight, pointed submachine guns in the faces of cashiers, grabbed the money and left in go-fast boats, drinking men in the rumshops talked about the robbery as if it were a promotion for the island. Camahoans were now worthy of the kind of heist they heard about on American TV or saw in the cinema. But when they raided the local credit union, it felt as if a first cousin had turned around and spat in our faces. It left Malan making finger circles on his desk for days.

We were having lunch in the office when a call came in. Pet picked up, said hello a few times. Frowning, she made a quick scrawl on the pad in front of her, then passed the handset to me, a finger on her lips. I put the receiver to my ear: very little background noise, just the occasional scuffle and a quick exchange of muffled words from a couple of male voices.

I pressed the secrecy button, lifted a finger at Malan. He hurried over. 'You picked up the number, Pet?' I said.

Pet raised the notepad and turned it towards me.

'422 is area prefix for the Flatlands,' I told them. I passed back the phone to Pet who kept it against her ear.

I told them what I thought. 'Some clever person phone us but they can't talk. They hoping we could figure this out from what we overhear. Hardly any background noise. No traffic, no wind… that mean is likely that the place closed-up: air conditioning, yunno. People in there, though; I hear a coupla coughs and a lil bit of shifting round. Three male voices.'

'Digger, stop flyin and land!' Malan said.

'I believe is a hold up. Could be a supermarket. I don think so though – not enough going on. Is most likely one of the banks down there in the Flatlands. The fellas I hear talking got Vincen Island accents.'

Lisa was already reaching for the phone. Malan lunged and

grabbed her hand. 'Nuh,' he said. 'Gemme the Coast Guard. Tell them I want one ov them sprint-boat they seize from dem Guyanese drugs-fellas coupla months ago. Fastest they got. I want Spiderface at the wheel. Tell Spiderface we going to Kara Isle.'

Malan rushed into the back room of his office and returned with a long canvas bag.

'What about the bank?' I said.

'I don't want the bank; is them Vincen Island man I want.'

In less than fifteen minutes, the wind was pushing into our faces and the go-fast boat with Spiderface at the wheel was leaving a trench of boiling spume behind it. Chilman had recruited Spiderface after we caught him with a bundle of ganja in his hold. He was in an underpowered tub of a boat and yet we only caught him when he ran out of fuel.

'The boy got talent,' Chilman said. 'To waste that in jail is criminal.'

Vincen Island was directly north of Kara Isle. Once the men left the bank, they would take to the sea. The rough waters of Kick em Jenny on the south-western side of Kara Isle was the fastest way back to Vincen Island.

We were on Kara Isle in forty-five minutes. Malan and I hit the jetty running while Spiderface sat in the boat with the engines turning over. We sprinted through the little town and up the chalky slope of Top Hill.

With a full view of the south-western approach in front of us, Malan withdrew his Sig Sauer, laid it at his feet and began to unpack the bag he'd brought with him.

'We twenty five minutes ahead,' he said. 'Give or take five.' He looked at me. 'I work it out, Digson. I work it out to the last 't'. Let them fuckers come.'

I could not help admiring Malan's thinking.

The gun was an M24-SWS. I'd only seen this model in the trade magazines that landed on my desk every couple of months. I did not know the Department owned one.

'Where that come from?' I asked

'I had it ordered.'

'Since when?'

'Since I decide we need it.' Malan laid the bag at his feet and, without taking his eyes off me, began reeling off the specs while packing the magazine with shells.

'SWS, that mean Sniper Weapon System, Digson. Bolt action. Five rounds. Twenty rounds per minute. A coupla inches under four foot long. This girl weigh sixteen pounds when you dress 'er up with optical sight, bi-pod and magazine on full load.

'338 Lapua Magnum bullets is what I feedin she today. Effective firing range just under a mile – that's what the instruction book say. Instruction book lie. With this,' he nudged the telescopic sight. 'I could make it reach a mile. Just watch.'

He settled himself on his stomach the stock of the rifle pressed into his shoulders, the muzzle steadied on the splayed bi-pods.

I spotted a grey dot emerging from around the cluster of little islands we called The Cousins.

'They coming,' I said.

'Digger, shut your mouth.'

The boat grew quickly. By the time I had a full frontal view, it was about three-quarters of a mile away and coming fast.

Malan raised his head just once, threw me a backward glance. Then he slipped a finger through the trigger guard.

The rifle spat once – a harsh metallic bark, convulsing Malan's shoulder. Malan came to his feet and stood with his hands on his hips. The boat came on, a widening scarf of water trailing behind it. I thought he'd changed his mind or missed. Malan was brushing his hands and attending to his clothes when the boat swung left in a tight half-circle and struck a swell full on. The waters folded over it.

Malan threw a quick dark glance across the water. 'Good driver,' he said. 'I give im that.' He lifted his chin at the town below. 'They have nice fry-fish down there, Digger. Ever try Kara Isle fry-fish?'

I remember watching him eat, fingers picking clean the bony fish. He caught me staring at his hands.

'Digson, what wrong?'

'I thinking about the report I have to write.'

'Easy, man!' Malan licked his fingers and grinned at me. 'Felons caught sight of us on the hill; they start firing. Me – in my capacity as Chief Officer and upholder of the peace, and in the interest of

174

public safety – I return fire. Besides, where you think they goin find dem in that shark-water there!' Malan raised a brow at me, 'Or mebbe you worryin where all dat money gone? Well, fella, money's ink-and-paper. They could always print more.'

I pushed the incident from my thoughts and descended Top Hill under a blistering sun.

I turned into the guest house, wondering where to start my inquiries on this little island of tight-lipped people who had no time for strangers.

Wilting bougainvillea – a fine coating of sand on their papery petals – lined the dusty driveway. Two arthritic sea-island cotton trees supported themselves against one wall of the building.

The elderly woman who owned the place looked as if she were made for the conditions here: dry-skinned and locked-in, scant words, prickly as a cactus. When she checked me in the day before, she barely looked at me.

She was in the kitchen when I walked in.

'You didn find them, not so?' The smile on her face threw me completely.

'Them?' I queried.

'Cuffy say you been lookin for your family?'

She smiled at my confusion. 'Cuffy the lil boy who bring me fish most mornings. His father got a boat. They my family. He say them Chilman is your people and you been askin about them?'

'Yes, Miss… erm.'

'Bucky. Bucky is my name. Is hundreds-a-years the Bucky famly been here. We blood not mix up and confuse like Camaho people. We blood pure.' She pulled open the fridge door, reached in, straightened up and put a Guinness in my hand. She nodded at a chair. 'Nice lookin boy you is. We Kara Isle people make pretty children. So, you say you'z a Chilman?'

'We connected,' I said.

Miss Bucky frowned. 'Well I happm to know that all them Chilman migrate. Long time. De easiest one to find is Chilly because he livin on Camaho, an he's a big-time policeman.'

She looked at me and smiled. 'Me an Chilman went same school. H'was one class ahead ov me. Long time before you born, yunno… long, long time. When I see him leave, I was upset.'

I watched her face soften, grow wistful. 'I was nineteen at the time when he start throwin pretty words at me. I give him a hard time. One time I upset him so bad, I make him cry.' She chuckled – a young girl's chuckle.

'But is only a fool who didn know Chilly had to go. Every time he look across at Frigate Islan, I could just imagine what went on in his mind. Rememberin, yunno?'

Miss Bucky was the kind who didn't require prompting once she got going. I sipped the Guinness and let her talk. No sign of an ole-fella around the place; no pictures on the wall of off-spring either. Earlier on, I noticed that the back of the guest house was a jumble of discarded wood and broken breeze-blocks. Cracked tiles ran the length of the balcony floor. The bathroom tap needed fixing. She'd been balancing two rice biscuits in a saucer when I came in, along with a cup of plain hot water. Lonely, and diabetic.

I realised that Miss Bucky preferred the past; if she could return to it she would. Not only had she left her youth there, but all the things she should have done and did not have the courage to do, like following Chilman to Camaho.

'Miss Bucky, you been saying Chilman left Kara Isle because…?'

She shook her head. 'Most people ferget now. Mebbe even Chilly ferget.'

I smiled at her, 'And you remember?'

'Uh-huh,' she said. 'Is the best ting I got – my memory. I remember like yestiday.'

Miss Bucky told me about a Friday afternoon when six boys left Kara Isle in their skiff to tend their goats on Frigate Island just offshore. There was talk of a minister of government throwing a curry-goat party for visitors from Chile. Problem was the minister had no goats. He dispatched the Coast Guard to Frigate Island. The police took the goats; the boys put up a fight. Their bodies were never found.

Miss Bucky went to the fridge and took out another bottle. Her back was turned to me when she spoke. 'Three of them boys was Chilman brothers. De other three was cousins. Chilman didn go with them that time because h'was sick with fever.'

Miss Bucky returned and placed the Guinness in front of me. I got lost for a while watching the sweat beads travel down the glass.

'Y'awright?' she said.

'I awright.' There was a small pulse in my forehead and despite the drink, I felt dehydrated. 'He had a daughter born here, not so?'

I thought I saw a new alertness in the woman's eyes.

'What you know bout de, erm, de daughter?' she said.

I shrugged. 'Not much. She's blood, so I ask. Word reach me that she kinda smart and erm…' I was about to add 'beautiful' but checked myself. 'She got a child, I believe.'

The grey eyelashes fluttered and when Miss Bucky spoke it was as if she were addressing something in the air. 'Yes, the lil girl is my granchile.'

I was bringing the bottle to my mouth. I rested it back on the table and cleared my throat. 'Grandchild?'

The woman worked her mouth into a tight twist. 'She never let me see de baby. I don't blame her. She didn ask for it, an Juba didn have no right to force heself on Chilly lil girlchile.' She dropped her voice – low and plaintive. 'After all this time people still saying he spoil her. But as far as I see, she not dead and she awright. De woman wouldn lemme see my own granchile. And is not as if…' – she raised aggrieved eyes at me – 'Juba didn pay for it. He spend nuff time in jail and he come out and he not causin no more trouble. And yunno, soonz he come outta jail, the woman tek up my one granchile and run off to Camaho!'

I glanced at my watch, stood up, steadied myself then dipped into my pocket. My stomach felt as if a stone had settled in it.

I took some notes from my wallet and placed them on the table. 'That cover yesterday and today, including tonight, Miss Bucky. I jus got time to catch the afternoon boat.'

'Everybody blamin me,' she muttered.

I dropped a hand on hers. 'My Granny used to say, you make your children; you don't make their mind. Thanks for the ole talk, Miss Bucky. I gone.'

As soon as I landed on the Carenage in San Andrews, my cell phone dinged.

*Dregs lukin 4 you. Call me l8r.*

It crossed my mind that I should buy a present for Pet.

My bank was a fifteen minute walk from where I landed. I asked for Mrs Dessima Caine.

Dessie came out, swaying like a Royal palm.

When I sat with her she discarded the smile, lowered her voice and leaned forward. 'What's happening out there?' She gestured at the frosted glass wall of the building.

'That's partly why I here, Dessie. I want to borrow money.'

All business now, she leaned back on her chair.

I told her the amount I wanted, what I wanted it for and why.

'It's a lot of money. Your job not supposed to pay for that?'

'They wouldn't,' I said. 'It's not in their interest.'

Dessie looked at me for a long time. 'Digger, this don't make good business sense. From what you told me, you might not have a job soon.'

'Add it to the mortgage on the house. Repossess me if I don't pay back. What's happening with you?'

'Don't look at me like that.' She fluttered a hand at me. 'I'm on the job.'

'I serious. Anything I could do, Dessie – as an officer or as a friend?'

'Digger!' she hissed; she looked distressed.

'Sorry,' I said and sat back.

Half an hour later, Dessie was seeing me to the door.

I made a quick trip to the pharmacy and hurried out of town.

*Digger, Malan here. What happen to your phone? We have to talk.*

The paper sat on a brown envelope on the top tread of my steps, anchored there by a stone. I unfolded the note. The other side was a typewritten letter from Malan.

A letter in the brown envelope confirmed the date of my 'hearing' at the offices of the Minister of Justice, at which the MJ, Commissioner Joseph Lohar, Chief Officer Malan Greaves and two 'concerned parties' would be present. I wondered who the 'concerned parties' were. That didn't matter as much as what the Minister of Justice would want them there for – no doubt to rubber-stamp whatever he had in store for me.

He'd given me fourteen days notice, effective from the date of this first letter. I had already lost two days in Kara Isle which meant I had twelve days to prepare.

I called Miss Stanislaus. 'You still in the bush down there?'

'G'day, Missa Digger. How are yuh?' Her greeting was measured, reminding me of my manners.

'I'm fine thank you, Miss Stanislaus. Are you, perchance, still residing in The Children of the Unicorn Spiritual Baptist Church on the banks of the Kalivini swamp?'

A string of chuckles filled my ear. 'Eh-heh, I still here. Missa Digger, when you comin?'

'Lil later,' I said

'For true?' She sounded delighted.

A couple of hours later, I was with her in a corner of the yard in the middle of which two glowing coalpots spat fire at the dusk. I smelled roasted sweet potatoes and Jonny-bakes. The children were animated shapes at the edges of the space, in a noisy tug of war with Watchman Pike. Pike's trick was to make them laugh so much at his antics they forgot to co-ordinate their efforts against him. In the end he let them win.

The Mother sat on a stool, an ebony Buddha whose tree-trunk arms were moving over a small mountain of flour in a big enamel basin.

A woman dribbled water from a big tin cup into the basin. I'd noticed her before – tall, high cheekbones, lean-muscled like an athlete – all pride and presence. This one, unlike the others, did nothing to conceal her awareness of my presence.

'Missa Digger…' Miss Stanislaus pinched my elbow. 'You got someting 'gainst de Modder?'

'What's the name of the woman pouring the water?'

'That's Adora,' Miss Stanislaus said, but not before I caught the slightest spasm of hesitation in her voice. 'Missa Digger, I been wonderin where you was.'

'Miss Stanislaus, we have to talk.'

First, I told her about the findings of the lab. 'Miss Iona was right; it wasn't Nathan we found in Easterhall.'

I saw myself again standing over a table of bones, Miss Iona beside me. 'Dat didn't come outta me,' she said, before hurrying out of the mortuary.

'I want to know, Miss Stanislaus, how a mother could glance at a pattern of bones and know is not her child's.'

'Mebbe is the way all that furrin-sick learnin make you see tings, Missa Digger. S'far as I know, a yooman been is more than bone. A pusson can't break down life to only that. Sometimes a pusson know tings, an they dunno how they know them tings. They just know. An it don't take no hifalutin learnin to unnerstan dat.

'Anyway, what make dat Trini place so sure is not Nathan? Trini people always get on like them know everyting. How come a likkle bit ov bone make them know so much?' Miss Stanislaus sounded fretful.

'You carry the people that come before you inside yourself. They there in the skin you scrub off when you bathe, in your spit; they even in your tears. Coupla thousand years from now, a pusson could find the part of yourself you pass on to all the children in your bloodline.'

I winked at her. 'So you see, Miss Lady, we like snail. We leave a trail behind until the end of time.'

Smooth brown fingers rested on my arm. I caught a whiff of nutmeg and lavender. 'Missa Digger, come siddown. I sure you not here to talk 'bout snail.'

I filled her in on my restricted duties, the pending inquiry, the worry I detected in her father and finally the news release.

'As far as they concern, Miss Stanislaus, you were never on that beach. That save Malan having to explain why a woman who not an officer could put a bullet in a preacher with a police gun. That's the good part; the bad part is…'

'Dey putting it on you.' She stood up, her bag clutched to her chest. 'Missa Digger, I have to…'

'Do nothing. Else you make matters worse.'

'But is de truth, Missa Digger. Is…'

'Miss Stanislaus.'

'You wasn even dere…'

'Miss Stanislaus!'

I laid an arm across her shoulder. 'Miss Stanislaus, I want you to hear what I have to say right now. Is important. In law, truth is what the facts support. Truth is evidence, y'unnerstand? In politics, truth is whatever people like the MJ decide to make others believe, and sometimes to make that happen, they got to lie. They got to hide the facts. Right now is politics we dealing with.'

'What Malan got against you?'

'I just the ball that Malan use to bowl his bouncer at your father. You should know by now how Malan stay.'

'That's de problem, Missa Digger. I dunno how he stay. I still workin him out. Missa Malan is like dat swamp-water across dere.' She pointed past the mangroves. 'Hard to see the bottom, and the more you stir, the more duttiness you bring up.'

An abrupt backward tilt of her head reminded me of that first time she confronted Malan in the office. The same slightly puckered lips, and unblinking eyes – now beautiful and disquieting with the reflected flames of the coal-pot licking at her irises.

'S'far as I kin see is trouble dem askin for, Missa Digger. Dem askin fuh people to put some, uhm, how y'all say it again?'

'Fire in their arse.' I smiled.

181

'Uh-huh,' she sniffed. 'A lil bit of that. Or mebbe a lot.'

'By my calculations, I don't have long to try to save my arse. And even then...' I decided not to say more – to tell Miss Stanislaus that it was a gamble. That I had to make myself believe she was not wrong about Miss Alice, Nathan and the children she thought belonged to Bello.

'Missa Digger, you say you got restrict from work?'

'Restricted duties, yes.'

'From what time to what time?'

'Nine to five – technically.'

'So after five you kin do as you please, not so?'

'Well, yeh...'

'So you not restrict at all. When we start – tomorrow?'

'Nuh, we start right now.'

I dipped into the cloth bag I'd brought with me and pulled out the swab kit I'd prepared at home: a dozen little plastic canisters, a packet of cotton buds, a handful of small self-sealing sachets and a permanent marker I'd bought in San Andrews.

I made my voice more breath than sound. 'Tomorrow, soon as you get the chance, I want you to take some swabs from the lil ones you say belong to Bello. Find a way to do it without too much fuss. Maybe you ask The Mother to help out?'

I slipped a cotton bud in my mouth, ran it along my inner cheek, placed it in the canister, closed it, then sealed it in the sachet. 'Like that,' I said. 'A different one for each child. Keep them separate. Is important. If you not sure, throw it away and start again.'

I looked into her eyes. 'You could be holding my future in your hands, mebbe yours too. You got all that?'

Miss Stanislaus nodded.

'Tomorrow, when I come back, I want to talk to all of them about Nathan and Alice.

I lifted my head at the women. They had doused the coal-pots and lit a bigger fire. A cast-iron pot, large enough to feed a village squatted on three hefty stones in the middle of the yard. Young children had made hammocks of their squatting mother's laps. Bello had left his mark on every one of them; the whip-strokes that ran the length of Miss Stanislaus's arms and legs were trivial in comparison,

I knew them all, not by name, but as part of the clay from which I too had been broken. From the moment my feet supported me, I'd grasped the hem of my grandmother's dress and followed her drumming feet in those beautiful and terrible dances of fire and release in Old Hope Spiritual Baptist Church.

I angled my head at the woman Miss Stanislaus called Adora, took in the steady, watchful eyes, the raised chin. I pulled away my gaze, found my eyes colliding with the steady stare of Mother Bello. I smiled at her.

Deacon Bello's wife did not return my smile. Instead, the woman lifted a hand and curled her fingers in our direction. Miss Stanislaus excused herself, walked over to the big woman who placed her lips against Miss Stanislaus's ear.

She was fanning herself when she returned. 'Missa Digger, I sorry to say The Modder ask for you to leave.'

I straightened up, dusted my clothes. A first-quarter moon had broken the hills, stippling the mangroves silver. I started walking to my car.

I heard my name and looked back.

Hers was a dainty walk down the path towards me.

'Missa Digger,' Miss Stanislaus said, peering at my face. 'Somefing botherin you?'

'Miss Stanislaus, Bello dead; why all them wimmen still so jumpy? What keeping them from leaving this church and going off somewhere else?'

'You not a woman, Missa Digger; these tings take time. Besides you not askin de right question.'

'What's the right question?'

'Where else they goin to go? You fergettin what some-a-dem lef behind?'

'Adora,' I said. 'Where she fit into all of this?'

'Why you ask that question, Missa Digger?'

'Because she not like the others.'

Miss Stanislaus was silent for a long while. I almost did not hear her when she spoke.

'Adora is the one who kill Bello.'

'Makes sense,' I said.

'Why?' Miss Stanislaus said.

Adora had moved to the far end of the yard, arms folded, face shadowed by her headwrap, her neck and shoulders sculpted by the firelight. A young girl leaned against her, hair pulled up in rough tufts and tied at the ends with bits of cord. Their aspects were identical. Faces closed against the world.

'Adora not the kind to take no shit from nobody. Not for long. And seeing that she got a girlchile…' I left the sentence hanging. 'What I want to know is why she don't move on.'

'Mebbe she tired moving on,' Miss Stanislaus said.

'Miss Stanislaus, you ready to tell me how it happen?'

Miss Stanislaus said Adora killed Bello for her daughter who'd run off with friends. The day before they left for Sadie Bay, the child had gone missing. Adora thought the girl had left the church, travelled back north to her great grandmother's place. Her daughter had done that before. When Adora went to get her, she wasn't there. The woman returned on the Sunday morning with no result, by which time the congregation had left the church for the Sadie Bay baptism. Adora met them on the beach. She asked Bello where her daughter was. Bello told her that she offended him. Adora insisted and he struck her. She hit him back. He knocked her to the ground and she stayed on the ground with a few of the Sisters tending to her. It was then that Bello turned on Miss Stanislaus, accusing her of trying to destroy his church.

'When Bello start draggin me to the water, Adora break loose and throw sheself on him. Dunno where she got the strength. Dunno where she got de stone to knock im down with. She hit im an he never get up.'

'Then you shot him to take the blame; I already work out that part.'

'Nuh, I didn shoot Bello to take no blame; I shoot im to make sure.'

'Don't tell nobody else that, Miss Stanislaus. S'matter of fact, I didn't hear you say it.'

## 33

I don't know how Miss Stanislaus managed it, but she got the samples from the children the same night I gave her the swab kit. She called the next morning, said she was at her place; did I want to collect them tings?

She was waiting at the side of the road when I got there, the cloth bag in her hand. I opened the passenger door to let her in.

'Missa Digger, you wearin new perfume?'

'Fellas don't wear perfume, Miss Stanislaus. Fellas wear cologne. Is cologne I wearing.'

She held out the bag.

'I want you to post them for me,' I said. 'How many you done?'

'Eight.'

I passed over the sample I'd taken from Bello, already wrapped and labelled. 'This is from Bello. I been keeping it in my fridge. I asking you to go to San Andrews later and post them special delivery to a fella named Ramlogan, Chief Lab Tech in Trinidad.'

I gave her the paper on which I'd written the address of the Forensic Science Centre. She dropped it in her purse.

'It should be in their hands late afternoon today or first thing in the morning. I'll call this evening and tell him to expect it. He'll let me know as soon as they receive it. Then you'll wire the fee to them.'

I passed her the paper bag of notes. It was all the money I'd saved, plus the four thousand dollars I borrowed from the bank.

Miss Stanislaus hefted the bag, dipped in a hand and fingered its contents. 'Is a lot ov money,' she said.

'My life worth more than that.' I told her about the Watchman in the market square the last time I was there. 'So you see, Miss

Stanislaus, even if they only fire me in the end – I still got a problem.'

'Is not right,' she said.

I touched her shoulder. 'I easy with that, y'unnerstan? Right now, everything make sense. I realise it wasn't Bello you was seeing when you shoot him; was some stinkin' fella name, Juba.'

She went still; her head dropped forward as if I'd struck her.

'You got no right,' she mumbled.

'You and Chilman drag me into something I didn't have no control of. Now I know what's behind all this, I feel better.'

'You still got no right.' Miss Stanislaus swung open the car door and got out. I sat there a while listening to her rapid footsteps up the path to her house.

'You forget to take the samples,' I shouted after her. I was answered by the heavy bang of her door.

The morning sun had just tipped over the Mon Tout Hills, I pulled out my phone, narrowed my eyes against the glare and dialled her number. It rang until voice messaging kicked in.

'I sorry, I upset you,' I said. 'But like I say, I had to unnerstan what I dealing with. I'll be at the church this evening. I need to ask the women some questions. If you not there, I'll assume you no longer with me on this.'

I took the bag of samples, and the money she'd left behind, secured them in the glove compartment and headed for the post office in San Andrews.

## 34

On my way up the West Coast Road, I thought of the places that Deacon Bello might have hidden Miss Alice and Nathan – that was, of course, if there was truth in what Miss Stanislaus said.

I ruled out Bello's own churchyard and the mangrove forest behind it. There was also the swamp, but he would have been observed by someone.

Beyond the circle of hills that hid The Children of the Unicorn Spiritual Baptist Church were the lagoons of Fort Jeudy, overlooked by the holiday homes of foreigners. They were tended by a small army of local gardeners. I doubted that Bello would take the chance to discard the bodies there.

In that state of mind, I saw the island differently – the potential of this buckled landscape for secrecy and hiding: the high mountain ridge that formed its spine; its gullies and ravines and rivers; its long leaf-tunnels created by the tight embrace of trees and ferns and vines.

It took me an hour to get to Lonnie's place. A wide sand road bordering the bay led me past wooden houses with their doors open to the ocean. Marais was like another country: closed-in, self-sufficient, its people as unpredictable as the sea on which they made their living.

Four red steps led up to a veranda on whose walls were potted spider-plants. I nodded at the woman sitting on the high step of the house next door, an aluminium basin of parrot fish between her feet.

I climbed the steps and tapped the door. Through the slatted blinds I could see the cushioned chairs, and just beyond, the kitchen. A plate lay covered on the table, a kitchen towel and a spoon beside it. Four chairs around the table. The woman on the step didn't appear to be watching me, but her hands were poised over the fish she'd been de-scaling.

I tapped the door with my keys and called, sat on the wall of the veranda and stared at the handle of the door. I would have gone in had the neighbour not now been observing me.

'Lonnie,' I said, 'if you in there, come out and talk to me. If I done you something, I sorry.'

No answer. Just the hum of the coconut tree above the house, the slap and sigh of the sea on the beach behind me.

I stood on the steps a while, staring at the neighbour – all muscles and tendons and tufts of uncombed hair.

'G'd afternoon,' I said. 'I lookin for Miss Lonnie. You could tell me if she around?'

The woman dropped the fish in the basin and made a quick backward jerk with her head, in the direction of the houses further back.

I stepped onto the path that would take me there, but she shook her head – a vigorous negation. I turned back.

'Tell 'er Digger, her erm boyfriend, came to see her.'

A chuckle left the woman's throat. My limbs went heavy and suddenly my mouth felt dry.

'Tell her that Michael Digson passed. Thanks.'

She turned down her head to her basin.

I reversed to the road. Sat in my car at the junction for some time, then made a three-point turn for home.

I was passing through Kanvi Town when my phone buzzed. The number was withheld. All I could hear was low and measured breathing.

I asked who it was and when no answer came, I said, 'You left your back door open when you rush out of your house to hide from me. Sorry to make you leave your food, Lonnie. I won't bother you again.'

I tossed the phone on the dashboard.

As I was entering San Andrews, the phone buzzed again. Number withheld.

I ignored it.

I was surprised to see Pet sitting on my step, a big brown envelope on her lap.

'What bring you here?' I said.

She stood up and dusted her skirt, her round face a mask of concentration. I appreciated Pet; she didn't bullshit and was not afraid of anyone when pushed. Malan told her once she was like me – pig-headed and insolent. She said she took that as a compliment. I remembered her fiery eyes and pouting mouth at that staff meeting when she responded to what was meant as a put-down.

'What sweeten you, Digger?' Pet sounded defensive.

'Remembering you and Malan falling out. Staff meeting August 5th last year.'

'Oh!' She passed me a vacant look.

'I'll make us something to eat,' I said. 'I hope you hungry too.' I opened the door and let her in.

Pet sat at the table and watched me for a while, then she began looking about her.

'Check out the house if you want,' I said. 'It belonged to my granny. I rebuilding it, or building around it, more like. How you got here?'

'A friend drop me off. I bring you some stuff I think you should hold onto, Digger, just in case.' She took the papers from the envelope and spread them on the table. Everything that concerned me and my job was there: my employment history, letters of congratulations and commendations I'd received after successful cases; Malan's communication with the Justice Minister. There was even a copy of my recent sick note to the department and Malan's written comment doubting I was really ill. He stated that he had good reason to believe I was off the island.

'I didn tell him anyfing,' Pet said. 'I dunno how he find out.'

'Kara Isle is a parish surrounded by water.' I said. 'So, technically, I didn't leave the island.'

'Why Malan want to set you up?'

I took out Malan's typewritten letter 'You know about this?'

Pet shook her head. 'Lisa must've typed it; is not on record.'

I shrugged. 'He's apologising here. Didn't intend for things to go this far, but procedures already start and is out of his hands now. He say he prepared to back me up. He want to meet me and talk over a coupla personal matters. He want me in the office.'

Pet flicked a dismissive hand at the paper. 'Is not on record; is not signed; no department letterhead. Malan could deny he ever write that.'

'You don trust him?' I said.

'It don't feel right, Digger. That's all.'

I shuffled a pack of CDs. Turned a couple of albums toward her. 'How you want it, soft or hard?'

'Soft,' she said, trying to hide the smile. 'Digger, the way you talk sometimes…'

I fed the player a Dennis Brown and Gregory Isaacs compilation, turned down the volume and brought the stewed fish and provisions to the veranda.

We sat and ate while looking down at the old cane valley. It was rampant with flame-coloured love vines. The air buzzed with the wings of ground doves heading for their roosts further up the valley. The sound of Old Hope rose and settled on the air, along with children's voices.

I told Pet about my visit to Lonnie earlier in the day.

'Where she from?' she said.

'Marais.'

'Marais!' Pet sounded surprised. 'You know what they say about Marais woman. They give you cook-rice to eat and you become their slave for the rest of your life because they make you chupid.'

'She done turn me chupid long time,' I said, 'and she didn gimme no cook-rice.'

Pet chuckled. 'It goin make it worse when she give it to you, then.'

Night fell quickly and with it an orchestra of insect sounds rose up and filled the valley. I was surprised at how comfortable the silence was between us. Somewhere down the hill a radio came on, then it was cut off.

'Digger, I, I could stay if you want.'

I knew it took a lot from Pet to say that. But, for me, there was a cost to every ill-considered impulse. Lately, it was not just Lonnie who'd been making me understand that.

'Pet, it will spoil the work – in the office I mean. And mebbe between you and me. Besides…'

'S'awright, Digger. Don't think that's what I come here for. I here to help you out, that's all.'

'You make nice company.' I said, and I hoped Pet knew I meant it.

'That woman from Marais, what's her name?'

'Lonnie.'

'I believe she still want you, Digger, but she got something she can't tell you. '

'What?'

Pet shrugged. 'Dunno. I not every woman; I just me. Mebbe she not the person you tell yourself she is. Mebbe you see what you want to see.'

And that was odd, because Lonnie once said the same thing to me.

I'd seen her sitting with a man at a bar on Lagoon Road a couple of months after we got together. I'd popped in for some food on my way home. I was surprised to see her there. They were leaned in close in conversation and she was giving him that smile that did funny things to my stomach. I stood at the doorway watching them. She must have sensed my presence. Lonnie rose from the table and came over to me.

'Digger, you look vex.'

I said nothing.

'That your man?' I said.

'I know him.'

'In what way?'

'You don't like it?'

'What you think?'

She turned up her face at me, closed a hand around my elbow. 'What you want me to do right now?'

'Do what you want.'

'Digger, tell me what you want? You want me for serious?'

'I been serious from time, and you know it.'

'I didn know for sure; you never tell me.'

She went over to the table, pointed her finger in my direction, said something to the man. Then she joined me at the counter.

That night, her head resting on my chest, I told her that I loved her.

191

She raised herself on her elbow and looked into my face. 'I didn know.'

'Who was the fella at the bar?'

'My cousin, Raul.'

'That's the way you talk to Cousin Raul?'

'People see what frighten them. Even if it not happening for real.'

She threw a leg across my stomach and rolled over to sleep.

★

Pet tapped me on the shoulder. 'Digger, I ready to go home.'

## 35

The churchyard was unusually quiet. The women followed my progress up the path with stony-eyed gazes. It was obvious that Miss Stanislaus had told them about the purpose of this visit.

By now, of course, they knew I worked with San Andrews CID, and whatever my connection was with Miss Stanislaus, it involved her carrying a gun and using it if she had to. The women did not seem to mind her – perhaps because she took the blame for what happened to Bello on the beach. They'd embraced her and her daughter completely.

With me – apart from Adora's brassiness – they adjusted to my presence the way water flowed around a stone.

Would they talk to me now? Would these women let me in on the intimate transgressions of this churchman who had held such power over them? Would they help me find Nathan and Alice?

I did not have Miss Stanislaus's faith in them. As I told her once, we – Camahoans – have no language for atrocity; or if we do, we cannot bring ourselves to use it. We'd rather make ourselves forget. I said that to her in the office, and pointed out of the window, which offered a full view of Fort Rupert. She'd followed my finger, quivered her lips and turned to her reading.

I was in no mood for niceties. I returned the women's stares and walked right up to them.

'We have to talk,' I said. 'We got a scandal waiting to bust open, and when it happen, it going sink this whole damn church and everybody in it. Lemme tell y'all why. First, the Deacon got killed in unusual circumstances. Nobody here look too sorry about that, in fact some of y'all look as if Carnival come early.

'I sure y'all know that it got people in high places who used to use Deacon Bello's services. I know one, for certain, who want the circumstances around his death investigated. Y'all done know what the results of that investigation going to show.

'Second, you got two young people missing. One of them, Alice, disappear almost four years ago; another – Nathan – gone for almost as long. Alice left her cell phone and her one boychild behind. She never been in touch with her son since, or for that matter anybody else. Y'all know that something wrong. Problem is y'all not talking. I dunno why. I don't understand it. As far as I can see, we have just one chance to limit the damage or hopefully avoid it. And that is by showing, if it comes to it, that what y'all did to Deacon Bello was the only way to protect y'all self from him. I believe that the best way to make that case for y'all self is by finding the two missing people.

'Now,' I pointed at the church door, 'I going in there, and I expect people to come sit down and try their best to help me find some answers. I can't force nobody. I don't intend to. Is up to y'all.'

Silence descended on the yard, filled by the whispering of fabric against skin, the soft metallic grating of the church roof soaking in the early evening heat.

On the periphery of the group, the two Watchmen looked on, as still as posts, their *fouets* resting easy in their hands.

I waited, conscious of Miss Stanislaus's eyes on me – a sidewise, almost surreptitious, appraisal of my face.

The Mother broke from the group and walked into the church. The others filed in after her.

In there, the smell of camphorated oil and incense. At the front, the altar with its Shepard Rod and staff, the Taria and Lothar vessels and the bell whose bronze multiplied the candle flames around the room. About five paces from the altar, the gaping door that led to the Mourning Ground.

Miss Stanislaus sat on the front bench, hands on her lap, knees pressed together, as if she were in the middle of a service. She seemed to be daydreaming.

Pike, the Watchman with the pointed beard, came in and placed himself in the corner to my left. I looked at him, then at Mother Bello.

'Is awright,' she said. 'Ask whatever you want.'

At the back of the room, Adora lit a candle, held the struck

194

match to her lips and blew on it. Iona was a shadow in the corner near the entrance.

'I want to start with Alice,' I said. 'I interested in anything y'all remember about her: what she look like, the last time anyone saw her, the last thing y'all saw her wearing. What state of mind she was in just before she disappeared. Body marks like scars, tattoos – that sort of thing. But first, anybody here was a close friend of hers?'

Thick silence; heads cocked as if they were all listening to something outside of the room.

Miss Stanislaus stirred, swivelled her body on the bench so that her face was partly turned toward the whole room.

Her voice was very, very calm. 'Mebbe,' she said, 'mebbe De Modder–' at that Miss Stanislaus smiled – 'who know her husband best of all, will try to help out first.'

I took Miss Stanislaus's cue and turned toward The Mother. 'Deacon ever used to go out on his own?'

'Nuh,' The Mother said. 'Before the car break down, he used to go with Pike or Popo to get the provisions.' She lifted her head at Pike. Pike nodded a vigorous confirmation.

'He never went out any other times?'

'Hardly.'

'No other times or hardly? Mother Bello, which one?'

'Hardly,' Pike said.

'Hardly meaning?'

Pike raised a hand, the way a school child might. 'Missa Digger, I could answer?'

'Course.'

'Deacon Bello go out once or twice in the car to collect water in Kalivini when we don't have enough. A coupla times he go off to give a politician or big shot a bush-bath to clear away de bad luck, or clean up his spirit, yunno. Or jus to fix im up.'

'Fix im up?'

'A bath with herbs; give him some strength, yunno. Specially if he got a young wife.' Pike was quivering an eyebrow and smiling at me.

'He go on his own those times?'

'Yes, Sir.'

195

'How long since the car broke down?'

'Last year, round September, October... Dunno,' The Mother said.

'Dunno don't mean nothing to me, Mother Bello. Somebody in here should know.'

'Third week in August last year,' Adora's voice cut in. She was leaning against the frame of the door, legs crossed, the box of matches poised between her fingers.

'You sure?'

'I sure.'

'How come?' I said.

'Because I remember.'

'You remember when Alice left too?'

'I wasn't around when that happen.'

'How come you remember when the car break down and the others don't?'

'They tell you that?' She sucked her teeth. 'Some people talk but they don' always *say*.'

'I don't understand.'

'A pusson could only dead once, y'unnerstan? Santopee don't frighten me. If it wasn' for my girlchile...' Adora tightened her headwrap and stalked out into the yard. I turned back to The Mother.

'How y'all manage for water and provisions after the car broke down?'

'Popo friend got a lil van.' She gestured at the older Watchman standing directly behind her. 'One of them go for the provisions every coupla weeks. Everybody carry water, including the children.'

'Mother Bello, I got a question to ask you: how come this carried on so long? Why nobody report it to the police, or say anything to anybody in the world out there?'

I watched the heavy face crumble, the moistening eyes and lowered eyelids. 'A pusson dunno what to do. You know dey goin come after you. You think all dis feel good? You think...' She began sobbing silently and openly.

I felt a hand on my shoulder. 'O-okay fe-fe-fella, I a-askin you to st-st-stop right now, please!' It was the older Watchman, the

196

silent one from whom I'd never heard a word before. The strength of his voice surprised me and the fact that he stuttered. I shot to my feet and turned to face him, felt my lips peel back, felt the heat of my own breath in my mouth.

'Don' fella me! And you never rest your hand on me again, not even as a joke. You do it next time I make sure you never use that hand again.'

I strode out of the church, quivering with a rage that I hadn't been aware of until that Watchman laid his hand on me.

The house was silent and I wondered where the children were. No sign of Adora either.

'Missa Digger.' A small breeze shook the top of the guinep tree that hung over the yard. Miss Stanislaus smelled of something lemony; she filled my head with Lonnie.

'Missa Digger. The Modder ask for you to eat with us.'

'I have to go. I got some things to settle.'

'Like what, Missa Digger?'

'Like my mind. I got to settle my mind.'

'When you say'z de meeting?'

'I got twelve days starting from tomorrow.'

'I kin post them swops today...'

'I did that this morning, thanks.'

Daphne appeared from the back of the church, wrapped her arms around Miss Stanislaus's waist. The girl looked up at her mother before fixing me. Brown as an evenly baked loaf. Clearwater eyes. At least, I thought, when Miss Stanislaus looked at Daphne she saw a younger version of herself. I wondered if that made a difference.

'You didn ask 'bout Nathan.'

'Alice feels more real,' I said.

Miss Stanislaus frowned. 'That mean?'

'I dunno,' I said. 'I dunno where to begin.'

She looked disappointed. 'None ov what them tell you help?'

'I can't say right now, Miss Stanislaus. I need something to... to kick me off. A spark, yunno. Something. I didn't get that from them. Or mebbe I got it, but I don't know it yet. By the way, what's going on with Adora – all this talk about centipede and her girlchild?'

197

'Adora is Adora. She a fighter woman who not feeling good about what she done to Bello. Missa Digger, killin is a stain dat can't wash out.'

'Miss Stanislaus, I been thinking you should go back to your house.'

'Why?'

'A feeling I got – that's all.'

She stared at the gaping doorway of the church for a while, then shook her head. 'Nuh! Not yet. Mebbe when tings start makin sense. Mebbe when I feel satisfy.'

## 36

I called Ramlogan in Trinidad and thanked him for the last job. A parcel should be with him that evening, containing eight samples. Did he think he could get the results back to me in ten days? And could he make sure that the return address was the PO Box I sent him, rather than San Andrews CID?

Crosschecking and analysis took time, he said, but he thought that he could do it.

I gave him Miss Stanislaus's number. 'She'll wire the money when you confirm receipt. The timing is important,' I said. 'A matter of life and death.'

Ramlogan said nothing for a while, then he told me, okay.

Wanting something to distract me, I turned to my grandmother's belt. I shredded the banana tree behind my house and was sorry afterwards, which did not prevent me from destroying the one beside it. I dropped the weapon on my kitchen table, stood looking out at Old Hope valley. I couldn't get Adora off my mind.

I reviewed my conversations in the church, reminding myself of Chilman's mantra, especially during our first few months of training: *Fellas, it got four ways an officer does get misleading information. First, the witness or guilty party tell you a barefaced lie intended to make you look the other way; second, the witness or guilty party not telling you what you need to know because they assume you know already; third – the one I won't forgive y'all for – is when the witness or guilty party tell you everything you need to know and you don't realise it.*

'And the fourth?'

'When I find out that one, Digson, I'll let you know.'

The trick was to examine every word I might have misunderstood. My list was very short.

'G'd afternoon, Miss Stanislaus. Can I speak to The Mother?'

Miss Stanislaus's voice faded. The background noises of the yard took over.

'Yes, Missa Digger!' The voice was sullen, deep.

'A question I want to ask you, Mother Bello. You said the men get the provisions every week – where they buy the provisions from?'

'They don't buy it; they collect it.'

'From?'

'The lands in Saint Davids. A fella up there name Crane wuk the land for us, keep his portion, an leave our share by de road. One of them collect it and bring it here.'

I sat back. 'Okay, thanks. Lemme speak to Miss Stanislaus.'

'Something wrong, Missa Digger?'

'Nuh, Mother Bello. Pass the phone to Miss Stanislaus, please.'

'Missa Digger, is me here.'

'Miss Stanislaus, give the phone to Adora, please.'

'Eh-heh?'

'Miss Adora, is Digger here...'

'I know.'

'Miss Adora, you always talk like that?'

'Go ahead an ask de question, Mister.'

I lowered my voice. 'You talking to me, but you not *saying* anything. What you want to tell me, Adora?'

'Missa Digger, thanks for the call. Ba-bye.'

## 37

Early evening, we took the road to Saint Davids. Miss Stanislaus was her old self – alert and cheerful, although she wouldn't look at me directly. When I picked her up she dropped a brown paper bag on my lap. I brought it to my nose and smelled potato pone. I rested it on the dashboard, smiled my thanks at her.

'You not eating it?'

'I waiting for your permission, Mam.'

She patted her green handbag and kept her eyes on the road.

An hour later, we were climbing through the colder, damper air of the Mardi Gras foothills. On the peaks above us, the deep-throated thrum of high winds; down below, the clotted green of vegetation speckled with wooden houses stuck against the hill-sides.

'What make you so sure is up here?' Miss Stanislaus wanted to know.

I quoted her: 'Sometimes a pusson know and they dunno how they know.'

She nodded, as if I'd just given the best possible explanation.

An hour later we topped the hill. 'The Lands', I explained, was anywhere in the mountains where a farmer grew cash crops – always treacherous to get to, but the richness of the soil made the trouble worthwhile. Here, the forest gave way only briefly. After a few months of neglect the place returned to bush.

We walked the grassy ridge above a banana plantation. I kept my eyes on the giant silk cotton tree that Pike, the Watchman, told me marked the western boundary of Bello's land. Miss Stanislaus strolled ahead, her handbag dangling from her bent elbow as if she was on a royal tour and the bushes around us were her subjects.

The misshapen shed of rotting wood and galvanise told us we were there. Directly in front, flowering pigeon peas, sweet potatoes and eddoes; halfway down the slope, earth mounds of growing yams, a field of sweet cassava. Beyond all that, a dense expanse of plantains and bananas.

The garden ended at a gully. From that point the ancient forest began its climb towards the peaks of the Mardi Gras. Treetops laden with a heavy weave of vines. A green Purgatory.

Miss Stanislaus must have felt the same thing – or something like it. I heard her slow intake of breath and when I looked at her she was dabbing at her eyes with a square of tissue.

'Miss Stanislaus, if it take me the rest of my days I will find them and bring them back.'

Miss Stanislaus took my elbow and steered me away.

At her gap, I gave her the money for the lab. 'When Ramlogan call and confirm that he's got the samples, you wire this to him.'

Miss Stanislaus got out of the car, closed the door and pushed her head through the window. 'Missa Digger, you still got girlfren troubles, not so?'

I shrugged and forced a smile.

'That girlchile got no sense. Don't forget the pone I bake for yuh.' Miss Stanislaus smacked her lips and walked away.

I ate the pone, licked my fingers, tapped my horn. Drove off.

## 38

A soggy Friday morning. A fine drizzle was misting the valley when I got to Bello's garden. I cleared out the clutter in the shed: the broken handle of a spade, a stack of dry wood along with the detritus of discarded root vegetables and dead leaves.

I took a break to call Caran.

'Digger what's happening? I getting news and it don't sound good.'

'What news?' I said.

'Word reach me that Dregs sell you out. That true?'

'Is not so straightforward,' I said. I filled him in as briefly as I could. Caran remained silent for a long time. 'Lissen, fella, watch your back. If I can't help you as officer, I help you as friend. Y'hear me?'

'I hear.'

Caran mumbled something and switched off.

I'd taken a spare car battery and adapter for my phone.

In seven days the results should be in my hands. That left me the weekend to digest it, make notes and prepare my case for the Monday meeting.

If the DNA results proved that Miss Stanislaus was right about the children being Bello's, that would not provide the winning argument. A man fathering a brood in every parish – with a different woman for each child – was no scandal on Camaho. In fact, it was a source of envy in other men. A father ignoring the existence of his offspring was as much a part of life as hot sun was. My own father was proof of that. But a man killing the mother of his child was a different matter altogether.

I started my search from the centre of the garden, prodding the soil with a slim, heavy iron rod. I worked in an outward spiral, stopping after dark and crossing out each day on a notepad.

The weather in the Mardi Gras was unreadable. An early morning sky would threaten rain, but the day turned out to be scorching. Sudden showers replaced sunshine without notice. Nights were always shivering.

When it rained, I threw a plastic sheet over my head and carried on. On blistering days I took off my shirt and worked bareback in my shorts. Evenings, I boiled a pot of plain rice, dumped a tin of sardines or corned beef in it and fed myself. I washed in the skin-chilling mountain stream that broke through the rocks further up the hillside.

Nights, I made notes, sifting through the streams of words from Miss Stanislaus, The Mother and the congregation.

I always came back to Adora. It was as if the woman was in some on-going conversation with herself while, at the same time, throwing words at Mother Bello.

I thought I understood that. A deacon's wife was the shield between her husband and the women of his flock. She slept with him and ate with him, was the ruler of the four corners of his bed. In every Fire Baptist church on Camaho, The Mother was the Watchman who watched her husband – the one whose job it was to temper his temptations and police his appetites.

I'd given Miss Stanislaus my new number. She kept in touch through text messages. She still hadn't got the hang of predictive typing, but occasionally I made out the odd word and because I knew it would fluster her, I entertained myself by sending back emoticons with pouting lips and throbbing hearts.

Pet left me several voice messages, asking where I was, reminding me at the end of every one of the date of the hearing. Nine o'clock, she said, MJ's office, Canteen.

By the fifth day, my limbs were numb, my hands sore from probing the earth. I checked my watch and saw that it was Tuesday of the second week.

I sat with the steel rod across my lap surveying the hills, the cresting vegetation, and the gully at the bottom of the land.

I remembered Kathy Jensen, a criminology tutor I adored, who talked rather than taught. She was obsessed with ideas – her own. Criminal thought is primitive thought, she said. Examine that part of yourself and you'll understand the way the mind of a criminal works.

Where in this place would Bello hide a pair of murdered bodies?

I took my notepad, drew a circle on a blank page, wrote HIDE in its centre. I began clustering words around it, creating a semantic field. The trick was not thinking while I did it. I scribbled *bury, under, dark, cover, shade, avoid*… building a widening constellation of word-associations and images.

I left the notebook lying on the earth, washed myself, boiled some rice and sat down to eat. An hour later I returned to the notebook, tore out the page and stared at the confusion I'd created. I circled the words that stood out for me, then tossed the paper in the fire.

By the next day, I had gone beyond the boundaries of Bello's land and would soon be crossing the gully where the forest began climbing towards the triple peaks of the Mardi Gras.

That night I sat up in the dark, not sure of what it was that pulled me out of sleep. Out there it was quiet. I felt for my belt and slipped out. A clear crisp night. The faint suggestion of a new moon directly overhead. A glimmer drew my eyes towards an unsteady flame progressing from the lower depths of the valley. Voices – sharp on the wind, then fading. The occasional yapping of a dog. Boys, no doubt, from the village below, hunting bush-meat.

I sat in the doorway following the climbing light until the kerosene torch became a yellow bloom above the gully directly ahead of me, never quite disappearing. I woke again close to morning, to the shuffling of dried leaves. I left the shed, pressed my back against the wall, stood there for a long time listening. Nothing but the chittering of night insects and the sloping grey silence down below.

I was up and working when Miss Stanislaus called, wanting to know if I was alright. 'What you eatin in dat bush up deh? You got fruit? A pusson body need fruit. You want me bring some sapodilla and star-apple? I got ripe fig too. What about a cake? Or p'raps some potato pone? Today is Thursday, Missa Digger; you call dem furrin-sick people in Trinidad to make sure?'

I said no to all her questions and thanked her for reminding me about the lab results.

I phoned Ramlogan. 'Digson here, Ramlogan. Results ready?'

'Hello, Mister Digson. How are you?' Ramlogan sounded cheery.

'It ready, Ramlogan? Gimme a straight answer.'

'Hold on, Mister Digson.'

He came back. 'We've done de screening, de extraction…'

'Yes, and the quantitation and the PCR and all them tings which should've happened in the first few days like you promised. You can't bamboozle me with your science. Is eight days now and I want to know if you finish the report and whether I getting it on time.'

'Everything done, Mister Digson. Is only the report not finish yet. Tomorrow, Friday, I will tie up everything for you; but like you know courier not available weekends. So I post it Monday and you get it Tuesday.'

'Tuesday too late.'

'Is a lotta work. We can't do better than Tuesday.'

'Tuesday no good.'

'I guarantee Tuesday, Sir. Is de best I could do.'

'No good.'

He must have heard my distress. 'Look, Mister Digson, I sorry. Is not the kinda ting you could take home and work on. I promise I come back to de office tonight and work on it. I promise.'

'And when I going get it?

'Monday morning, I'll go personally to Piarco Airport, put it on Islander Airlines with one of them air hostess girls I know. You pick it up Monday morning.'

'No good.' I said. 'Monday morning is the meeting.'

'You trust Missa Ramlan wuds?' Miss Stanislaus wanted to know.

'I have to.' I said.

'And you say he say he goin be at the office tonight?'

'That's what he say.'

'Office same address you did ask me to send the package to, not so?'

'What you thinkin, Miss Stanislaus?'

'I not thinkin, Missa Digger, is a question I asking you.'

'S'far as I know, yes.'

'Missa Digger, you alright?'

'Miss Stanislaus, why you keep on askin me that question, especially now?'

'I call you later, Missa Digger.' Miss Stanislaus hung up.

*

Ramlogan's response forced me to see the impossibility of what I'd set out to do. I looked about me. For all my efforts the garden looked untouched, the blue-black hills just as detached and impenetrable as the climbing forest.

I began tidying up my mess and sorting out the luggage I had brought with me.

Finished, I cast an eye on the aluminium case I'd leaned against the doorway – my 'murder bag' into which I'd slotted foam compartments and packed with phials, measuring tape, preservatives, viscera boxes, anticoagulant, needles, syringes, toothpicks, self-sealing sachets, brushes, lifting tapes and small medical instruments. There were plastic spoons and forks in there, empty 35mm film canisters, sea salt, small bottles of over-proof rum, vinegar, surgical spirit – in fact, whatever substitute I could find for the necessary things I could not obtain or afford.

I walked the land once more, crisscrossing it first, then retracing my steps till I came once more to the old forest – cool, filled with the ticking of dried leaves and insects, but still heavy with an ancient silence that could not be replaced by any sound on earth. Dusk was purpling the vegetation when I got back to the shed.

I boiled some rice, tried to eat, but did not have the appetite.

My phone rang, I picked up.

'Missa Digger?' I could barely hear Miss Stanislaus for the roar and clatter that invaded my ear.

'What's happening in that church? I could hardly hear you.'

'Missa Digger, I call you to tell you dat Missa Ramlam back at the office seven o'clock.'

'Ramlogan, not Ramlam. He tell you that?'

'Uh-huh, so I waitin around a bit.'

'Waitin aroun… Miss Stanislaus!'

'I come to collect dem tings. Missa Digger you there?'

'I here. Where you say you…'

'I by de office waitin for Missa Ramlan.'

I felt a light-headed, breathlessness. 'Miss Stanislaus! Miss Stanislaus – you – you the greatest woman in the world, y'unnerstan? You – you the top of the topmost!'

She chuckled brightly in my ear. 'Watch your mouth, Missa Digger. Yunno, Trinidad not bad. Everybody a little crazy here, but them awright. I see you soon, Missa Digger.'

'Where you stayin?'

'Missa Ramlam tell me he up whole night to write the report. I goin keep im company. Missa Digger, you make any progress?'

'Nuh,' I said. 'Was a waste of my days. I out of here tomorrow.'

'This goin have to do, Missa Digger.'

'Yes, but only if…'

'Is so, Missa Digger. I believe is so. Ba-bye.'


I got up early, dragged my things out of the shed and prepared myself for the downhill journey to where I'd parked my car.

On the top of the incline above the garden I stopped, held there by a nagging reluctance to leave – that and the certainty I'd felt about this place as Bello's site of concealment.

Far below on my right, I caught a glimpse of the hill village from which the boys had climbed the night before. I visualised the journey of the masantorch on the other side, above the gully, the abrupt uphill turn a little way past the silk-cotton tree, avoiding no doubt what looked like a vine-covered rock-protrusion that would have stood between them and the upper region of the ravine. Avoiding the difficulty of the climb from there.

I dropped the bags and began walking back down the hill, the case on my shoulder.

I crossed the gully, scrambled left.

The stones stopped me, a dark receding bed of boulders over which the great protruding rock-face hung. I could still see the slipping footprints of the youths, veering uphill.

I dropped my case, took out my torch and began making my way over the stones, some almost as tall as me. The place was so deeply shaded, I had to pause to adjust my eyes to the gloom.

A clearing was at the foot of the rock-rise and what looked like an abandoned coal-pit. I made my way towards it and switched on my torch. With the blade of light I traced the outlines of the subsided earth, the darker shade of soil around the edges of the depression. With a small shovel, I probed the soil for compaction, felt the yield of the earth under its blade and stepped away.

I took photos of the scene, then placed soil samples in a solution of baking soda which confirmed for me that it was alkaline.

The subsoil was dry despite the rains – sheltered as it was by the overhanging rock. Already, from the soil sample, I had a reasonable idea of the state of the body if anything was there.

By early afternoon I had made a trench around the space and removed most of the covering earth. Finally, for that last series of brushstrokes – that awful moment of revelation – I paused and braced myself.

Death is not a pretty thing, however much you dress it up. I couldn't help imagining what this young woman was before, as I looked down at what lay in front of me. It took something out of me, always, to confront this – the wasteful indifference of death.

I was no pathologist. I had no training in forensic anthropology or anthropometry. My understanding of entomology was sketchy. The equipment I had was basic.

But I would do my best to identify these remains, keep what was left of this female as whole as I could. I would take her back to people who would recognise and claim her. I would do this to help fill whatever void this woman's disappearance had left in them. It was the best that I could do.

It took me all weekend. I made notes, took photographs, made more notes, collected bone and tissue samples including arthropods that had colonised the body. At this stage they were mainly mites and rover beetles.

Sunday evening, when I phoned Caran, my head was throbbing. He answered straight away.

'Is Digger here. I need your help.'

'Where you deh exactly?'

I gave him directions.

'Gimme two hours, Digger. I busy right now.'

'Bring a stretcher when you come.'

'Bring what?'

'A stretcher, Caran – you not hearin me? A body-bag too.'

'A what?'

'Body-baaag.'

'Hold on, Digger, I coming right now.' Caran hung up.

An hour later, the big man appeared with two of his men behind him, their hands covering their noses. I filled them in as thoroughly as I could.

Caran threw his keys at one of his officers. 'Okay fellas. Go to my place, tell Mary to send hot food. Bring soap too. Digger, you need a bath.'

Caran watched me while I packed up, a square of cloth masking half of his face. He'd gone so quiet, I barely remembered he was there until he cleared his throat or adjusted his position.

I showed him a sample of the insects I'd retrieved. There are people in the world, I said, who could look at these lil creatures and work their way backward to the month of this body's passing, even the manner of her death. Did he know that?

I felt Caran's hand on my shoulder. It took a while before it registered that he was pulling me away from the hollow at my feet.

I let my big friend hold me while I struggled not to cry.

Caran guided me up the slope to the stream, threw water over my head and scrubbed me with his bare hands.

He fixed sheets of plastic on the earth-floor of the shed for me. I lay down and slept.

## 39

Sunlight was spilling over the rim of the hills when I woke. Caran had gone down to his vehicle and passed the night there. The mist had peeled off the peaks of The Mardi Gras, now inky-blue above me. They appeared so close I felt that I could land a pebble on their summits.

I went back to the site. By now, the MJ would be sitting in his office with Malan, the Commissioner and two 'interested parties'.

I sent Pet a long message telling her I had to finish what I was doing and it would take me all day. I thanked her for everything, then I switched off my phone.

Late afternoon, I stood up. I told Caran that I had all the samples I needed; I was leaving the rest to him.

The big man helped me to my car.

I was shivering with exhaustion. I felt as if a swarm of flies had invaded my head. Hands helped me out of the vehicle when I got back to the church. I was aware of Miss Stanislaus's voice imploring and commanding at the same time.

I woke up on a mattress on the church floor surrounded by the smell of crushed nutmeg, camphor and other odours I could not place. They'd wound a cloth around my head. My back and shoulders throbbed. I found myself looking straight into Miss Stanislaus's eyes.

'You back,' she said softly. 'You been all day on that mattress, Missa Digger.'

Miss Stanislaus sounded aggrieved. She dropped a hand at the side of my neck and thumbed the pulse there. 'De Modder say you catch a chill. I tell her you tired. Missa Digger, I been missin you.' She folded her dress around her legs and leaned forward. 'Miss Pet call me from the office. She say she couldn get hold of you and she been desperate.' Miss Stanislaus pulled a tissue from under her sleeve. 'Missa Digger, I got de papers.'

'Pet,' I said. 'What she said?'

'Missa Ramlan is a nice man. I decide mebbe I show you Trinidad next time. Is not bad.'

'Miss Stanislaus, what Pet say?'

'She say, seein as you didn make de meeting, people get vex. They decide…' Her lips worked around the words. 'Yunno, Missa Digger, I been thinkin that you'z a bright fella. And besides, you nice. You could get work anywhere. If them don't want you here, I believe Trinidad goin take you. I goin phone Missa Ramlan tomorrow…'

She turned away from me.

'Miss Stanislaus,' I prodded her on the shoulder.

She didn't look at me.

'Miss Stanislaus, I believe I found Alice.'

Those brown eyes held mine for a long, long time.

'Missa Digger, you… you too much!' Miss Stanislaus shot to her feet and ran out the church.

A woman-shape in the doorway. A pause, a few steps, another pause.

'Adora,' I said.

Adora strolled over and stood over me. She dropped her voice, 'What you find?'

'I not sure, Adora. Not yet.' I sat up and untied the wrap around my head..

'What you find?' she insisted. I looked into large, darkly intense eyes, traced the beautiful arch of the woman's neck and wondered again what it was that had brought her here.

'Come to church tonight, Adora. We'll find out together.'

She lowered herself beside me. 'I see the way you watch me; you treat woman good?'

'Sister Dora, leave the man alone.' Mother Bello had pushed her head through the doorway. 'Missa Digger, Pike bring you some food to ketch your strength.'

Pike was standing just behind her, his beard like the needle end of a compass in front of him. He walked to the table near the altar

212

and rested a covered bowl on it. 'Fish-broth,' he said. 'Nothing make you better quicker. How you feelin, Missa Digger?' Pike's hand was warm on my forehead.

'A bit better.'

'Fever gone,' he said. 'You a strong youngfella.'

The two women left the room.

'What you know 'bout all this, Pike?'

''What you mean?'

'You a Watchman. Watchman see and hear everything. How come…'

'Even Watchman have to sleep, Missa Digger. And if people intend to hide tings from me, ain' got nothing I could do. Besides, if tings happm, dem happm inside deh.' He swung his head in the direction of the Mourning Ground. 'I never go in dat place, because I not suppose to.'

'Thanks for the food.' I said.

Pike slipped me a sideways glance. 'Everybody want to know if you got a result.'

I blew on the spoonful of hot soup and sipped it. 'I dunno what I got yet, Pike. We'll find out at the same time – all of us. Tell the Mother to take the children somewhere else or keep them in the house.'

## 40

They sat me down on a chair in front of the altar. Candlelight filled the room with an amber shine. Mother Bello was a hulking presence at the edge of my vision. Other women spread themselves around the small incense-filled space. Most stayed on their feet, shoulders propped against the wall.

Adora said she wanted her daughter to be there. The other children were in the main house playing a muted game of hide and seek.

Someone had lit a fire in the yard; the smell of lemon grass and wild pine blessed the air.

I'd already interpreted Ramlogan's report for Miss Stanislaus.

Seven of the children's DNA profile matched Deacon Bello's. Ramlogan concluded a 99.9 percent probability of parentage. The profile that puzzled him was Amos's and he said so in an additional note. Not sufficiently matched to conclude with certainty that he was Bello's offspring, but enough markers to link him genetically to the Deacon.

'You right about the children,' I told Miss Stanislaus.

'You don' have to tell them nothing about all that,' she said.

'I don't intend to,' I told her. 'No sense in telling them what they know already.'

'Missa Digger, you ready?' The Mother said.

I said 'Yes' and took in all the faces in the room. Pulled out my notepad and held it near the light. 'Young woman between twenty-one and twenty-four years old. Black jeans with v-pockets, gold thread at the seams, a dragon pattern on the right back leg of her trousers. She's the height and size of that lady in the back there.' I pointed at one of the women in the far right-hand corner of the room.

'That young woman used to suffer from toothache. She wear a cowrie shell around her neck, hanging from a shoelace. And – I guessing now – she didn't walk straight. Stiff left shoulder.' A few women at the back of the church had broken into murmurs. I did not look up.

'She had a broken shoulder blade. That account for the way she walked. She was still growing when that happened – probably in her early teens – judging by the way it healed.'

I stopped and scanned the faces in the room. 'Anybody y'all know fit that description?'

'Is she,' Iona said. She covered her face and turned her back to the room.

'I need somebody to gimme the name that fit the description I just gave.'

'Ali', someone said.

'I want the full name.'

They murmured among themselves. 'Alice Massy.'

I repeated the name, waited for confirmation, then wrote it down.

'Thanks,' I said. 'In a few days from now, y'all can reclaim Miss Alice in San Andrews mortuary.'

Miss Stanislaus was at my elbow when I walked out.

'I ferget to tell you Malan come to see you.'

'Where?'

'Here. You wuz sleepin. I tell im to go way.' She raised her chin at me, her face a soft sheen in the firelight. 'Missa Digger, you strong enough to go home? I ask because…'

'Because?'

'Is for the best. I-I see how Miss Adora eyes fall on you. I fink you know it too.'

'And?'

Miss Stanislaus shook her head. 'I don want to upset you, Missa Digger. I sayin is for the best, dat's all.'

## 41

I unhooked my windows and swung them open. I wished for wind, rain, a hurricane – something cleansing and redemptive to hit the island. Shake it up a bit, dig up its secrets and spit them out like that river in Les Terres that had pulled the Indian girl from its bank and handed her back to us.

I stacked the evidence I'd collected into the small fridge bought for that purpose. When I finished it was almost full. My report took me the rest of the night. I went to bed at daybreak and slept right through till evening.

Night had fallen when I called Pet. She picked up immediately; sounded so angry she could barely speak. I waited till she ran out of breath.

'Pet, I need you right now,' I said.

She went dead quiet.

'It mean we have to go into the office tonight. Late as you can make it.'

'You hear from Malan?' she said.

'Not directly, no.'

'He fight for you, Digger. At the meeting I mean. I never see him so upset… so…'

'Tell me, Pet, you doing this or not?'

'Of course!'

'Okay, I pick you up just after midnight. That alright?'

'That alright, Digger.'

I put down the phone, gathered my papers and sorted them. Malan phoned. I stared at the screen until voice messaging kicked in. There were nineteen waiting to be picked up. I hadn't bothered to retrieve them.

10.30 next morning, I parked outside the ministerial complex – a glass and concrete construction looking down on what used to be a zoo.

A security man I didn't know came up to my car and shoved his head through the window.

'I could help you, sah?'

I still had my ID. I pushed it under his nose. 'I here to see the MJ.'

'He expecting you?'

'Homicide.' I replied. 'The MJ very interested in this one.'

I said the same thing to the women at reception; they pointed me to the lift.

The MJ's office was on the third floor. I followed the signs, tapped his door with my keys and walked in.

It was freezing in there. 'Air condition working overtime?' I said to the young woman at the front desk. She raised a broad, impassive face, looked me up and down, then reached for a folder. 'You have an appointment?'

'Nuh. But the MJ dying to see me. Tell him Michael Digson here.'

The woman stiffened. 'What's it about?'

'Murder,' I said. The tight mouth tightened even more. I stared her down.

'Hold on,' she said and got up.

Her voice came through the walls of the office. An answering grumble. The secretary's again, pitched higher. Defensive. Another grumble – more sustained.

I got up quickly, turned the handle of the door and slipped in.

Deep brown pupils set in yellow irises settled on my face. Even in the freezing room the MJ wore short sleeves, his black tie loosened around his collar. Meaty, hairy arms; the rest of him thick as a bluggoe.

'You walk into my office without an appointment. You want to get arrested?'

'No, Sir.'

'What happened yesterday? You had a meeting with important people. You didn't have the decency to call…'

'I wasn't ready, Sir. I apologise. I was gathering evidence pertinent to the outcome of the meeting.'

The MJ raised a brow. 'You already have an outcome, young man.'

'You promised a public announcement at the end of this week, Sir, concerning the circumstances surrounding Deacon Bello's death. I'm here to present you with the facts.'

The MJ steepled his hands, leaned back against the chair. I'd never felt so diminished by a look before.

'You here to beg for your job? Well, you going about it the wrong way.' He reached for the phone.

'I here to tell you, Sir, that if you go out there tomorrow and make a public announcement supporting Deacon Bello, you'll be allying yourself with a murderer. I have the evidence to show.'

He withdrew his hand from the phone.

'You already know from Chief Officer Malan Greaves that Deacon Bello was the casualty of a police operation. He was in the process of drowning a woman. It was clear that members of his congregation could not get him off her. My judgement, as a trained officer, was that the use of force was necessary.'

'So you shot him?'

'That detail is not necessary, Sir. The autopsy will have confirmed that the weapon used belonged to the Department. It has never left the possession of the department before or since.'

The MJ showed his teeth – yellow like his irises. 'You fancy yourself a lawyer? Well, Michael Digson, I'm the lawyer here. I asked CO Malan the same question. He wouldn't answer me outright. He said he did not have the full facts. In the meantime people are out there waiting for answers. I promised them answers; they will get answers.'

'You don't understand, Sir. I not taking the blame.'

He spread his hands, rolled his eyes and smiled. 'Nobody's called your name.'

'Yes, by implication.'

I dropped my report on his desk. 'First five pages show that Deacon Bello fathered at least seven children with under-aged girls in his church. One as young as fourteen. Statutory rape. You're a lawyer, so you know that.'

The MJ flicked a couple of pages, glanced up at me and chuckled.

'You trying to make a case with that?' He rose to his feet – slowly, heavily and planted his palms on the desk. He sounded almost friendly. 'Go down to the lobby, young man. Have a look at the pictures of all the Prime Ministers who served this island. Take a good look at the first one – the Saga Boy. He was in office the longest. How many children you think he got?'

I shrugged.

The MJ chuckled. 'Some people say two hundred. Others say more. In every parish in the island. That guaranteed him the male vote. Look at Putin and those strongman virility grand-moves he keeps making for the Russian people all the time. You think he doing it for joke?'

Thick fingers tapped the folder. 'Anyway, Mister Digson, you miss the point. This is not about the misdemeanours of a preacher. It is about his death in questionable circumstances.'

'I'm willing to accept responsibility on condition that you make it known that officers received a distressed call by Deacon Bello's wife and that he was intercepted drowning a member of his congregation. Furthermore...'

'You writing my speech?'

'Just presenting you with the facts, Sir. I have further evidence to implicate Deacon Bello in the murder of Miss Alice Massy. She was a member of his congregation.'

I reached into my folder and dropped eight pictures of Alice's body in front of him.

He looked at the topmost one for a long time, then without raising his head made a shooing movement with his hand. I'd forgotten the secretary behind me. The woman stepped back, lingered at the doorway before pulling the door behind her.

'What's that?' The MJ looked as if he really wanted to know.

'Positively identified by Bello's congregation as Alice Massy. Killed by your friend and spiritual councillor, Deacon Bello. The man you fired me for. Look at the neck, Sir. I marked it out for you. Cervical vertebrae, numbers five, six and seven from the top smashed. Hyoid bone in the neck broken, which leads me to believe the woman was strangled after she got the other

219

injuries. I got eighteen more here to show you. From every angle.'

Beads of perspiration were settling in the creases of his brow. The office next door was very, very quiet. I pressed my back against the wall and waited. Finished, the MJ raised his head and cleared his throat. 'Where's the link?'

'What link?'

'Basic principle in criminal law. You can't incriminate a suspect, far less convict them without linking said suspect to the crime.' He grinned at me. 'Where's the link?'

'Circumstantial evidence good enough for my purposes. More than enough for the public who keep you sitting in this freezing office. Rumour will do the rest. After today, I dare anybody to go out there and make excuses for Deacon Bello. Or to call my name.'

'You here to beg for your job, not so?'

'To hell with the job. I already tell you what I want. As far as I can see you got a choice between two kinds of embarrassment: admit you made a big mistake and apologise, or go down with Bello.' I pulled open the door. 'Keep the pictures, Sir. They might come in handy.'

'You still don't have a job,' he said.

'I not finish yet,' I threw back. 'Just watch.'

## 42

It was one of those sizzling afternoons that narrowed the eyes against the glare from the high white walls and sprawling concrete mansions in Morne Bijoux.

I hadn't seen him in five years. The last time I heard his voice was on the phone when I asked him to pay for my tertiary education. When I told him how much it cost, he chuckled in my ear and I put down the phone on him.

I'd paid a few boys to wash my car and bring it to a shine. I wore a pressed long-sleeve cotton shirt with cuffs rolled back, my best trousers and patent leather shoes. Dressing had been an effort.

The Wife was in the veranda. It seemed as if, in the five years since I visited, the woman hadn't moved from the same latticed metal chair, except this time her hands weren't in her hair but in that of a teenage girl's sitting on a mat in front of her. The girl had her mother's high cheekbones and the long, fine-boned face of the man who called himself my father.

The woman leaned over the veranda wall and smiled. 'Mistuh Farringdon?'

'Nuh,' I said. 'Mistuh Michael Digson.' I pointed at the two folders in my hand. 'I'm here to see the Commissioner.'

The woman's face glazed over. She rose from the chair, shuffled backwards, the hand with the comb straight down at her side.

The girl shot up from the mat and rushed through the open glass door.

I watched the woman *not* watching me. I felt relaxed and easy.

The elder sister came out, barefoot and beautiful. Wide-spaced eyes, a mouth like mine. Slim-limbed, with a head of hair that stood up like a black bush-fire.

'Michael?'

I nodded.

She took my hand, looked me in the face then rested an index finger on her chest. 'Lucia,' she said.

'I know.'

'Dad – *our* dad's in the study. I'll get him.' She'd flashed a hard glance at her mother.

The younger of the two hung at the side of the sliding door, legs crossed at the ankles, staring at me from under long, fine lashes.

'You Nevis, right?'

She said yes with her eyes, lifted her shoulder from the wall and was no longer there. The woman brushed past me and ambled down the steps. I followed the slip-slop-slipping of her flip-flops until she disappeared behind the house.

Nevis returned with a glass of cherry juice and held it out. Before I could say thanks, she'd spun on her heels and disappeared.

My father had grown a small paunch. Hair gone grey – even those on his legs and stomach. A deeply lined face. Brown, translucent eyes.

'Come in, Michael.'

'I rather sit out here, Sir. It's work-related.'

'As you wish.' He pulled up a chair, rested his glass of fruit juice under it, and nodded at another chair.

I sat with the folder on my knee. He took his time looking me over. When he'd finished, he leaned back and clasped his hands across his stomach. He angled his chin at the shadowy figures of the girls behind the curtain.

'What you make of that, Michael?'

'I'm here to talk about work, Sir.'

He held my gaze for a long time, then crossed his legs. 'Have it your way. But before you start,' he lifted a rigid finger. 'You put me in a very embarrassing position yesterday. I want an apology and an explanation.'

'What I was doing was more important, Sir. I said the same thing to the MJ.'

His eyebrows shot up.

'I told him what I'm telling you now: I'm not going to be used even if I have to take him down with me... I...'

222

The Commissioner raised a hand. 'Hold on a minute; you threatened him!'

'Yessir.'

'The MJ!'

'Yessir.'

He shifted in his chair. 'That's how your grandmother brought you up? That's…'

'Don't talk to me like that, Sir. You have no right.'

His mouth opened and shut. He made to get up then sat back.

'I'm here to brief you on a matter relating to work. That's all.'

He grumbled something, got up from the chair and went into the living room.

The girls were staring at me. I nodded at them and sipped the juice. I looked out past the whitewashed walls towards the bungalow next door, shaded by a giant mahogany, its lawn dotted with stunted Julie and Ceylon mango trees.

A yard-boy, who looked about forty, was unspooling a long green hose across the grass.

My throat felt full and tight. I could barely swallow. I sidled a glance at the girls. Lucia looked close to tears.

He returned with a glass of liquid in his hand – a large white tablet fizzing at the bottom. He placed the glass close to the foot of the chair and sat back.

'Okay,' he said. 'Talk.'

I began to take out the documents from my folder, aware of him following every movement of my fingers. Then I raised my head at him.

'I didn't make the meeting because I was uncovering the body of a young woman that Deacon Bello buried in the Mardi Gras mountains. I've also gathered evidence of serious sexual abuse by him of seven or eight under-aged girls in his church. I had a choice between coming to that meeting or completing the job. I decided to complete the job.'

I pulled out some photographs and dropped them in his lap. I watched his fingers falter, watched him wither with the inspection of each image. When he raised his head he looked ill.

'The marks you made on these, what are they for?'

'They point to probable cause of death; they're also for iden-

223

tification. Miss Alice was, at most, in her mid twenties. I narrowed it down to twenty-three.'

'How?' The question sounded like a challenge.

'Wisdom teeth not yet emerged. Sutures on the skull not fully closed, plus a few other indicators. Deacon Bello really wanted Miss Alice dead.'

The Commissioner looked up at me with a tortured, puzzled gaze. 'What's behind all this, Michael? How a man could do this to… to anybody. And even think it's alright…'

'Miss Stanislaus believed that Alice was going to expose Bello. Her behaviour changed a couple of weeks before she disappeared. More outspoken. Defiant. She lost the fear. Something brought that on. I think I know what it was.'

The Commissioner leaned back. 'I'm not sure I want to hear, but tell me all the same. I s'pose you have to.'

It was one of the things I didn't tell the people at the church. I saw no sense in causing more distress.

'She was pregnant again, Sir. I-I prefer not to go into the details.' I held out the report. 'It's all in here.'

He took it with hesitant hands. 'Where you learned all that – the science, I mean?'

'I had an education, Sir. I sent myself to school.'

'Go on,' he grunted. 'Rub it in. You can't help it anyway. What about the woman, Chilman's daughter?'

'Miss Stanislaus?'

'She's as good he says she is?'

'Better than good, Sir. She points and I follow the pointing finger.'

'She's got Chilly brains then. We have a joke: Chilman gets drunk only from his shoulders down. I thought it was his conscience trying to make up to his daughter for all the grief he…'. He stopped abruptly, then looked away. 'You like this job?'

'Not really, Sir.'

'You good at it, Michael. Much better than you realise. Why you dislike something you so good at?'

'I don't want to stop feeling.'

A long breath escaped him. He raised himself from the chair. 'I want you to eat with us. The girls would like that.'

He angled his head at his daughters. 'Do that for them, if you can't for me.'

'Nuh thanks. I got other things to do.'

He held me with a long hard stare, his mouth tense with irritation. His lips barely moved when he spoke this time. 'Chilman told me why you joined the Force.'

'Coercion,' I said. 'He didn't give me a choice.'

'You lie to yourself. You actually…' He sounded disappointed. 'How far you got?'

'Got where?'

'You've been doing some digging, haven't you?'

I almost asked him for what, just to hear what he would say, but I did not answer.

I switched my gaze to his wife at the far edge of the lawn, bent over a ring of red and white anthuriums. The sunlight fell across her hair and shoulders creating the illusion that she was sliced in half.

He raised his shoulders and dropped them. 'When you said you were coming, I was er, hoping we would clear this up.'

'I got as far as Boko Hurd,' I said.

He'd gone still. I knew he was waiting for something more.

'So you got that far. You want to know what happened after?'

I shrugged.

'I called a meeting a couple of days after the shooting. Just three of us. Chilly would've been the fourth if he wasn't on leave. They voted we bide our time – sensible thing to do because Boko was protected. I voted to kill him. Lucky fella. He got away.'

I remembered what Pablo John said about a vehicle that ran over Boko Hurd. I shrugged; said nothing.

He did not try to push it further. Instead, he raised a brow at me, a trace of a smile on his lips.

'What happens if you need to have the MJ on your side one day?'

I shrugged. ''S'far as I see, I didn have no choice…'

He cut me off with an impatient movement of his hand. 'What I'm really asking is – you think confrontation is the only way to win a fight?'

'I didn say so, Sir.'

225

He showed me his teeth. 'When you shame or disrespect a man in high office, you make of him an enemy. There are better ways. Keep that in mind.' He tapped the folder. 'I'll show you what I mean.'

He turned for the door. 'Give me a couple of days to digest this. And that *boy*, Malan Greaves: tell him I say that after this, he's on my list of things to do.'

He parted the curtains and disappeared.

Lucia and Nevis followed me to the gate, Nevis cradling a black and white rabbit in her arms. 'We call her Michael.'

Lucia grinned. 'We didn't know it was a girl. Sorry. We could change it if you wish.'

'How long since she got that name?'

'From birth. She was too tiny to tell.'

'Name suits her.' I fluttered my lashes at them.

I left them at the gate shaking with giggles.

## 43

Early Wednesday morning, the Commissioner took over the six o'clock news, spoke for thirty minutes about the history of politics and law enforcement on the island, and purely to impress the population, I thought, he slipped in words like kleptocracy, megalomania and political presumptuousness, evils of which Camaho was fortunately devoid; devoid too of individuals tempted to conflate important ministerial duties with the humble business of law enforcement. At which point the Commissioner paused, excused himself and blew his nose.

If he hadn't introduced himself, I would not have known it was the man I'd sat with a couple of days before. This voice was for the public, each word rolling off his tongue and dropping on the ear like a polished stone.

In his capacity as Commissioner of Police, he said, he had reinstated forthwith the Officer who had been dismissed – understandably so, in the light of the misinformation circulating at the time – while in the pursuit of a case concerning one Bello Hunt, Deacon of The Children of the Unicorn Spiritual Baptist church. Furthermore he, The Commissioner, was appointing to San Andrews CID, another officer. A woman. He did not need to point out the shameful lack of female representation in San Andrews CID and the Force in general, did he? And he was assured of the understanding and – dare he say – support of the MJ in his commitment to rectifying this imbalance in The Force.

If time would allow, and in the interest of transparency and accountability, he, The Commissioner, would like to preface the distinguished MJ's announcement on Friday with some facts about the case in question – facts that had only recently come to the attention of both the MJ and himself.

The Commissioner presented my report in full, reducing the technical language to simple words. Even for me – hearing him read in a voice riding on a barely suppressed indignation – it was shocking stuff.

At the end of the report, he barely paused for breath. 'I hasten to add that at the time of the officer's suspension, the MJ was not aware of Deacon Bello's crimes against the seven children.' The Commissioner paused on 'children'.

'Nor did the distinguished gentleman have in his possession Detective Constable Digson's report along with photographs of the murdered woman. The MJ, I've been informed, is still digesting its contents and will, I'm sure, be referring to it in his statement on Friday.'

The Commissioner thanked everyone for listening and signed off.

I switched off the radio.

My phone rang on the hour, every hour, until midday. I left it lying on my kitchen table. The pattern of the ringing changed to every half-hour or so.

Several hours later, I got off my bed, picked it up and strode out to the porch.

'Yes, Pet!'

'Yuh radio turn on?'

I moved the handset a couple of inches from my ear. 'Nuh.'

'Keep your fuckin radio turn on,' she said, and rang off.

I tuned into the biggest commercial station. Outside, through the thickening darkness, I heard the raised voices of women hurrying their children to finish off their chores before nightfall.

In the houses down the hill, transistors were on full volume – the Commissioner's words repeated as news, as commentary, followed by phone-ins. I heard occasional bursts of indignation from the women in the houses down below.

The MJ came on the late news – his voice thick with shocked outrage at the contents of the report that he'd only just finished digesting. He thanked the Commissioner and commended the exemplary work of San Andrews CID .

I listened to the man and chuckled. I was still smiling when I heard my name. I switched on the outside light and stepped out to face three boys and a big-toothed, bright-eyed girl I knew as Pinny.

The shortest, Marcus, greeted me under his breath, resting the basket he was carrying on the lowest rung of my step. It was packed with fruits and vegetables.

'Mammy send that,' he said. 'She say she want back the basket.'

They said g'night and melted in the dark.

Chilman phoned. I picked up. The old goat chuckled in my ear, cleared his throat and switched off.

## 44

The scandal around Bello was still making the rounds when Miss Stanislaus and I returned to work.

A memo sat on our desks informing us of the Commissioner's decision to employ more staff and complete the restructuring of San Andrews CID. Furthermore, despite his retirement from the force, but given his experience and demonstrable expertise in the matter, DS Chilman would be tasked to oversee the aforementioned restructuring and recruitment.

In the meantime he'd granted Lisa Crawford, Malan's PA, the paid leave she'd requested the year before. Furthermore, in the meantime, and from henceforth, Miss Kathleen Stanislaus and Michael Digson would report directly to him.

Miss Stanislaus made a show of folding the memo and dropping it in her purse. Her theme today was butterflies – or rather pretty things that flew. Her maroon skirt had a small menagerie of hummingbirds and dragonflies probing the blood red petals of hibiscus flowers. She'd pinned a little silver feather in her hat, and a butterfly broach to her collar.

Malan could not take his eyes off the butterfly.

It was his mistake to involve the MJ in Department business, he said. Man is not God; Man is flesh so Man does make mistake. But at least Miss Stanislaus and Digson here resolved a crucial case and the Department was very pleased about that.

'I don see the connection between the trouble you cause, and us absolvin Miss Alice case,' Miss Stanislaus replied.

'Well, let's just say it speed up matters.'

'How?'

'Like I just say, we resolve the Bello case…'

'Nuh, case not finish. Missa Nathan still not 'counted for.'

Malan wiped his brows and shifted in his seat. 'He not up in the Mardi Gras for sure. We spend a week up there; we done dig up the whole damn place. No sign. Anyway, is my duty to welcome you as staff member, Miss Stanislaus. So as CO of this department, I say welcome.'

Miss Stanislaus gave Malan a pretty little smile. Malan smiled back.

He hadn't been watching her eyes.

Lunchtime, Chilman paid us a courtesy call. He dropped a small bag stuffed with rotis on my desk, congratulated the department on the 'steerrrling' results achieved *so far*, and strolled back to his car. The vehicle coughed a couple of times before clattering into life. The little Datsun must have travelled halfway across the island before I could no longer hear it.

'Who de fuck he think he is,' Malan snarled. He remembered Miss Stanislaus, threw a quick look in her direction, before stalking back to his office and slamming his door.

'Boy!' Miss Stanislaus muttered, rolling her eyes at Pet.

We ate the food, licked our fingers and watched Malan prowl his office space.

Pet followed me to the sink.

'What your Marais woman look like, Digger?'

'Dark-an-smooth. Same height as you; mebbe lil shorter. Quiet.'

'Red-strap sandals?'

I dried my hands and turned around to face her. 'How you know that?'

Pet's eyes glassed over and she shrugged.

'Pet, you talking to me or not?'

Malan killed the conversation by strolling over and handing me my special issue.

Pet glared at him so hotly I wondered what had gone on between them in my absence.

'Leave it on my desk,' I said.

'We could have a chat after work?' Malan said.

'Missa Digger, you promise to take me to buy some fish in Beau Sejour Bay,' Miss Stanislaus said.

'I didn't remember,' I said. 'But that's fine.'

We took our time driving up the West Coast Road. Miss Stanislaus bought her fish, stood beside me watching the incoming twenty-footers pleating the waters.

Her expression was distant.

'Missa Digger, one day I make pepper-fish soup for you. You never goin ferget it.'

'You thinking about Kara Isle?'

'Mebbe,' she said and smiled.

We drove back through a fine drizzle. Miss Stanislaus was at rest beside me, her head turned sideways, her hands on her bag. Small trucks and vans littered the Carenage. Inter-island ferries hulked over the sidewalk. Crewmen with their elbows planted on the high railings of their boats were shouting down words at the upturned faces of women who'd managed to squeeze their flesh into lycra suits designed for infants.

I braked for a cluster of school boys tussling over a basketball in the middle of the road. I leaned out the window to shoo them off. Through the gaps between their limbs, I glimpsed a flowered frock, a braceleted wrist, then the smooth ripe face turned up to a man's.

Lonnie must have felt my eyes on her. She shifted her shoulder, held my gaze a second, then dropped her head.

'Missa Digger, you holdin up traffic!' Miss Stanislaus's voice was like a slap in my ear. I didn't realise I'd braked.

When Miss Stanislaus spoke again, her voice was softer, almost pleading. 'Missa Digger, let's go.'

I drove on. The drizzle had begun to slick the road while the last of the evening sun threw a wash of yellow on everything.

'I didn know you know Lonnie,' I said.

'Uh-huh.'

'Since when?'

'Since Miss Petty tell me 'bout she an Malan.'

'How long ago was that?

'Since I start puttin two-an-two togeder.'

Once clear of the traffic, I eased the car onto the side of the road. I pressed my head against the seat closed my eyes and forced myself to breathe. 'So why you didn't tell me, Miss Stanislaus?'

'Missa Digger. Nobody did want to tell yuh. Not even Miss Pet, cuz she say she didn know what you would've gone an done.'

I'd never heard Miss Stanislaus sound so defensive.

'I see how Pet loss respeck for Malan. I ask her what the problem is. She tell me, but she aks me not to tell you.'

'You s'pose to be my friend.'

'Miss Pet not your friend too? Missa Digger…' She rested a hand on my arm. I shook it off, watched the wheels of passing vehicles lifting spray off the road.

'Mebbe that's why Miss Lonnie ask you for baby?'

'You, you talk to her too?'

'Yes, Missa Digger. I was worried 'bout you. You didn look yourself. I went to find Miss Lonnie. You was in the bush up dere lookin fo Miss Alice an Nathan. Sh'was in her house. I ask she what the problem was, same like I ask Miss Pet. She tell me everyting.'

'In other words, you went digging up my business.'

'What I know, Missa Digger, is dat luv not always straightforward and woman tink funny sometimes. When Miss Longy come ask you fuh baby is because she feel dat Malan goin leave 'er alone if she carryin baby fuh you. Sh'was Malan woman before you. Mebbe she love you more, but she just don't have the strength. S'far as I unnerstan, she was a lil girl when he start interferin wid she. He plant imself in she head from small. He break 'er out. Miss Longy grow up takin orders from Malan. Mebbe she can't help it? Mebbe is better so? What happm if you an she married an Malan come round to order she about? Den is murder dat goin happen, not so? On dis islan y'all man use de law to suit y'all self. An 's'long as dat don't change, problem never absolve.'

She turned fierce, unblinking eyes on me, 'What I don' unnerstand, Missa Digger, is why you so full of grievin all this time. Cuz as long as that girlchile in your head, she goin be ridin you like donkey. Nice fella like you, you got no problem gettin gyulfren.'

She mopped her face and sucked her teeth. 'Or mebbe you got a problem, yes. Mebbe you can't stand losing woman. Mebbe since yuh modder gone an don't come back…'

'My mother not your business! Y'unnerstand!'

233

'Missa Digger, you shoutin.'

'I shout loud and long as I want; is my car. You got no business in my business.'

'But you got bizness in mine? You take boat and go all the way to Kara Isle to find out about me, not so? Well, I damn well got a right to find out 'bout you too. Yuh modder lef' you an you vex. You vex to bust all yuh livin life.'

'You any different? Lemme ask you this: Since Juba lay his hand on you, you been feeling good 'bout yourself? And if so, how come you never go near man since?'

She fumbled for the handle of the door, pushed it open and stepped out. Miss Stanislaus stood against the bonnet her head lowered against the rain.

I got out of the car and stood beside her, heavy-hearted and choked. 'I shouldn've said that. I sorry, Miss Stanislaus.'

'Gimme yuh hand.' She reached out and grabbed it. Hers was cool. I felt the pulse in her wrist.

She placed herself in front of me, wide-eyed, fierce.

'Missa Digger, I askin you a favour. Is important. Tomorrow, you let Malan know you know about him and Miss Longy. Nothing more. Then I asking you to carry on like if nothing happm. You could manage dat?'

She must have felt me heave.

'I askin you, please. But mebbe you don have the strength?'

'Strength! What strength! I'z a big man!'

'Den tomorrow, show me.'

'I not as bad-minded as you think, y'unnerstan...'

'Yuh *fink* you not!'

She got back in the car; I followed. She turned her face toward me, 'Missa Digger, I hurt your feelins and you hurt mine. We balance now?'

'We balance.' I said.

We drove the rest of the way in silence.

At her gap, Miss Stanislaus made her usual preparations to get out. I nodded at her, forced a smile. With a movement so swift it caught me off-guard, she reached over and pulled me towards her. For a moment I felt her breath on my face, her hand inside

234

my shirt. Then just as smoothly, she eased back and I saw that she had my special issue in her hand.

She dropped the revolver into her bag and was out of the car before I caught my breath. I sat staring at the road ahead, stunned – not so much by the unexpectedness of Miss Stanislaus relieving me of my weapon as the shock of her skin on mine.

I fixed my shirt, blinked at the two top buttons that her fingers had unhooked; took my time driving home.

## 45

I realised they planned it – Pet and Miss Stanislaus – leaving Malan and I in the office and going off to the market square.

I'd bent my head to a crossword puzzle. Malan was on his cell phone. Occasionally I heard a chuckle burst from him and I couldn't stand to hear him enjoying himself. I strolled over to the window, pressed a shoulder against the frame and looked down on the Esplanade.

A tourist liner was edging backwards from the jetty, its engine creating a small storm-surge that threw water over the sidewalk onto the street.

I heard my name, shifted the angle of my gaze to see Malan at the periphery of my vision. He was making beckoning movements with his hand.

I returned to looking down on the Esplanade.

Malan approached, stood a little way behind me.

'Digger we have to talk.'

'About?'

'The erm, the Guinness, yunno – Lonnie.'

'So you got personal, like you promised – right?'

'I come to see you coupla times to talk man-to-man about me and she, yunno. Man even come to that Fire Baptist bush-church to find you. But she,' he flashed an evil glance at Miss Stanislaus's desk. 'She tell me to haul my arse.'

Malan moved to touch my arm. I stepped back.

'Easy, fella.'

He spread his fingers, 'All I saying is things happen, yunno. Is life. I should've let you know from the time you start with she; it don't matter which fella Lonnie go with, she still mine. She always go be mine. I know her since she small, yunno.'

I looked him in the eye. 'In some parts of the world man get jail for that. What about your wife?'

He clenched his brows. 'What wife got to do with that? Digger, you tryin to tell me someting?'

'Yep!' I uncrossed my legs and took my shoulder off the window frame. 'What I telling you is, when Man play with my head, Man give me permission to play with his too. Y'unnerstan?'

'So, what you sayin…'

'You heard me first time. Don't ever raise that kinda talk with me again. Let's stick to work.'

I returned to my desk.

I was settling down to my crossword puzzle when the glass door swung open and Pet rushed in, eyes wide and streaming, her body heaving. I shot to my feet.

'Digger-Dig… Miss Stanislaus, she…'

'What happm? Talk to me, Pet!'

'Fella in the market chop up his woman. Miss Stanislaus try to arrest im. Now he got Miss Stanislaus…'

Malan erupted. His desk drawer banged open, his office in-tray hit the floor and he was out of his office with his SIG Sauer in his hand. He headed for the entrance of the driveway. I took a hard left, vaulted the wall of the compound and hit the road sprinting. All I had to do was listen out for the uproar. I spotted the tightly packed bodies at the western end of the market square.

I jumped the railing when I got there, began making my way along the edge of the crowd.

Rivulets of blood had darkened the concrete. High above the din, the rake of a man's voice. I recognised it instantly: Cocoman, the coconut seller. I pushed past sweating torsos and resisting shoulders.

I spotted Malan on St John's Street above the square, sidling along the railings, his gun hand across his chest, the muzzle of the pistol tilted upward.

From the buzz of words I picked up that Cocoman had turned his machete on his woman. She was a stall holder herself, and the day before she'd left him for another man.

Miss Stanislaus had witnessed the attack and tried to arrest him. Cocoman turned his rage on her.

I broke through the circle, my belt in my hand. Miss Stanislaus's back was pressed against the man's chest. The coconut seller had an elbow locked around her throat. The man's body was slick with sweat, his string-vest clinging to his skin, his mouth frothing with obscenities. The machete in his other hand made glinting arcs above her head.

Miss Stanislaus flowed with the man's movements, almost as if she'd become boneless from the waist up. She didn't have her purse.

Malan had positioned himself on the other side of the street, in my direct line of vision. He'd pressed his back into a corner of the Syrian storefront, his face wiped of all expression. I risked a quick shake of my head, hoping he would read my signal to stand down. Malan didn't seem to notice.

As long as the man was facing me I could not move on him. As if Malan knew what I was thinking, he shouted something, his voice derisive, goading. Then he fired in the air. The crowd spread out abruptly. Cocoman's head swivelled round, Miss Stanislaus stumbling with his movement. I threw myself across the space, driving the buckle of my belt forward. It buried itself in his shoulder, sent the machete helicoptering through the crowd.

The sonuvabitch stiffened with the shock, rocked backwards, began howling like a scalded dog. I was on him in a grunting, hollow-headed frenzy – the shouts around me echoing and smeared. I felt arms around my waist, my shirt ripped off my back, my body dragged backwards. Then a man's voice in my ear, 'You hit im one more time, Sah, you kill im. That what you want to do?'

It sounded like a tease – an invitation. I allowed myself to be pulled to my feet.

Miss Stanislaus had slipped into the crowd as soon as the man released her.

'Y'awright?' I said.

She nodded.

I looped my belt around my waist and strode back to the office.

At the sink, I washed off the grit, stared into the mirror at a face I barely recognised – a tight-lipped, bare-chested man with a bruised cheekbone and half-crazed eyes.

238

I was looking out the window again when Malan returned. He opened his drawer and slid in his revolver. From the corner of my eye I saw him pick up his in-tray from the floor and lay it on his desk, his movements gentle, as if careful not to disturb the quiet in the office.

He turned his attention to Miss Stanislaus when she came in. She'd managed to retrieve her bag, and that bright-eyed serenity had returned to her face. She sat back in her chair both hands folded in her lap. I felt her eyes on me.

Half an hour later, Pet shouldered the door, tripped in and dropped a parcel in front of me. 'Sixty dollars,' she said.

I handed her the money.

Miss Stanislaus got up, took the packet off my desk and returned to her seat. She unfolded it, extracted the pins from the new shirt and spread it on her lap. She passed a palm along the creases and unbuttoned it. Pet followed every gesture, Malan too. Miss Stanislaus came over and held out the shirt to me.

'Miss Stanislaus,' I muttered. 'You still got my special issue. And look what *almost* happen.'

Miss Stanislaus leaned over and dropped her voice. 'Missa Digger take the shirt. We goin take a lil breeze togedder after work?'

Miss Stanislaus sat beside me, looking out across the water. In the distance, San Andrews town was just a scattering of lights at the foot of High Lake mountain range gone blue-black with the oncoming night.

She'd asked me to take her to this quiet place of trampled grass and scuffed earth, which used to be a colony for lepers. Now it was a communal love-nest for San Andrews.

A genleman offer to take her here a lil while ago, she said, and she was curious about the place.

'Then he wasn't a genleman if he want to take you here,' I grinned.

Cars arrived, rising and dipping over the uneven ground, their headlights doused. We watched them manoeuvre until their windshields faced the ocean.

Miss Stanislaus turned bright interested eyes on me. 'Missa Digger, people don't have bed?'

'Mebbe they just taking some fresh air, Miss Stanislaus. Or mebbe is more exciting outside here. I dunno. Why you don't go and ask them?'

'They won't mind?' Miss Stanislaus reached for the handle of door.

I lunged over and pulled it closed. 'I not advising you to do that.'

She raised a brow. 'Is so San Andrews people take fresh air?'

'Uh-huh.'

'How you know?'

'Know what?'

'That is more exciting?'

'Is only guess I guessing, Miss Stanislaus. I can't say for sure. You ready to go home?'

'Nuh. You don't mind me watchin people take de breeze a lil longer?'

'Miss Stanislaus, which part of the world you from?'

A chuckle bubbled out of her. 'Missa Digger, why you take everything so serious?'

'Didn't sound like you joking. You ready to go home?'

'Nuh.'

'Enjoy yourself then. Wake me up when you finish.' I adjusted my seat and settled back.

Miss Stanislaus prodded my rib with an elbow. 'Missa Digger, Adora left the church.'

I sat up. 'When?'

'Few days ago. I wasn' dere. The Modder say she left in secret, and after she left she call and cuss them stinkin. She say all ov them is cockroach and they goin stay cockroach for the rest ov them life. She say that me an you – we like bat in daylight.' Miss Stanislaus pushed herself forward and looked me in the face. 'Missa Digger, them is hurtful words from a Sister ov the church.'

I felt a sudden blood-rush in my head, sat still for a while.

'Miss Stanislaus, tell me again what Adora say.'

Miss Stanislaus repeated what Mother Bello told her.

'Them is clever words, Miss Stanislaus. Right now I feel ashamed; I feel as if I let Adora down. I underestimate the woman. I...'

'You goin stop runnin yuh mouth an start talkin sense?' Miss Stanislaus's lips were quivering with irritation.

'Easy, Miss Stanislaus.'

She folded her arms and stared stiffly out of the window.

'She said the same thing in the church before she left us in the room and walked off. No centipede – or rather santopee – could frighten her. Now she's calling y'all cockroaches.' I leaned forward. 'You ever see what happm when a centipede is in your house?'

Miss Stanislaus shook her head.

'Well, every part of the house come alive with the insects that been hiding in the cracks and crevices of your place, especially cockroaches. Miss Stanislaus, if you want to know what frighten look like, then watch cockroaches running from a centipede. What Adora been saying is that me and you – we're like bat in daylight because we don't see the centipede in the house.'

Miss Stanislaus raised enigmatic eyes at me. 'Missa Digger, you just gimme a picture of how I been feeling about this church from time. But I just couldn wuk it out.'

She was quiet for a while. 'The santopee Miss Adora talk about, you know how to catch it?'

'Yes,' I said.

'You goin tell me how?'

'You smoke it out, Miss Stanislaus. Is smoke you smoke it out.'

I spent the night sitting at my worktop, feverish with thought. I dug out my notebooks and reread everything I'd observed and written since the case began. I reviewed the photographs of the first body we'd found in Easterhall, my measurements and the topology of the stresses and damage the bones had sustained: fractured upper ribs, adjacent vertebra and shoulder blade. A pattern of cracked bones along which I could run a line from one extremity to the other. I was astonished at my carelessness. Now I saw the way this body linked with Alice's, not just by the nature of the trauma to the bones, but also by the fact that Alice's body, like the first one, had been disposed of face down.

I called Pet.

241

'Digger, what you want now; you know what time it is?'

'G'night Pet, you could run a check for me tomorrow?'

'On?'

'Bello Hunt. Find out as much as you can about him and his family, starting with his parents.'

'That might take all day.'

'Clear it with Malan. If he ask you what we up to, tell him we chasing Nathan.'

'You still on that case?'

'I never dropped it, Pet.'

'You mean Missa Chilman never let you.'

## 46

It took two hours of crawling up a dizzying road before I found myself in the mountains where the soil was always wet, and trees were ten times the size of those in the lowlands.

The two-roomed house was as decrepit as the woman who rested her elbow on top of the closed half-door.

'Adora not here,' she said. 'Nobody hardly hear from she. Adora foot too hot; she never stay one place. Mebbe she gone to her first cousin place in Kanvi. Them two always help out each other. Adora not the kind ov woman a fella like you should be askin for. She don't take no lash from no man. Adora temper turn her chupid.'

I searched through my pockets and pulled out a few dollars and a handful of coins.

'Is all I have,' I said handing everything to her.

The old woman looked surprised.

'Take it, Granny. Please.'

She nodded as if she were doing me a favour.

On the way back, I called Miss Stanislaus to say I would pick her up from the office at eleven.

It was one of those mornings when the sea breezes travelled inland and took the sting from the sun.

Miss Stanislaus threw a quick look at my face when I turned into the old mud track that would take us to the church. A spell of rain had fallen in the night that made the going tortuous. The mangroves were unusually loud with the lapping of the waters between their roots.

'The santopee? she saïd. 'You goin to smoke it out now?'

'I might have to light the fire first and let it burn a while. Miss Stanislaus, we been careless.'

'How?'

'We been ignoring Amos, we been forgetting Mother Bello and that first body we found in Easterhall. Well, let's see what happens now.'

I got out the car and opened the door for her. The air was peppery with the fumes of burning wood.

I greeted the two Watchmen with a wave and a nod. Pike gave us a thumbs up; the other watchman pretended he hadn't seen us.

Miss Stanislaus curtsied, then turned her attention to a smiling, animated Daphne, handing over a little multicoloured rucksack to her daughter. 'School start Monday. Me an Missa Digger drop you off at Miss Grace.' She bent down and whispered something in Daphne's ear. The little girl nodded, shouldered the bag and went to sit in my car.

The Mother stood at the church door, one hand planted on a hip; in the other she held the bell.

'I looking for Adora,' I said to The Mother.

'Adora gone home fuh a while, I fink.'

'You think! You not sure?'

'I sure.'

'And her little girl?'

Mother Bello frowned. 'She take de chile with her, ov course. What you fink…'

'I not thinking right now, Mother Bello. I asking questions. When she left this place?'

'Three days ago.'

'Four,' Iona said. 'Counting the night she left.'

'Anybody saw her leave?' I looked at the faces about me. They shook their heads.

'Mebbe she didn want nobody to know she leavin,' Iona said.

'Miss Iona, when last you been to your house?'

'Church business keep me kinda busy, yunno.' She was scuffing the earth with her feet.

'Who feed your dog, then?'

'Dog know how to look after imself.' She gave me a brief underhand look.

'I could take you home to feed your dog,' I said.

'Nuh – s'awright.'

244

I let it drop and turned to The Mother. 'Mother Bello, where's Amos?'

The Mother shouted the boy's name. He came running down the steps of the house to stand before her.

I reached into my pocket, took out a dollar. I held out the coin to him, following the quick shift of his head before he plucked the money from my palm.

'Amos, what's yuh age?'

'I ten,' he said.

'You remember Nathan?'

The boy nodded. 'Uh-huh. He use to give us sweetie. He an Missa Jason.'

'Missa?'

'Jason – Jason gone long time,' The Mother said. Her face relaxed into a smile. 'He used to give the chilren sweetie. Jason was here for a coupla months, an then he go. People don' always stay. Sometimes hard times bring dem here and when dem catch demself, dey tell we thanks an leave.'

'He tell you thanks before he leave?'

She shrugged. 'It don't matter; thanks or no thanks, we do God work same way.'

'H'was friends with Alice?'

The mother lifted her shoulders and dropped them. 'I don meddle in young-people bizness.'

'What business, Mother Bello?'

'What all dese question for?' She was suddenly fuming, the big body shifting in the doorway. The Mother's voice retreated down her throat, like low thunder.

I had begun to dislike this woman. 'Mother Bello, you really want to know what all these questions for? Well, I guessing Jason left the same way Alice left. I guessing that the same person who kill Alice, kill that youngfella too. And it wasn't your husband who killed Alice, Mother Bello.'

I stopped, taking in the faces, the complete stillness of these women. 'Is the pattern of the damage to the bones that tell me that. And if y'all think I making this up, lemme tell y'all what Jason look like: he was a slim fella, brownish curly hair, which most likely mean that he was light-brown in complexion. Nice

245

teeth, so I guessin he had a pretty smile. He had *beke* features too – straight nose, that kinda thing. About same size as Nathan. Good-looking I think, at least in the eyes of Alice. Is jealousy that kill Jason. Some fucker with a fouet…'

I was about to turn around to point when a fiery snake of pain exploded across my shoulder. It arched my body backwards and dragged the scream out of my throat. I hit the stones, rolled over, glimpsed the downward arc of an arm. The fouet caught me across the chest. Pike stood above me, the knotted whip quivering in his right hand like an aroused snake.

I saw the flash of teeth. 'Y'all couldha save y'all self – you an she. I goin deal wid she after I finish with you. Y'all shouldha leave what don't concern you. Y'all too fuckin faas and stupid. Now yuh go dead.'

I heard the fast scuttle of feet around me, voices shouting the children back into the house.

I kept my eyes on the whip, my body still quivering from the shock. When the Watchman lunged again, I followed the swing of his arm with my body, throwing myself down the slope at the side of the house towards the swamp. Pike followed me, the whip-arm straight out, his bare feet peddling the slipping earth – a quick, dim spider-shape above me.

I struck mangue-water, scrambled over the mesh of roots towards a spread of brightness seeping through the mangrove. I pressed my back against a mangrove tree and watched Pike approach, crouched, lips locked down. He swung. I ducked. The whip hummed about my head like a hornet. I slipped around the tree and clawed my way onto the path that led up to the hill overlooking the church.

Not wanting to turn my back on him, I began backing up the hill.

Over there, in the yard, it was silent. A still mid-morning. On the mud track down below, between the mesh of trees, I caught a glimpse of yellow.

Pike's teeth flashed as he got nearer. I followed his rising hand, his body's backward arch. At the height of his swing, I dragged the belt from my trousers, convulsed my arm. The leather leapt; the buckle struck his elbow; bit; snapped bone. Even then Pike did not

246

cry out. He staggered back, face twisted with the shock. He righted himself and leapt. I sat back abruptly on the slope, snapped the buckle at his ankle and threw him off his feet.

I saw him rise, heard the shot, watched him grab at air as if it were something he was trying to hold onto. The Ruger barked again, the sound flat and defined like a solid thing. Then three shots in succession, almost as if the weapon had lost patience.

Miss Stanislaus stood halfway down the hill, left leg forward, knees slightly bent, shoulders up to her ear. Her arms stretched out, full and rigid. I wished I could see her eyes.

I looked down at Pike laid out on the earth, his body dark and angular like a fallen shadow.

Miss Stanislaus adjusted her hat, dropped the pistol in her bag and hurried toward me.

'Missa Digger,' she said, her face so close to mine it was as if she were sampling my breath. Then she pulled away.

I phoned the office to update Malan. Could he arrange to have Pike picked up? He told me to leave it to him.

I limped along beside Miss Stanislaus to the churchyard. My right shoulder throbbed. The skin along my rib-cage felt singed. She'd poked my shoulder and my back and decided I would live. I had been moving when Pike struck and that saved me from the full impact of his first blow.

Miss Stanislaus wanted to know what made me so sure that it was Pike.

'The pattern of the damage to the bones of Jason and Alice,' I told her. 'Dunno how I missed it. The impact from that knotted whip is not just in one location. The only thing that I thought could do that is a fouet.

'Then my trick with Amos and Iona: when I gave the boy the money, he wasn't sure if he should take it, he looked at Pike as if h'was checking for approval. Same with Iona – I offer to take her home to feed her dog. She looked back to see Pike's reaction. She was afraid. All of it was unconscious.

'Miss Stanislaus, after what happened to Bello on the beach, Pike locked them down. None of them was leaving there without his permission and it was getting worse – which explain

247

why Adora crept out in secret with her little girl. Adora took a risk, you see, when she talked about the centipede. When she realise we didn get the message, she knew she had to run. She chose the middle of the night through all that mud and darkness.

'I didn see none ov it and I been right in the middle. How come?' Miss Stanislaus sounded distressed.

'Pike is a special case, Miss Stanislaus. We'll talk about him later. I'spose you work out by now that he is Amos father, and that Alice was the one he believe he own. Right?'

They were in the yard when we returned – the children quiet and still-eyed, leaning against the adults. There was no sign of the sour-faced Watchman.

Mother Bello stood in the middle of the space, tying and untying her headwrap. Daphne threw her arms around Miss Stanislaus's waist.

'Y'all know what connection Watchman Pike had to Deacon Bello?'

Silence.

I turned to the Mother. 'You know?'

She would not look at me.

'Half-brothers,' I said. 'Same father or same mother. I'll know for sure tomorrow. Pike never got introduced as Deacon Bello brother to any of y'all? How come, Mother Bello?'

The women's eyes were on her. I watched the readjustment of their postures and I knew that Mother Bello would not be among them for long.

Iona's throat was working as if she were struggling to swallow. She turned her head in the direction of the church door, still swallowing hard. Then she levelled stormy eyes at Mother Bello.

I edged over to her, dropped my voice. 'Mebbe Adora take over? She'll do a better job. I sure.'

Iona shook her head. 'Is the Sisters who decide. But she – she good as gone. You want to bet me?'

'Nuh.'

## 47

Thursday night, Dessie sent me an emoticon with an inverted face and a red glistening teardrop just under its right eye. Whichever way I turned the phone, it looked the same. As soon as I could, on Friday afternoon I went to the bank. The teller I spoke to left her post and busy-stepped towards a glass door at the back. She knocked on it, then tentatively turned the handle. A woman came out after her, with the walk of an air hostess, her white collar bracketing her ears like butterfly wings.

'Can I help you? I'm standing in for Mrs. Caine,' she said.

I read her name, Passiflores Arielle, on the gold rectangle of her tag. 'You're Luther Caine's PA; not so?'

'Mister Digson, I can take care of it, I'm very sure.'

I looked in her eyes. 'Miss Arielle, I got good reasons to want to see Dessima.'

'She's not here.'

'When's she coming in?'

'Mister Digson, Dessima is not here.'

'You just done tell me that. Where *is* Dessie?'

The woman wouldn't look at me. 'Sir, I can't…'

I slipped out my ID and pushed it towards her. 'Just tell me.' The woman looked down at the card.

'She, she's in hospital.'

'Where?'

She looked around her quickly. 'I can lose my job for this, Sir.'

'Relax. Pretend you serving me. What happen to her?'.

'I can't say, Sir.'

'What happen to her?'

'It's… I can't, I really…' She turned to leave.

'Miss Arielle,' I said. 'You forgetting something.' I offered her a sour smile. 'You forgetting you'z a woman too.'

I watched her start to walk away, the swing in her shoulders gone. I was about to leave when she turned around and came back to the counter, picked up a slip of paper, scribbled on it, and handed it to me.

I took it and told her thanks.

I went back to the office, phoned directory enquiries in Barbados. After that, I spent an hour or so making calls.

At work the next day, I emailed scans of my letter of employment, my salary slip, my passport and my police ID to the Cave Hill Clinic in Barbados. They called back and I spoke to a Doctor Philips for at least twenty minutes. After, I drove the five miles to Saint Paul's.

Mrs. Shona Manille grew cattleya orchids and butterfly jasmines in the front garden of their old, white, colonial house, with gables and awnings and a veranda with delicate latticework.

Damson and plum trees created circular islands of shade on well-tended grass. White translucent curtains fluttered through big bay windows. There were books and photos of family everywhere in the living room.

Dessie had inherited her mother's beauty. The woman floated about the veranda like a dancer, dressed in a loose flowing forest-green dress with enormous sleeves. Her thick cotton-white hair was scooped into a mound, held in place by an elaborate tortoise-shell comb.

'Raymond's shopping in Miami,' she said 'He's back next Tuesday. You can talk to me.'

When I'd told her what I knew, she went to the phone and called Raymond-in-Miami.

She blew her nose into a white handkerchief patterned with pink hand-embroidered roses. 'We didn't know,' she said. 'Dessima told us nothing. Luther said she was taking a break in New York.'

'Maybe Dessie wanted to spare y'all the embarrassment… Socially, I mean. I take it that you don't know about last year too. Between January 5th and 17th?'

She grew still, pulled up a wicker chair and sat down. 'You talking about the baby she lost?'

'That's what Mister Luther told you?'

She gulped. I thought the woman was having a stroke.

'Overdose.' I said. 'That's all the clinic was prepared to tell me. Had to send my ID and a couple of other documents to confirm who I was.'

I wrote down the address of the clinic and my number and placed it in her hand.

'I'm getting the plane this afternoon,' she said. 'We have family in Barbados. I'll stay with them.' She leaned forward, all dripping eyes and trembling lips. 'Luther doesn't know what he's playing with. When I finish with that boy…' She straightened up, shook the tears from her eyes and was suddenly calm again. Her self-control was frightening. Old money; I thought, old power. The Manilles owned the rum factory in the south, a couple of cocoa plantations, the biggest hardware store in San Andrews, and probably every string-puller worth pulling on the island. Them kinda people – a pusson don't want to cross them. No, Suh!

'I have to go,' I said.

'What did you say your name was?' She was waving the paper at me.

'Digger,' I said, and left.

## 48

I admired the small miracle of Miss Stanislaus walking the mud-path to the church in a fine white linen dress and matching strappy sandals without getting a speck of dirt on her clothing. She wanted to see The Mother, she said, before our debriefing at the office.

Miss Stanislaus strolled into the church, looked around her briefly, pulled up a chair and sat in front of Mother Bello. I noticed that she hadn't done her usual curtsy.

It was Saturday – usually a time of elaborate preparations for the all-day Sunday service – yet the yard was empty. It was odd how the absence of human sounds transformed the way I saw this place – just a pair of shabby buildings buried among the bushes on the edge of a festering swamp. Mother Bello was inside the church. The stammering Watchman sat on a narrow bench at the back. I saw no sign of his whip.

'Mother Bello, what Miss Alice was to you?' Miss Stanislaus looked agitated.

The Mother said that Alice was like a daughter. Life did not bless her with children of her own. Alice was nine when she took her from her grandmother in that hill village in Saint Johns, named Malaise. The old woman couldn't manage the child anymore and so she offered to take her.

'Amos is ten,' Miss Stanislaus said. 'Not so?'

The Mother said yes.

'That mean,' Miss Stanislaus leaned forward, her elbows on her knees, both palms pressed together. 'That mean Alice had Amos when sh'was thirteen. From what Missa Digger tell me, that… that was the year after Edmund Hill Prison let go Pike and he come straight to the church. Not so?'

In the silence, I looked back at the Watchman. He seemed asleep or was pretending to be.

'So, why you never let nobody know?' There was a new quality to Miss Stanislaus's voice – fretful, impatient.

'As God is me witness…'

'Don't waste God time and ask him to do your dutty work for you. Answer me! Why!'

'Deacon mek me.'

'Mother Bello, you lie. Miss Alice never try to tell you what go on? Eh? You never notice no change in she behaviour? You wasn watchin she; you never use to bathe she or dress she, or comb she hair? You never use to talk to she. Eh? How come you didn know what yuh husban brother doing to she? And when it hit you that she thirteen years and she with child for a harden-back jailbird, what you do?'

Miss Stanislaus was on her feet and in the woman's face. I thought she was going to strike her. I closed my fingers around her elbow and urged her outside.

Miss Stanislaus covered her face with her hands and pressed her head against my shirt. Soft sobs shook her shoulders. I held her until she quietened.

'I going back in there,' I said. 'I not finish yet.'

We left the church at noon. The briefing was not till late afternoon so I took my time. Miss Stanislaus's eyes were still swollen; I was wary of engaging her in conversation.

'You talk,' she said, when we got to the office. We were five minutes late.

Chilman had taken my desk. The old man grinned and winked at me.

'I here at the behest of the Commissioner.'

Malan looked relaxed. Pet was throwing covert glances at Miss Stanislaus and I.

'Okay, Digson, shoot,' Chilman said.

'That's an invitation, Sir?'

The old geezer scratched his cheek and grinned.

Malan shuffled his papers and tapped his feet.

'Okay,' I said. 'These are the facts as I see them: In summary: four murders – three committed by Pike Hunt, Deacon Bello's brother. Pike's victims are Jason Cullman, Alice Massy and Nathan Kurl, in that order. The last victim, Deacon Bello Hunt, was… well… I'll come to that later.

'Pike was Bello's half-brother. The third of five brothers. All of them same mother. Apart from Bello, each had a record: harassment, criminal damage, threatening behaviour and various public order offences involving cutlasses, bootoo, stones, lengths of chain and knives.

'Every one of Pike's convictions refers to his temper, or to actions pointing to his temper. Basically, when Peter "Pike" Hunt goes berserk, he is capable of anything. On top of that he was pathologically jealous.'

'Keep it simple, Digson,' Chilman grumbled.

'For most of his adult life Pike been in and out of jail for aggravated assault. His first son, Christopher Russ – aged nine – died from trauma to the lower spine. Pike was arrested on suspicion of murder but the boy's mother – a woman from Moyah village – would not speak. They released Pike because of lack of evidence.

'Pike was released from jail six and a half years ago for GBH – his victim was a school boy. He went straight to Bello's church. Bello took him in and made him a Watchman.

'Pike lay claim to Alice when she was twelve.' I slid a look at Malan, but the Chief Officer had his eyes on the floor. 'Alice was thirteen when she had his child – Amos. She was nineteen when she started selling provisions from Bello's land in San Andrews marketplace. That's where she met Jason, who came from Saint Mark's parish to San Andrews looking for work. I got his phone number off Alice's phone, and his details from his service provider. Alice brought him to the church. I don't know if she ever told him about Pike or was using the fella as a shield between herself and Pike. In fact, Alice tried to run away once. Pike caught her and beat her up so bad he broke her shoulder blade with that whip of his. As a matter of interest, Pike always strike across the shoulder first.

'The Mother confirmed that Jason left without notice. Now we know why.

'Jason suffered major damage to the back of the head. There

254

was no evidence of him having on clothes, which leads me to believe he was naked when he died. He was probably with Alice at the time.

'Two months later, Alice was gone. People thought she went chasing after Jason – that was until The Mother found Alice's phone.'

I paused and looked at them. 'I s'pose y'all wondering why Pike killed her? Well, Alice was pregnant and she either told Pike the child was Jason's, or he worked that out himself.'

'Where Nathan fit into all of this?' Chilman said.

'Nathan an Miss Alice was good friend,' Miss Stanislaus said. 'He the first to suspeck somefing happm to Miss Alice. H'was a brave lil fella; he face up to Pike.'

'The Mother confirmed a drastic change in Nathan's attitude to Pike after Alice disappeared,' I said. 'Very hostile. Not long after, Nathan wasn't there no more.'

I held up Alice's phone. 'This is what kicked off things. When Amos spotted the phone in Miss Stanislaus's hand and said it was his mother's, Bello was not the only one who heard. A few of the women did and they got suspicious.

'The Mother say where she find it?' Chilman wanted to know.

'I had a hard time getting that out of her,' I said.

'I interested, Digson. Tell me.'

'In a minute. Bello wanted to know who gave Miss Stanislaus the phone. The Mother never told him and Amos was so afraid of the man, the child's mouth used to lock up in his presence.

'I believe Deacon Bello had a crisis. He saw the scandal coming, the church falling apart. He also realised that Miss Stanislaus was no ordinary member of his congregation.'

Malan flicked his pen, 'Time to land, Digger. You say you got doubts about who kill Bello Hunt?'

'Yes. What kept bothering me was the absence of the Watchmen and children on the beach during the baptism. That's not normal.

'What I know now is that the Watchmen stayed at the church with the children. That was the understanding between Pike and his other woman.'

I left them with that; went to the sink to wash my face. When

I returned, Miss Stanislaus was squinting at me and Chilman's head was shaking. Pet looked puzzled.

'His other woman?' Malan said.

'The Mother. It was an open secret that Bello and the Mother slept in the same room, but that was all. She admitted to finding Alice's phone under Pike's pillow and that it was her decision to ask the Watchmen to stay with the children. She wouldn't tell me why she made that decision.

'As far as I could see, Pike was running the Mother for years. The woman literally gave Alice to him. When she killed Bello, she was ripe for it.'

Miss Stanislaus was shaking her head at me.

'It wasn't Adora who killed Bello,' I said.

'Missa Digger, that's not true.'

Malan shifted in his seat, his eyes switching from Miss Stanislaus's face to mine. Chilman went completely still as if he was listening to something outside our words. The red eyes never left my face.

'Miss Stanislaus, you prepare to swear to me that you actually saw Adora strike down Bello? That you saw the blow that knocked him down?'

She said nothing for a while then frowned. 'I thought...'

'Adora admitted to throwing herself at Bello, and wanting to tear the flesh off his face, but Mother Bello was in the way. I believe Adora.'

I raised my head at them. 'The Mother carry that stone all the way from the church yard. I could prove it. She had it on her person; it wasn't obvious because she not a small woman. Is not Adora kill Bello. Is The Mother.'

'So we got an arrest to make,' Malan said.

'Nuh,' Miss Stanislaus said.

'How you mean, nuh!'

'Let's vote on it,' Chilman cut in abruptly. 'Who favour arresting the woman who kill she husband for raping seven girl-children in his care and being complicit in the murder of three members of his congregation and, after all that, attempting to drown an officer.'

Malan raised his brows. I saw him stifle a smile. Chilman

pointed his pen at me. 'You been making sense so far, Digson, except the logistics. How Pike manage to carry them people to them places...'

'The Volvo in the yard. Pike used to work as a bus driver. The Mother knew that too,' I told him.

Malan said he wanted it noted that he had one concern.

'Wozzat?' Chilman said.

'We could not interview Pike Hunt because he got five bullets for the price of one.'

Chilman crossed his legs and chuckled.

'I don't see the joke.'

'That's because you think is a bad thing, Malan – right?' Chilman looked like an old rooster preparing for a fight. 'So what you expect?'

'How you mean what I expect!'

'Okay, Malan, lemme put it this way. That incident in the market square that none ov y'all bother tell me about: if Cocoman knew the way DC Stanislaus use a gun, you think he would've tried to cut 'er throat in the middle of the market square because she is a woman trying to arrest him? And look what happm – you and Digson had to run from y'all desk and go play Bruce Lee to get her out of trouble. So what would've happened if y'all wasn't around? Eh?'

Chilman stood up, his body swaying. 'Y'all should advertise the fact. Make every badjohn and henchman on this island know that once she raise that gun and point it at their arse, they good as dead; no escaping it; they dead – not once, Malan; not twice. They dead five fuckin times. I done talk.'

'You getting worse in your old-age, Sir.' I said.

Chilman laughed. 'You not doing too bad yourself, Digson. I bet that never cross your mind? Anyway, I travelling with y'all to Easterhall. I want to survey the damage meself.'

When we stepped out into the yard, there was a cameraman at the door and a young woman with a microphone from Island Voice TV. Did we have a statement to make about the second body we found in Easterhall?

Malan stepped forward. Miss Stanislaus tapped the young woman's shoulder.

'Missa Digger'z the one who know all about it. Or mebbe you talk to both ov us, because we wuk togedder.'

Malan fixed her with that dark-eyed glare he reserved for her father. He was probably going to shoulder her aside. I felt my lips peel back. 'Yuh even breathe on her, you'll wish you never born.'

He pretended he didn't hear me. I kept my eyes on him until he moved aside.

## 49

Now that the Dry Season was upon us and the mint grass shrunk down to stumps, we could see the field of stones – black pock-marked protrusions that ran all the way down to the ocean.

Somebody had made chalk marks on the boulder at the foot of which they'd uncovered Nathan, and yes, Nathan had been wearing his brown leather sandals like Miss Iona said and there were remnants of his khaki shorts.

It would take them several days to comb these stony acres for whatever else Pike might have buried here. But for now it was enough to know that we'd found Nathan and secured the scene. Later tonight, or at some unholy hour in the morning, I would return and interrogate his bones.

Chilman made his way towards the excavation with a floundering urgency. The old fella stood for a while over it, the wind pulling at his clothing and making of him a scarecrow. Miss Stanislaus and I remained on the road.

She raised inquiring eyes at me. 'You know 'bout dat?'

I told her, yes, I knew about Frigate Island.

'Missa Digger, it look to me like everybody on Camaho searching for somebody.'

Maybe loss needs something to attach itself to, I told her, something it can see or touch before it's able to put whatever is lost to rest.

'You goin tell me about your modder?'

'Nothing much to report, Miss Stanislaus. Demonstration in San Andrews. Fella named Buckman Hurd shot them up so bad, they couldn't let the public see the carnage. So they decide to chalk them. It is the only explanation.'

'Chalk?'

'You make a mark with chalk – one wipe with your hand and it's gone. The first coupla years they claimed she wasn't at the demonstration. When the papers printed pictures to prove they lied, they changed their tune and said she fell off the sidewalk into the sea and drowned. Tide took her. Problem is the Carenage don't have no tide.'

'What you goin do now, Missa Digger? You finish wiv it?'

I looked away; said nothing.

Chilman returned, cleared his throat and focused rum-reddened eyes on his daughter, then on me. 'Digson, you'z a dog.'

'Same back to you, Sir.'

'Precisely,' he said, and winked at me.

The old DS turned his back on us and strolled over to his car. We watched the tail lights of his vehicle grow dim in the distance then disappear.

'He like you, Missa Digger. He, erm, he like you a lot.' Miss Stanislaus was staring beyond the rocks at the sea. 'But he dunno how to say it.'

'He love you, Miss Stanislaus. A lot. But sometimes, yunno, life is a bitch; it take over.'

'What I don unnerstan, Missa Digger, is why Pike hide Miss Alice in the mountain up there and a different place for Nathan and Jason.'

'Mebbe he couldn't stand the idea of another man near her, even in death. I dunno, Miss Stanislaus.'

'Missa Digger, you tired?'

'Lil bit.' I said. 'Why?'

'I been thinkin dat we go relax. Me an you.'

'What you got in mind?'

'Ristorant, mebbe, with knife-an-fork and nice plate, and waiter-boys-and-gyuls servin us. Yunno?' She glanced at me, smiled. 'You wear your perfume. I dress up lil bit – put on someting nice. Den we go take some breeze, remind weself dat life not bad. That awright?'

'That very awright, Miss Stanislaus. We could, erm, take Daphne with us?'

'You want ter?' I could not read her expression.

'I been thinking about Daphne,' I said.

I remembered the child being always beside Miss Stanislaus or one step behind her whenever we were at the church. She would rest her head against her mother as soon as she got the chance. There were times when Miss Stanislaus dropped her hand across her daughter's shoulders and Daphne's face became blissful.

I watched Daphne change the rules of a game of Po-Man-Po so that the younger ones could join in and enjoy themselves. And this, more than anything, made me see her differently.

'Mebbe we can take her out, yunno? After work. She like ice-cream? Mebbe a glass of cold cane juice down in the mall in the Drylands. Or the cinema, a dance show, a play, or even the airport – she might like to watch them planes coming and going. Give 'er something to dream about.'

Miss Stanislaus reached down and adjusted the ankle strap of her sandals. 'What you sayin, Missa Digger?'

'That's all I'm saying, Miss Stanislaus. Nothing more.'

She straightened up, passed a tissue across her eyes. 'I remember tings sometimes, Missa Digger, then…'

'Then what?'

'Tings not finish yet, Missa Digger. I got to go to Kara Isle an finish it. That's all I have to say.'

Miss Stanislaus fanned her face, glanced at me and chuckled. 'An' I have to say, Missa Digger, I like it. I like it very much.'

'What you talking 'bout now?'

She tapped her bag. 'Uhm, when you catch Missa Malan watchin me cross-eye, an you growl at him like dog, I have to say you sound very fierce indeed. Very fierce an nice! You take me home right now?'

'As you wish.'

'Then what you waitin for?'

## 50

My head was ripe for nightmares, so I didn't go to bed but followed the progress of the night by the sounds of the world outside: crickets stopped their chorus around three, after them the bats – in a final feeding frenzy – made me dizzy with their chittering. The wing-whisper of owls returning to their roosts took over, followed by the early-morning seawind rolling up the valley, stirring the trees.

I showered and dressed, boiled some cocoa, dropped in milk and sugar and sipped it until the cup went cold in my hands. I read and made notes for three hours, left my house at nine and answered a phone call from Dessie's mother on my way to Wax Apple Hill.

I sat on the wall above the courtyard of Luther Caine's church until the Sunday morning service was over and the congregation had their fill of gossip and handshaking. I kept my eyes on him back-patting fellow congregants – hair slicked back, a blue long-sleeve shirt with gold cufflinks, patent leather shoes polished to a high shine. Bright wide smile.

I wanted a clearer picture of the face behind the cruelty. I found it hard to square the Luther Caine I saw with his wife recovering from an overdose in a clinic in Barbados. Why was there no law in Camaho that made the mental torture he put her through a crime?

Shona Manille had called from Barbados to thank me. The grimness in her tone made it plain they would destroy Luther without touching him. Here was Luther – smiling, laid-back – unaware of what was about to hit him. It left me wondering at the ways in which a life can be so readily dismantled.

Back home, I unsealed the taped-down pages of my black

notebook. Thick as a Bible and just as heavy, it used to be my mother's. I was fourteen when I dug it up from the pile of her belongings that my grandmother could not bring herself to throw away.

The first forty pages were notes to herself about my father, as if she were at war with her own feelings about him.

As a boy, I'd been uncomfortable reading the details of their intimacies, my mother's expressions of desire. What struck me now was the way she wrote about his house. His bed was theirs, the living room not just a place she cleaned and tidied, but one she sat in, watched television and had him feed her fruits.

Then came the break when his wife found them together. She wrote of the hurry with which she'd dressed and left. I detected no shame in my mother's words, only defiance and regret. She'd dedicated nine short lines to a man named Prince who took her sometimes in his car to a quiet beach in the south, but it was clear to me now that my father had occupied some place in my mother that could not be breached.

I'd sealed the pages when I could not bear them anymore. What happened between humans frightened me. They still did, but when I closed the book, I did not reseal the pages.

My mind drifted back to Pike and Alice Massy, then Dessie – Dessie drowning and reaching out to me.

I got into my car and drove through one of those thunderstorms that were as sudden as they were violent, my wipers a crazy blur. Some things Lonnie had left in my house – a bottle of Nivea lotion, a cream nylon slip she used to come to bed in, and a yellow sleeveless body-hugging top – were on the passenger seat beside me.

When I got there, the beach in front of Lonnie's house was drowned in a layer of seething foam and broken coral.

She was on the veranda with two women – one with a head of thick unplaited hair, let loose to the wind making a small tornado in the veranda. She was combing Lonnie's hair. The other was thin, light-skinned, with rust-coloured hair and brownish-golden eyes that reminded me of the pictures I've seen of lions.

The women stepped back, one with her shoulders against the door frame, the other close beside her.

I nodded to them and held out Lonnie's bag. 'Coupla things you left behind.' I tried to smile.

Lonnie looked at the bag, then at my face.

I hadn't planned what I said next. 'I don't regret nothing, Lonnie. You been good for me.'

I turned and started walking back to the main road. Through the wind I heard my name. I looked round to see Lonnie hurrying along the path, the red comb in her hair.

She stood before me, breathless. 'Digger,' she said. 'I – I awright now, yunno. I straighten out myself. I straighten out from… since… since…'

'So stay straighten out then! These things take time.' She blinked at me as I patted her arm.

As I pulled out onto the road, I thought how fear – along with all the ways a fella tried to own or control a woman – might make her stay, but it could not make her love him.

I might say that to Miss Stanislaus later – impress the lady, yunno. But come to think ov it, she been tellin me that in her own watch-y'arse, don'-gimme-no-bullshit way. From time!